On Our Own Behalf

On Our Own Behalf

Women's &.&. EDITED WITH AN INTRODUCTION

Tales from Catalonia

&.&. & NOTES BY KATHLEEN MCNERNEY

&.&. *University of Nebraska Press: Lincoln and London*

The paper in this book meets the minimum require-
ments of American National Standard for Information
Sciences – Permanence of Paper for Printed Library
Materials, ANSI Z39.48–1984.

Publication of this book was aided by a grant from the
Program for Cultural Cooperation Between Spain's
Ministry of Culture and United States Universities.

Library of Congress Cataloging-in-Publication Data
On our own behalf.
(European women writers series)
Bibliography: p.
1. Catalan literature – Women authors.   2. Catalan
literature – 19th-20th centuries.   3. Women – Literary
collections.   I. McNerney, Kathleen.   II. Series.
PC3925.05   1988   849'.9301'08352042   87-12465
ISBN 0-8032-3122-9 (alkaline paper)

For Maria-Antònia,
Caterina, and Clementina
And Some—Not Many—Others:
A Poem in Dedication
to Forgotten Women Writers

I knew that you could,
in spite of many things,
always explain to us
pieces of whatever we wished.

I knew that you knew
much more than you wrote;
that you were much more daring
than the bravery you needed.

I knew that behind so many restraints,
so many obstacles,
so many doors learned and closed,
there was a fountain to quench thirst and desire.

I knew that you offered morsels of every kind
(I have known it almost always,
beyond the silent ridicule)
that saved me too many words.

I knew that I had to search for you
(to rummage through editions impossible to obtain)
faithfully and closely to read you,
precedents of our reckless lives.

By Marta Pessarrodona.
Translated by H. Patsy Boyer
from *Poemes 1969–1981,* "A favor nostre"
(Barcelona: Mall, 1984).

Contents

Introduction

The democratization of Spain since the late 1970s has brought about many significant changes in Spanish life, particularly in regions whose language and culture differ from those of Castile. In Catalonia, suppression of the language was harsh during the Franco era, but the new home rule laws of 1979 have encouraged a kind of renaissance of letters. At the same time, the women's movement has strengthened and Spanish women have won several new rights. An exciting result of these changes is the appearance, in Catalan, of many works by women writers. Montserrat Roig, Isabel-Clara Simó, and Carme Riera have recently won important literary prizes, and others have had their works reprinted several times already. Some have returned to Spain after years of exile to reimmerse themselves in their native Catalonia. Mercè Rodoreda's book *La Plaça del Diamant* (1962) has been made into a film and translated into English.

The choices in this collection as well as my critical comments focus on works of high literary quality and on themes dealing with women: the friendships among women, for example, in the work of Helena Valentí and Carme Riera; the contrast between young and old women and their relationships in Montserrat Roig; the treatment of older women in Maria-Antònia Oliver and Riera; violence against women in Isabel-Clara Simó and Oliver. These and other interrelated themes are of interest to all women. The universality of the topics underscores some of the problems women have in common across cultural and national divisions; they also offer some interesting new solutions and insights.

These authors often address the difficulties of women's lives and feminist issues in original and refreshing ways, without sacrificing such literary qualities as lyricism, imagery, suspense, style, and elegance. Carme Riera's "I Leave you, My Love, the Sea as a Token" (1975) is a case in point. In a state-of-the-art short story she deals with the topics of female adolescence, incipient sexuality, lesbianism, and teacher-student relationships and at the same time produces a rare combination of lyricism, delicacy, beauty, and truth. The sea represents at once the love of two people and their separation; the voice of the narrator is exquisitely nostalgic, appreciative, and hurt, but without rancor. The triad of love, death, and new life comes together in the somewhat ambivalent ending in an aura of softness and sweetness that bespeaks the "feminine" voice in literature.

This important group of writers is barely known outside of Catalonia. For example, *The New Catalan Short Story* (edited by Porqueras-Mayo et al., 1983) has excellent selections, but not all of the stories are translated (and of those that were, none are by women). *El feminismo ante el franquismo* (Feminism vis-à-vis the Franco Regime) by Levine and Waldman (1980) is a book of interviews with prominent Spanish feminists in various professions. Only Mercè Rodoreda is fairly well represented in literary scholarship. *La rateta encara escombra l'escaleta* (The Little Rat Still Sweeps the Stairs) by Gabancho (1982) is a brief look at several women writers but lacks a clear thematic focus. Unfortunately, and typically, the bibliography on these Catalonian writers consists almost entirely of book reviews and personal interviews, with the repeated assumption that their work is all autobiographical. There is little critical analysis, a situation that might be corrected as their works become available in English and more widely known.

THE FICTION World literature is replete with novels of male adolescence, *Bildungsromans*, picaresque tales, and the like. But until recently, few books have dealt with the female counterpart, and even fewer can claim the authenticity of having been written by women.[1] Several Catalan writers deal most effectively with this subject. In her delightful novel *L'òpera quotidiana* (The Everyday Opera, 1982), structured like an opera, Montserrat Roig weaves together several interrelated stories. One selection included here recounts the growing up of Mari Cruz, a poor and simple Andalusian girl working as a maid in the Barcelona of the 1970s. She marks time in a convent school, where all the girls, starved for male attention, worship the few fathers who come to visit. Her first sexual explorations take place at the school with the gardener who takes advantage of the innocence and needs of the girls. Although physically unmarred by this experience, she is nevertheless discovered and ostracized by nuns and companions alike.

Muller qui cerca espill (Women Who Look for Mirrors, 1982), a television screenplay by Maria-Antònia Oliver, deals with the theme of female adolescence in a different way. In this work, Mariona is engaged to Martí, and wonders why she is not more excited to see him when he comes over every day. She recognizes that he is a good catch, and surprises herself and others with her bad humor toward him. She is unsure of her feelings for him: "no em fa cap il.lusió que vengui . . . Però i si no vengués? Què faria, si no vengués? Em posaria trista?" (I'm not at all excited that he's coming. . . . But what if he didn't come? What would I do? Would I be sad? p. 80). She

3

recalls the excitement of only a few years ago when she was the belle of the ball and several men paid court to her, but she cannot seem to find that excitement in Martí. She wanted to be an actress or a movie star. All those beaux, and even a few of her girlfriends, have gone to the university, but that was not possible for her. She reprimands Martí for being so conformist; she is much more ambitious than he but has no outlet for her energy. Martí is a "bon noi" (good kid), dependable, somewhat intimidated by her but a believer in the double standard. With scarcely any choice except to marry him, she tries to convince herself that she loves him, despite all evidence to the contrary.

Sebastiana, the young Majorcan of Oliver's *Estudi en lila* (Study in Lilac, 1985), is victimized more directly. Raped, pregnant, and alone in Barcelona, she is found by the detective Lònia at the request of her island relatives, a proud and conservative Catholic family. Lònia supports her economically and emotionally, letting her know about alternative possibilities of solving her crisis. The scrupulous feminist detective suggests abortion without pushing, but Sebastiana's relatives, with the sureness of being right that precludes any scruples, convince her that that would be a terrible sin. Sebastiana does not have the strength to withstand the pressure.

The young women characters we have discussed, though they come from different backgrounds and have very different life-styles, share a sense of frustration with the few possibilities open to them, the stifling upbringing, the prison of being a female in a patriarchal society.[2] Mariona will have a comfortable but completely unfulfilled life; Mari Cruz ends up "col.locada" (kept), still looking for some vague fantasies suggested to her by the delirious old Senyora Altafulla, half-mad from her own disillusionments.

Carme Riera's *Epitelis tendríssims* (Very Tender Epitheliums, 1981), a collection of erotic short stories with

Majorca as a background, features women protagonists of various ages: a teenager who writes very explicit love letters but does not send them—they represent more an exploration of her own sexuality than a message to anyone; a mature woman who falls in love with a voice on the telephone, which she hears by accident, and who subsequently has an affair with the voice rather than with its owner; and a somewhat older woman who leaves behind a notebook full of very erotic poetry to be found after her suicide. In an eerie tale, included here, depressing for the lack of progress in women's status that it reveals, an investigative reporter doing research on the Inquisition finds herself in a compromised position with an elderly man. He had promised to give her historical fact, but only recreates his own fantasy of love for a young woman who was burned at the stake by his medieval ancestor. Parallels between the "witch" and the reporter are inevitable. One of the most curious stories, called "Una mica de fred per a Wanda" (A Cool Breeze for Wanda, included here), involves a young man's lust for his father's lover. The sensual Wanda is willing to satisfy both men, but the young viscount introduces technology into the relationship in an effort to gain the upper hand, and pays the price of eternal frustration.

Sexual exploration, eroticism, autoeroticism and lesbianism are not lacking in this body of literature. Carme Riera's "I Leave you, My Love, the Sea as a Token" (included here) is one of the most lyrical of the pieces to emerge in recent writing, exploring female sexuality with delicacy. Núria Serrahima's unnamed protagonist, a liberated woman indeed, lists her lovers in her "agenda," in "Amants," one of the three novellas contained in *L'olor dels nostres cossos* (The Odor of Our Bodies, 1982). In the story, she evokes the tenderness of this one or the joyful playfulness of that one, preserving the letter *K*, not a very romantic one, "per a mi, per a les meves masturbacions, que mai no dedico a ningú, sino a mi mateixa" (for myself, for my masturbations, which I never dedicate to anyone, just to me myself, p. 138).

The theme of solitude also appears in several of the works by the younger generation of Catalan writers. It is, sadly but realistically, much more pervasive than the theme of solidarity among women. Helena Valentí's "L'altre" (The Other, included here) in *L'amor adult* (1977), though much more subtle and less violent, reminds us somewhat of Jorge Luis Borges's story "La intrusa." It is a story of male bonding among the lover, friend, and son of the female protagonist, a relationship that excludes her. "Desarrelament" (Uprooting), in the same collection, adds exile to the loneliness of the female character. In *L'òpera quotidiana*, Mari Cruz needs nothing so much as a friend to talk to. Though she has superficial relationships with several people, she never has an opportunity to speak intimately with anyone. In Oliver's *Vegetal* (1982), Marta speaks occasionally to her dead husband, and she insults her only friend Fina as well as her son Charles and his mate Julia. Her only real companions are her plants, with which she fills up the house. (Two acts of this play are included here.)

Marta's plight is a common one—she is an older woman, a widow, who has never worked outside the home, and she feels worthless.[3] She agonizes about having been nothing but a decoration all her life, not unlike her beloved plants. Her final decision, after trying unsuccessfully to make herself useful to society, is to accept her role as merely decorative, joining the ranks of the flowerpots. Oliver addresses the themes of the loneliness and the feeling of uselessness of older women in an extremely poetic and beautiful short story whose title echoes that of the screenplay "Muller qui cerca espill les mans s'hi talla II" (Women Who Look for Mirrors Get their Hands Cut) in the collection *Figues d'un altre paner* (Figs from a Different Basket, 1979). Unable to accept her mother's death—par-

ticularly painful because she had not seen her for years—
Marta fills her house with calendars and clocks in an effort
to thwart the passing of time. Her husband and son, believing her to be crazy, lock her up in the house, but she
escapes to look for her mother and for the village of her
childhood, across the sea.

Older, lonely women are the protagonists of several
of Carme Riera's stories in *Jo pos per testimoni les gavines*
(I Offer the Seagulls as Witness, 1977). "Es nus, es buit"
(The Knot, the Void, included here) is a monologue by a
woman who finds herself free for the first time in her life
when her husband dies. She loses this freedom when her
relatives, convinced that she is deranged, commit her to a
home when she throws away her wedding pictures and the
postcards her husband had written to her years before. In
the bitterly ironic "Unes flors" (Some Flowers, included
here), a woman loses both husband and child in a divorce
resulting from her attempt to get her husband's attention.

In Riera's "De jove embellia" (She Was Pretty Once), a
once-beautiful woman never marries and lives in self-im-
posed isolation, carrying the stigma of a sexual assault she
experienced years before. At first, she is so paranoid that
she puts furniture in front of her door, but as the years
pass, she comes to wish in vain that someone would come
into her lonely room.

There are two interesting older women characters in
Roig's *L'òpera quotidiana*. I have mentioned in passing
Senyora Altafulla, who hires Mari Cruz as a maid and
companion. In her idealized youth she loved only the gal-
lant soldier Captain Saura who was executed for desertion
toward the end of the Civil War. To her, no one else could
be as noble, and she spends her life fondly remembering
the little contact she had with him. Senyora Miralpeix,
Mari Cruz's other employer, enjoys the companionship of
Senyor Duc and listens, very nurturingly, to his anguished
memories of the past. He marvels that he is able to open
up to someone as he does to her. But she explains it to

him in these words: "Es lògic: amb mi, no li cal dissimular. No em veu com una dona, ja no pot sentir cap mena de desig. Tinc un peu al calaix" (It makes sense. With me, you don't have to pretend. You don't see me as a woman, since you don't feel desire. I have one foot in the grave, p. 142). And she is right; Senyor Duc cannot seem to deal with younger women on any basis other than sex.

Nor do these writers shy away from dealing with the difficult issues of abortion and violence against women. Anna's abortion leads directly to her solitude in Valentí's *La solitud d'Anna* (1981), for her lover abandons her as a result of her difficult decision. Her mother can only criticize, not support her. In Roig's *El temps de les cireres* (The Season of Cherries, 1977), Natàlia's botched abortion nearly causes her death, and her brother reacts in much the same way as Anna's mother. One of the most interesting treatments of this problem is found in Carme Riera's novel *Una Primavera per a Domenico Guarini* (A *Primavera* for Domenico Guarini, 1980), in which the reporter Isabel Clara Albern's soul searching about whether to become a mother or not coincides with her investigation of the mysterious attack on Botticelli's painting. She finds both her answers in the enigmatic work itself.

Violence against women is the subject of Maria-Antònia Oliver's story "Broken Threads" (included here) as well as the full-length novel *Estudi en lila*. A detective story by genre, this novel addresses the aftermath of rape. The author contrasts the reactions of two victims: a very young and vulnerable Majorcan, and a fashionable fortyish antique seller. Oliver emphasizes the opposite reactions of the two victims, with the feminist detective in between in years and sympathy. The very self-assured Senyora Gaudí, of a certain means as well as age, reacts with outrage and seeks the aid of a detective to carry out her plan of vengeance. The young Majorcan Sebastiana is doubly victimized in that her reactions are feelings of shame, fear, guilt, and helplessness. She is sought out by the detective

8

agency at the request of a relative, who sharpens her sense of worthlessness and tendency to self-destruction.

Rape is also the subject of two shorter pieces by Catalonian women. The sarcastic title of Maria-Josep Ragué Arias's "Les flors d'un home delicat" (Flowers from a Sensitive Man) in *I tornarà a florir la mimosa* (The Mimosa Will Bloom Again, 1984) is a story of "date rape," the kind which leaves the victim with no defense since she did enter the criminal's apartment. Núria Serrahima, after a long and mostly joyous list of lovers in "Amants"—she assigns each one a letter of the alphabet—leaves the last episode unlettered, since it is too horrible to name. The story begins, "A tu, t'odio i t'odiaré sempre. Tu em fas tornar al record de l'hivern del 1965 . . ." (As for you, I hate you and I'll hate you forever. You make the memory of the winter of 1965 return to me, p. 170).

The violence against women in a short story and a novel by Isabel-Clara Simó takes on a different form. In both cases the violation or mutilation is a result of the weak socioeconomic situation of the woman vis-à-vis a powerful man. In *Júlia*, a factory worker may become the wife of the owner, but only if she agrees to sterilization. In this collection's "Melodrama in Alcoi," a poor woman agrees to kinky nonpenetrative sex to earn a little money for her children. The more conventional violence comes when her jealous husband finds out.

Many of the stories display a sense of humor, defying the silly stereotype of humorless feminists. Without trivializing the issues, and indeed making the point most eloquently, Maria-Antònia Oliver turns the tables on the oppressor, who says girls cannot compete for entry into the Writers Guild in "La confraria del Cavaller que matà un Drac" (The Brotherhood of the Knight-Slaying Dragon) in *Figues d'un altre paner*. She turns the girls into boys, and they win every contest hands down. The boys, of course, accuse them of having cheated by using disguises. Oliver's novel *El vaixell d'iràs i no tornaràs* (The Ship

That Never Returned, 1976) is full of good humor involving sex, and again, changes characters from one gender to the other. Margarida Aritzeta's science fiction novel *Vermell de cadmi* (Cadmium Red, 1984) also uses sex changes and a healthy dose of laughter. Isabel-Clara Simó's humor is of an earthy sort, which complements her preoccupation with people of the working class and underscores her wish to be read by its members.

It is not surprising that, in addition to feminist themes, many of these works also focus on the question of Catalanism. Sometimes the two are linked, both for writers and for their characters. In Roig's short story "Before the Civil War" (1983), Catalonia has to be defined and explained again and again by a Catalan woman living in England. In Riera's "Helena, Helena" of *Jo pos per testimoni les gavines*, dedicated to "tots els exiliats del meu país" (all my country's exiles, p. 27), a woman separated from her husband during the war finds that he is alive years later after she has begun a much happier relationship with another man. Sometimes the themes are in a curious opposition, as in *L'òpera quotidiana*, in which Senyor Duc insists on Catalanizing his young Andalusian wife Maria. He does it so successfully that she becomes radicalized and passes out forbidden bulletins, over his desperate protests, and the quarrel ends their relationship. Senyor Duc is tempted by the younger Mari Cruz, who so resembles his Maria that he is driven away from her.

Literature by women and literature by Catalans have been neglected throughout history for different reasons, but one reason stands out in particular—the oppressed status of the writers. With this new body of literature, we now have a chance to overcome that neglect and gain fresh insights from a continuing production of works of distinct literary quality. Some of these novels and short stories have been translated into Castilian, and a few are being considered for English versions. The topics are relevant, even urgent, and the writing is excellent. It is fortunate for us all that at least some of these works are finally finding their way into the mainstream.

This project came about as a result of a long-standing love of Catalonia and its people and literature, a watchful eye on the growing Spanish feminist movement, and several recent business and pleasure trips to Barcelona. Delighted at the proliferation and quality of the work produced by women, I decided to look into the possibility of having some of these works translated and published. I spoke with the authors themselves, finally interviewing the five I had chosen, to ask them about their work, their reactions to criticism or the lack of it, and their involvement in the parallel movements of feminism and Catalanism.

Not everyone reacted favorably to my work; in fact I often found myself defending the project to people who questioned the exclusion of male writers, or Castilians, or earlier writers. There was even a Catalan from Barcelona who thought I should not include Majorcans and Valencians. At social gatherings, everyone had an opinion, usually negative, or at best bewildered. Why would I want to waste my time on these works? I took these reactions to be quite political, especially as most of these cocktail party critics had not read the works in question. One young man told me he was not interested in literature by women unless he knew the writer and liked her personally. I did not bother to point out what such a criterion would do to literature if applied to nonwomen writers.

But many others were supportive and helpful, beginning with the writers themselves, who went well beyond professional courtesy and cooperation. The translators did excellent work; my own West Virginia University generously helped with a grant from the Faculty Senate. Other friends in Barcelona helped in various ways—Cristina Enríquez de Salamanca, Mari Chordà, Carme Junoy, and Jaume Fuster, who made for me the best *truita* I have ever tasted. Here, too, I found much-needed support and help from Judith Stitzel, Christopher Wilkinson, David Connell, Victòria Codina, Sara Blanch, and especially from John Martin.

THE WRITERS   In Barcelona in 1984 and 1985, I discussed several themes of interest with each of the five authors represented in this anthology. I asked about the present state of criticism, their current projects, their status as outsiders, conflicts among the various roles they play, how they got involved in feminism, role models and who influenced them, and many other concerns. Here are some of their answers from transcribed tape recordings, with my translations of the direct quotations.

On Criticism   Everyone laments that at present, criticism, especially of women's work, barely exists outside of book reviews and interviews, in which personal remarks about the authors are often given more attention than their work.[4] Carme Riera points out that people who write book reviews usually have other time-consuming jobs and cannot devote the necessary time to in-depth reviews. She also notes the machismo of some critics—those who fail to see the eroticism in *Epitelis tendríssims*, for example, because it is not male eroticism. She believes that "the type of eroticism which is the insinuation of desire, more than of its realization, is feminine," and that this distinction may make it difficult for some male critics to respond to her work. Female critics within the patriarchal mind-set might make similar mistakes. Maria-Antònia Oliver finds misogyny in some of the critics, too; the tendency to assume that everything written by women is autobiographical implies that women can only describe, not invent. Oliver finds that this problem is especially severe when women write about intimate topics. Helena Valentí and Isabel-Clara Simó agree that the role of the critic needs to be clarified, and both see a certain elitism and cliquishness among the critics. One of the constant criticisms of Isabel-Clara Simó's novel

Júlia and other works by women with female protagonists is that even though the realization of the main character is very good, the minor characters are not well developed. Most of the minor characters are men, of course, as are most of the critics. Would anyone think to criticize Cervantes for not developing more interesting minor female characters? Montserrat Roig is concerned, too, that because her work and that of other committed women writers has a political content, some critics might find it easy to consider it "pamphlet" literature. She feels that it is important for feminists to avoid the pitfalls of some social realists who, in creating their worker protagonists, depicted people who were perfect in every way. That tendency has to be avoided, even though we might feel a need for heroines. What is important is to create a real world for people to move in, and let them act out their lives in a natural way. She bristles, understandably, at the critic who says that now that we have seen Montserrat Roig's view of the world, let us see the world itself. "What does that mean?" she wants to know. "Is the world that I see not the world?"

On Feminism, Catalanism, and Being an Outsider   All five of the authors consider themselves feminists, though none is associated with any particular group. Carme Riera shares the worry of Montserrat Roig that her work might be considered "de tesis"; writers have no obligation whatsoever to deal with social problems in their work, though Riera feels her writing may help diffuse feminist ideas. Roig and Riera agree that pamphlets have an important role, and that sometimes a particular one may achieve status as literature, but for the most part such writings do not. Both writers have feminism on their minds often, but would not sit down to write a "feminist" novel.

Riera is particularly concerned with women's language, and in fact has written an article about it. She feels strongly that women have to develop a language of their own, for every other language is misogynist. She is hopeful, though, that the kind of difference documented in Robin Lakoff's 1975 work is losing ground, and she cites recent studies that indicate that schoolgirls know just as many bad words as schoolboys, and that the boys are just as sensitive to color words as girls.[5]

Roig underscores the machismo of the Latin-based languages, in which the masculine form of nouns and adjectives are the norm from which one forms the feminine, not unlike Eve coming from Adam's rib. She, like many others, was drawn to feminism in college, where she reacted with bad humor to the sexism she saw, even among the most radical political groups. Since feminism has become part of her life, she has learned much from women, especially from observing ordinary women in their everyday activities. Roig fears that some "successful" women have erred in imitating men. What is truly revolutionary, she believes, and therefore threatening to people, is for people to live as women, with women's values, rejecting the structures and institutions that have been imposed upon us by the patriarchy. Simone de Beauvoir and her Catalan counterpart Maria-Aurèlia Capmany were not really models for Roig. Though intellectually inspiring, she could not identify with them. She rejects the idea that women should have to choose between careers and children, for example, and she has taken both challenges upon herself.

Helena Valentí is the only one of this group who has lived for a long period outside of Catalonia. Her most militant period was during her ten-year residence in England, where she did her first writing for the British feminist magazine *Shrew*. She is very interested in relations among women and the efforts of women to have good relationships with men. She sometimes feels uncomfortable with her more radical lesbian feminist friends, who may feel this interest is not worth the trouble, not a valid quest for a feminist. She rejects the manless world they would create, but she does want to break into male bonding and create a female version of it.

As far as a male or female writing style is concerned, Valentí believes it is a question of writing within a certain tradition or trying to create another; she is not convinced that there is a "female" style. One reviewer of her work mentioned that although Montserrat Roig's work could have been written by a man, hers could not have. To this, Valentí replies that it could be "merely that Montserrat Roig follows certain conventions and I follow others that aren't known here. I don't know, frankly, whether I invented them, but surely Montserrat Roig is more Catalan than I am, for I had spent ten years in England and my style probably seemed a bit strange—it could be that."

Maria-Antònia Oliver came to feminism and Catalanism through a need to relate directly to the world, not through a man or another country. These are two parallel lines for her, and she sees the search for identity in colonized people as a necessary starting point for rebelling against the oppressor and redefining the self. Even though men and Spain may not think they are oppressing anyone, the struggle to avoid being defined as the other by the one is paramount.[6]

Oliver and Valentí both see conflicts between Catalanism and feminism. For Valentí, Catalanism is the defense of the language and territory, but no more. Because the Catalanist movement is dominated by men, and not particularly enlightened ones at that, women who try to espouse both Catalanism and feminism often run into difficulties. Isabel-Clara Simó believes very strongly that all antioppression movements must work together. The Valencian Simó is, of these writers, the one who exhibits the strongest sense of identification with and militancy on behalf of the working classes. "It's not possible," she affirms, "to defend the liberty of a social class, but only the masculine part of that class. . . . It's the liberty of the human being, as a whole." For her, liberating one without liberating all makes no sense. The closed atmosphere of antifascism in which Simó grew up made her a leftist almost automatically, but the feminism came later, on her own. She feels her Valencianism keenly in Barcelona and this contributes to her sense of isolation within the cultural life of the city. Interestingly, she contrasts Valencian politics with Barcelona politics in this important respect—in Valencia if you are "nationalist" you are leftist; in Barcelona among the Catalanists, there is a whole range of allegiances from left to far right.

On Their Work, Their Plans, and Other Subjects   People who are committed to causes are usually very busy people, and these five women are no exception. None can afford the luxury of writing only, and of course it is extremely difficult for writers to live exclusively from their work. In spite of the prizes, reprintings, and general popularity of these authors, they are writing for a small audience. All of them know Castilian, of course, and they are sometimes asked why they do not write in the language that offers a far greater number of potential readers. Their answers are that they are writing in their own language; Spanish has some great writers and it is hardly in danger of extinction. Montserrat Roig finds it easy to write in Castilian for journalism, but not for fiction. Helena Valentí's first writing experience was in English, but she feels that English speakers do not need her voice. Carme Riera translated some of her own stories into Castilian, but does not intend to repeat the exercise.

Teaching, translating, journalism, and parenting are the jobs these writers do when they are not writing. Carme Riera is completing her doctorate in literature, raising a son, and teaching at the Universitat Autonoma de Barcelona. She specializes in Golden Age literature, but her doctoral dissertation is about the writers of Barcelona who wrote in Castilian during the 1950s. She has written literary criticism, but not on a regular basis. As a kind of extension of her work in Golden Age literature, she is also very interested in the chronicles, letters, diaries, and journals relating the "discovery" and conquest of the New World.

Helena Valentí became so influenced by Doris Lessing, whose work she was translating, that she was finally glad to set it aside. After all, she says, one cannot write like Doris Lessing, can one? She prefers to translate into Catalan, but economics sometimes dictates that she work in Castilian. She has translated other British feminists as well, including Virginia Woolf, and very much appreciates the work of Marilyn French. Valentí is also raising a daughter, has another novel finished, and her head full of ideas for new stories.

Maria-Antònia Oliver has also translated from English, including Melville's *Moby Dick*. She writes to invite people into her world, "and that's just what I like, and that's possibly why I write, to invite my readers into the game." She is happiest when writing, perhaps because that is when she is most herself. She also loves to do nothing once in a while, and often feels guilty as a result, though she recognizes her lack of activity at certain times as a need for mental space, a need to let what she has written sit for a while before revising, or to let the next project mature in her mind. Oliver commutes between her apartment on a busy Barcelona street and a hideaway in the Pyrenees, for she needs both the stimulation and the tranquillity. She has also written for television, which she describes as very different from fiction writing, as the former is team work and the latter necessarily solitary.

Isabel-Clara Simó has had impressive achievements involving teaching, translating, reporting, and raising children. She teaches philosophy; she directed and contributed a good deal of material to the cultural periodical *Canigó* for ten years; and she has translated novels from the Italian. She is also raising a family, and she sometimes sees herself as a prisoner of her own great love for

17

them. Translating and journalism have helped her with creative writing through the discipline of working every day and in developing a clarity and preciseness in her prose. She has been influenced by several writers, among them Rodoreda, Dickens, Joyce, and the noted Valencian intellectual Joan Fuster. She was raised in a very closed environment because of her father's reaction to the Civil War, but does not repeat that kind of environment for her children.

Montserrat Roig's nonfiction writings have been in journalism, but she would like to try translating as a way of learning new techniques and working with language. She feels a necessity to write, and wants to compose the perfect novel as her contribution to Catalan culture. She does well in aspiring to greatness, and an awareness of her own limitations and the impossibility of the task never keep her from fantasizing. It will be an urban novel, she believes, because she deeply feels her ties to Barcelona's urban core. She would emulate, in this endeavor, her distinguished predecessors Mercè Rodoreda and Narcis Oller.

CONCLUSION   This latest rebirth of literature in Catalan is not without precedent. Somewhat neglected for both historical and linguistic reasons, Catalan literature followed an evolution roughly parallel to the literature of other Romance languages until its period of Decadence from about 1500 to the early nineteenth century. Because of its cultural and linguistic ties with the South of France, literary production began somewhat later in Catalonia than in other Western European countries, and it did not flourish until the fifteenth century, when it enjoyed a brilliant period of activity, particularly in the old Kingdom of Valencia. During the long period of Decadence, when Catalan intellectuals wrote in Castilian, Catalan language and culture nevertheless remained active, and another renaissance of Catalan letters began in the nineteenth century. The disruption of intellectual life during the Franco era and the exile of many survivors of the Civil War, as well as the government's anti-Catalan laws, resulted in the virtual disappearance of Catalan literature during most of this century. The present energetic revitalization is in a way a reaction to those events, but the feminist nature of much of this recent literature creates a new link not only with other European and American literatures but also with incipient feminist writings from many other parts of the world.

NOTES

1. For an analysis of the female adolescent in literature in English, see Patricia Meyer Spacks, "The Adolescent as Heroine" in her *The Female Imagination* (New York: Avon, 1972), pp. 143–201.

2. For an exploration of the effects of the patriarchal system on choices and personal relationships, see Rosalind Coward, *Patriarchal Precedents: Sexuality and Social Relations* (Boston: Routledge and Kegan Paul, 1983).

3. Simone de Beauvoir and Zoe Moss, among others, deal with the problems of older women in society from a feminist perspective. See Simone de Beauvoir's *The Coming of Age* (New York: Warner, 1973); and Zoe Moss, "It Hurts To Be Alive and Obsolete: The Ageing Woman," in *Sisterhood is Powerful*, ed. Robin Morgan (New York: Vintage, 1970), pp. 170–75. For a specific treatment of *Vegetal*, see also Janet (Díaz) Pérez's "Plant Imagery and Feminine Dependency in Three Contemporary Women Writers," in *In the Feminine Mode: Essays on Spanish Women Writers*, ed. Noël Valis (forthcoming, Bucknell University Press).

4. Several articles have appeared in the 1980s about the state of criticism with reference to works by women. For literature from Spain, see Maria-Lourdes Möller-Soler, "La crítica feminista, una parenta pobra de la crítica literària?" *Serra d'Or* 274–75 (July 1982): 49–50; Maria-Lourdes Möller-Soler, "Caterina Albert o la *Solitud* de una escritora," *Letras Femeninas* 9, 1 (1983): 11–21; Margaret E. W. Jones, "Las Novelistas Españolas Contemporáneas ante la Crítica," *Letras Femeninas* 9, 1 (1983): 22–34; Linda E. Chown, "American Critics and Spanish Women Novelists," *Signs: Journal of Women in Culture and Society* 9, 1 (Autumn 1983): 91–107; Janet (Díaz) Pérez, ed. *Novelistas femeninas de la*

postguerra española (Madrid: Porrúa, 1983); Beth Miller, ed. *Women in Hispanic Literature: Icons and Fallen Idols* (Berkeley: University of California Press, 1983). See also the American feminist classics: Elaine Showalter, "Feminist Criticism in the Wilderness," in *Writing and the Sexual Difference*, ed. Elizabeth Abel (Chicago: University of Chicago Press, 1982), pp. 9–35; Catharine R. Stimpson, "Feminism and Feminist Criticism," *Massachusetts Review* 24, 2 (Summer 1983): 272–88.

5. Riera's article was the second of three to appear in *Quimera*; the series began with Marta Traba's "Hipótesis sobre una escritura diferente," *Quimera* 13 (September 1981): 9–11. Riera followed with "Literatura feminina: ¿Un lenguaje prestado?" *Quimera* 18 (April 1982): 9–12; the final piece was by Evelyne Garcia, "Lectura: N. Fem. Sing. ¿Lee y escribe la mujer en forma diferente al hombre?" *Quimera* 23 (September 1982): 54–57. Many articles and books have addressed this question, for example, Robin Lakoff, *Language and Woman's Place* (New York: Harper and Row, 1975); Mary Hiatt, *The Way Women Write* (New York: Teachers College, Columbia University, 1977); Mary Jacobus, ed. *Women Writing and Writing about Women* (London: Croom Helm, 1979); Sally McConnell-Ginet et al., eds., *Women and Language in Literature and Society* (New York: Praeger, 1980); Annis Pratt, *Archtypal Patterns in Women's Fiction* (Bloomington: Indiana University Press, 1981). Several articles appeared in the summer 1981 issue of *Feminist Studies* (7, 2) and the 1981 issue of *Yale French Studies* (62) about this question. Finally, see Elizabeth Abel, ed. *Writing and the Sexual Difference* (Chicago: University of Chicago Press, 1982); and Mary Midgley, "Sex and Personal Identity: The Western Individualistic Tradition," *Encounter* 63, 1 (June 1984): 50–55.

6. Oliver explains the idea of parallel colonizations literarily in her 1985 novel, *Crineres de foc* (Manes of Fire), in which a young woman's struggle for freedom and identity matches the collective one of the nearby town. See my review in *World Literature Today* 60, 2 (Spring 1986): 298–99.

Bibliography

For a list of the creative works of each of the five authors whose work is included in this book, see the author-specific introductions.

Abel, Elizabeth, ed. *Writing and the Sexual Difference*. Chicago: University of Chicago Press, 1982.

Aritzeta, Margarida. *Vermell de cadmi*. Barcelona: Laia, 1984.

Beauvoir, Simone de. *The Coming of Age*. Tr. Patrick O'Brien. New York: Warner, 1973.

Chown, Linda E. "American Critics and Spanish Women Novelists." *Signs: Journal of Women in Culture and Society* 9, 1 (Autumn 1983): 91–107.

Cotoner, Luisa. "*Una Primavera per a Domenico Guarini* de Carme Riera." *Mirall de glaç: Quaderns de literatura* (Spring/Summer 1982): 52–57.

Coward, Rosalind. *Patriarchal Precedents: Sexuality and Social Relations*. Boston: Routledge and Kegan Paul, 1983.

Feminist Studies 7, 2 (Summer 1981).

Gabancho, Patricia. *La rateta encara escombra l'escaleta*. Barcelona: 62, 1982.

Garcia, Evelyne. "Lectura: N. Fem. Sing. ¿Lee y escribe la

mujer en forma diferente al hombre?" *Quimera* 23 (September 1982): 54–57.

Hiatt, Mary. *The Way Women Write.* New York: Teachers College, Columbia University, 1977.

Jacobus, Mary, ed. *Women Writing and Writing about Women.* London: Croom Helm, 1979.

Jones, Margaret E. W. "Las Novelistas Españolas Contemporáneas ante la Crítica." *Letras Femininas* 9, 1 (1983): 22–34.

Lakoff, Robin. *Language and Woman's Place.* New York: Harper and Row, 1975.

Levine, Linda Gould, and Gloria Feiman Waldman. *El feminismo ante el franquismo.* Miami: Universal, 1980.

McConnell-Ginet, Sally, et al., eds. *Women and Language in Literature and Society.* New York: Praeger, 1980.

McNerney, Kathleen. Review. *World Literature Today* 60, 2 (Spring 1986): 298–99.

Midgley, Mary. "Sex and Personal Identity: The Western Individualistic Tradition." *Encounter* 63, 1 (June 1984): 50–55.

Miller, Beth, ed. *Women in Hispanic Literature: Icons and Fallen Idols.* Berkeley: University of California Press, 1983.

Möller-Soler, Maria-Lourdes. "Caterina Albert o la *Solitud* de una escritora." *Letras Femininas* 9, 1 (1983): 11–21.

———. La crítica feminista, una parenta pobra de la crítica literària?" *Serra d'Or* 274–75 (July 1982): 49–50.

Morgan, Robin, ed. *Sisterhood is Powerful.* New York: Vintage, 1970.

Pérez, Janet (Díaz), ed. *Novelistas femininas de la postguerra española.* Madrid: Porrúa, 1983.

Pessarrodona, Marta. *Poemes 1969–1981.* Barcelona: Mall, 1984.

Porqueras-Mayo, Albert, et al., eds. *The New Catalan Short Story: An Anthology.* Washington, D.C.: University Press of America, 1983.

Pratt, Annis. *Archtypal Patterns in Women's Fiction*. Bloomington: Indiana University Press, 1981.

Ragué-Arias, Maria-Josep. *I tornarà a florir la mimosa*. Barcelona: 62, 1984.

Riera, Carme. "Literatura feminina: ¿Un lenguaje prestado?" *Quimera* 18 (1982): 9–12.

Rodoreda, Mercè. *La Plaça del Diamant*. Barcelona: Club Editor, 1962.

Serrahima, Núria. *L'olor dels nostres cossos*. Barcelona: 62, 1982.

Spacks, Patricia Meyer. *The Female Imagination*. New York: Avon, 1972.

Stimpson, Catharine R. "Feminism and Feminist Criticism." *Massachusetts Review* 24, 2 (Summer 1983): 272–88.

Traba, Marta. "Hipótesis sobre una escritura diferente." *Quimera* 13 (September 1981): 9–11.

Valis, Noël, ed. *In the Feminine Mode: Essays on Spanish Women Writers* (Lewisburg, Pa.: forthcoming, Bucknell University Press).

Yale French Studies 62 (1981).

Carme Riera

Carme Riera, photo by Rose Marquetz

Carme Riera *Majorca, 1948*

Creative Works *Te deix, amor, la mar com a penyora*. Barcelona: Laia, 1975.
Short stories.

Jo pos per testimoni les gavines. Barcelona: Laia, 1977. Short
stories. Some of the stories in these two collections were
translated into Castilian under the title *Palabra de mujer,
bajo el signo de una memoria impenitente*. Barcelona: Laia,
1980.

Una Primavera per a Domenico Guarini. Barcelona: 62,
1980. Novel, winner of the Prudenci Bertrana Prize.
Translated into Castilian by Luisa Cotoner, under the title
Una Primavera para Domenico Guarini. Barcelona: Norte,
1981.

Epitelis tendríssims. Barcelona: 62, 1981. Short stories.

Carme Riera does not like mirrors. But the imagery in her
work offers us a dazzling series of reflections: a look at
oneself through others, a narcissism which becomes an in-
terior voyage, a trip to the center, a deep self-analysis on
the part of her protagonist. The artifacts she uses to
create the images are many—the eyes of the beloved, or
those in a painting; the body of a same-sex lover, a per-

son's two lovers of the opposite sex which become two halves of a whole in a superimposed reflection; the mercury necessary to reach the inner space of alchemy; and repeatedly, the sea.

Much of her work evokes delicate memories of childhood and adolescence in Majorca. A vision of life seen through windows—views of a nearby convent, passersby and children playing, and the Mediterranean. Riera's aversion for mirrors seems a lack of confidence—her mother was good-looking but her father was not, and since she was told as an adolescent that she resembled her father, she made the obvious assumption . . . besides she hated her ponytails and did not want to see them. At the same time she professes a fascination for the Narcissus theme, and she does love to see herself reflected in the calm sea, with the pines, early in the morning.

The various reflections in Riera's novel *Una Primavera* are complex, forming concentric circles. Isabel Clara Albern, reporter, investigates the mutilation by Domenici Guarini of Botticelli's famous painting. She discovers Guarini's fascination with a young woman, whose violet eyes evoke for him both Petrarch's Laura, whose name she shares, and the figure of Flora in the painting. By analyzing the painting and searching her own soul, Isabel Clara finds the answer to both internal and external mysteries. Flora represents the fertility of the new springtime, as well as Isabel Clara's own pregnancy. Isabel Clara's dialogue with herself is a mirror in her process of interiorization, culminating, with the help of the symbolism of the painting and of alchemy's great work, in the understanding of the role of Mercury—the ability to change base matter into gold, a secret revealed only to those, who, like Cloris or the Graces of the painting, are capable of transforming themselves. The final duality—that of love and death—is embodied in Laura, loved and destroyed by Guarini in a ritual of crime against the only possibility of happiness: communication.

The tendency toward a polarity of vision is apparent in some of Riera's short stories as well. In "Marc-Miquel," a woman needs the love of two men—husband and young lover—to be able to love either of them. Alone, neither can inspire her love; together, they complement each other, forming a whole. Inevitably, she calls them by each other's names. The names in the title of another story, "Helena, Helena," refer to the same person, but in different circumstances, different times.

Riera's beloved Mediterranean is at once the unifying force and the separation of the lovers in "Te deix, amor, la mar com a penyora," the first story in this section. A young student, in love with her teacher, is sent away from her home in Majorca to study in Barcelona. She yearns for the clear sea of her island and the smooth body of her lover—remembering "the beauty dissolving in your-my image when I looked at myself in the mirror of your flesh."

Translated by Alberto Moreiras from *Te deix, amor, la mar com a penyora*, © Carme Riera 1975.

I Leave You, My Love, the Sea as a Token

Here, from my window, I cannot see the sea. Only some sick-colored clouds fading into nothing, and the tip of the Tibidabo church steeple. Nothing good. Tall, ugly apartment buildings with decaying flowers on the balconies and yellow awnings damaged by the sun.

I cannot see the sea because it lies far away on the other side of the city. A mourning, greasy, almost stinking sea. Like a wet-nurse, it shelters merchant ships, yachts, and the *golondrina*-boats anchored at a corner of the harbor. This sea does not resemble ours. It is a metal board, with no transparencies or changing colors. Clotted, hardened up. But I miss it. I miss it only because when I see it I know that you are on the other side of it, and that from sea to sea, from shore to shore there is less distance than from city to city.

I miss the sea, I miss the blue immensity, the little blue immensity that seemed to invade the cabin through the porthole that spring day on our way to the island. Forgive me. I was going to ask you if you remember it, just for the pleasure I feel when you tell me that you do, when all of a sudden your eyes are awash with the bewitching blue of our sea, and you get lost in a breath of faraway and some-

31

what stagnant memories. How many years ago was that trip? I refuse to count those years, because I might end up giving you the exact number of hours, minutes, and seconds, as if it were a problem of basic math. Don't be surprised that I've made myself a personal calendar in which the years, months, days begin at the very moment when the blue was perfect, your silky body warm, sweet, soft, the light filtering through.

We were younger, less conscious, full of a perverse, almost wicked innocence, the innocence of rebellious angels. I do not like using these words, because you will get the impression that I feel remorse, that I am not comfortable with my conscience. I was fifteen years old—a song by the Duo Dinamico, the fashionable group then, talked about girls as tender as flowers, and you used to sing it to me, to spite me. I was fifteen years old, and my age was partly why we broke up. But, on the other hand, I like to think that I encountered you in the most critical moment of my adolescence, when I was starting to become a woman, and that you had a great influence in my getting to be the way I am now. During that year, tenth grade, I started wearing stockings instead of colored socks, I had my first pair of high-heeled shoes and an evening dress. It was a velvet dress, red, slightly low-necked. I wore it every Tuesday, to go to the concert at the Teatre Nou. We used to have the free tickets that the Society of Friends of the Arts sent to our school. You did not like the way that provincial orchestra mistreated the music. They did all they could with their violins, their horns, their kettledrums . . . and yet the results were off key, almost howls. But you came and sat down on a seat near our box, you closed your eyes as the lights went off, with only the stage lit up. Little by little I noticed your eyelashes wink, you opened them slightly and gave me sidelong glances. One day, as we came from listening to Bach, you told me that I was staring at you. You asked me what I meant by looking at you that way, as if I were searching for your soul. I answered—I cannot believe my frankness—that I always looked that way at people I thought interesting. And it was then that, for the first time, you put your hands on my hair. You made me shake all over and I was embarrassed.

I liked your hands so much! They are so beautiful still!—long fingers, white skin, manicured nails. I felt happy when you took my hand and we walked like two lovers in the city. You showed me many places that you had discovered when as a teenager you started taking walks in the evenings, long walks through lonely sites. My eyes, which were your eyes, for I saw the world as you looked at it, perceived nuances, colors, shapes, details that you thought surprising and new. It flattered me so much to interest you that I tried to guess and translate your reactions, making them pass as my own, almost unconsciously. And even now, eight years later, it still thrills me to wander mentally through the fisherman's neighborhood of el Carme and el Putxet, whose slopes, stairs, fishy smell reminded you of some place in Naples, on the left side of the docks. Children went around naked, playing with cans and cats, and shabby women chattered in loud voices out on the porches. Or I can also—almost as if I could touch you—follow your lazy steps through the old cobbled streets with elegant facades, toward the Cathedral. I cross Porta del Mar, it smells like incense. . . .

We went out to the country some afternoons. Water gushed in the irrigation ditches and the almond trees had just created a snowy sky among their branches. I visited two abandoned villages with you: Fosc lluc, from which emanated fear and Biniparraix, ruined by a storm. We used to find them after a good hike uphill, through little groves of oaks and pine trees and thickets of shrubs and rosemary. . . . We almost never talked while the hike lasted. Your arm caressed my back. Sometimes I leaned my head on your shoulder and you kissed me as nobody has ever done it.

I was discovering the world the same way love was dis-

covering and appropriating me. It was not in books or
films that I learned to live the story of our history. I was
learning to live, I was learning to die little by little—but I
did not know that then—when, embracing you, I refused
to let time go by. I wanted to remain forever at your side,
to feel the touch of your lips, of your skin. And from your
arms the world was as beautiful and sad as we were, it had
an indefinable color, somewhere between blue and lilac,
under a phosphorescent makeup.

The fog is dying out, thick and slow, it melts away
through the sewers, it fades out between the parked cars.
The sadness of these hours, frozen on our temples, frozen
in our frozen tears, takes me back to you. I am greedy
above all for the clarity filled with kisses that we loved so.
We loved so many things!

The wet soil after the rain, the abundant poppies
among the wheat, the sun-filled café terraces, children,
swallows, deserted beaches, the nights of our imaginary
dates, and love above all, the love we never at that time
talked about.

Our relationship lasted exactly eight months and six
days. It was broken off because of the public scandal and
because you were afraid to face a double responsibility.
You did not have enough strength yourself, nor enough
confidence in me. You were obsessed by the idea that
someday I would reproach you for the love we then called
friendship. They threatened you in the name of morals
and good manners, they talked to you about perverse behavior, child abuse, you received anonymous letters full of
sickening insults. . . . I had to put up with snickers and
whispered comments; more than once my schoolmates
changed the subject of conversation when I approached
them, but nobody, except my father, dared to talk straight
to me, facing reality. I still remember the grimace that
contorted his face, the bitter tone in his voice, but I forget
his words, I only remember two sentences, which have
often echoed in my mind like the insistent slogan of a

commercial that gets into your head and you unintentionally repeat over and over in your mind: "This is the way to depravity. I'll send you to Barcelona if this goes on for just another day." Now I can tell you about it. Back then it would have hurt you, and I wanted to spare you suffering any way I could. I lied to you. Nobody had said anything to me. Everybody behaved as usual. My father was sending me to spend the summer away from Majorca as a prize for my good grades at school.

They were days filled with gall, wounded by absurd frenzies of rage. I felt empty, barren, distant, I almost failed to recognize myself. I began to hate people, the city, and the tender summer just starting. And all the love, that immense capacity for love, was nourished by you and returned to you undisputed. The last evening we were at the seafront and your car was parked in front of the harbor. I started crying—there were so many reasons!—looking for shelter in your arms, which rejected me. The dance of a thousand lights reflected on the bay tickled my eyes. Through my tears I could see fragments of boats and shards of the sea. Your nerves were frayed; the very tension that was wearing you out gave a tragic expression to your face. You did not want to look at me. Finally you turned toward me and with a gesture of desolation you stroked my hair like the first time. I closed my eyes and told you that I loved you. You told me not to say anything; then, as if you were an automaton, words came out of your mouth.

"This cannot go on. We have to bring this senseless relationship to an end."

Suddenly the smell of the sea drew my thoughts out into the waves. Water was knocking upon the glass of the porthole. The sky's calm reflected on it, an intensely blue color stabbed my vision and I did not know whether it was the color of the sea or of your eyes. We were on the berth. We were alone in the cabin, which was big enough for eight people. Sea foam, gulls' wings, dolphins' spurts entered through the round, full-mooned glass, noon-moon of our porthole. You slowly started undressing, you took off your clothes without looking at me, assuming an air intended to seem natural but which I can now guess was pregnant with a sickly innocence. You covered up your body with a sheet: maybe you feared my fear on seeing it naked, perhaps you had imagined me running away, scared by the sight which was offered to me for the first time. I assure you I was not alarmed. My pulse was beating fast, and inside I was unveiling the most beautiful adolescent dream. I had always thought your body splendid. Now I felt curiosity and the desire to satiate my eyes looking at it for as long as I wanted to. That is why I uncovered you. And you looked—I was feeling creative, for my eyes were the ones seeing it so—statuesque, perfect. My fingers, as in a ritual, the slippery dance of my fingers on your skin outlined your lips and every one of the shapes in your body. Then you asked me—with your touch rather than with your voice—for permission to undress me. You wanted to do it, you insisted, to slowly relish the moments that separated us from the instant in which you would finally see me naked. You wanted to make those moments long, in spite of the urgency of your desire. Every passing second—the clock of our veins was the fullness of noon—my trembling body caressed by your hands, brought us nearer to some mysterious, ineffable place that imperiously summoned us. A place out of time, out of space (noon, a boat), made to fit our measure, into which we would inescapably fall. Without salvation, for that was the only way for us to be saved, because down there, in the realm of the absolute, the inexpressible, beauty was waiting for us, beauty dissolving in your-my image when I looked at myself in the mirror of your flesh. And in the safe shelter, in the most intimate cleft of your body, there the adventure began; an adventure not of the senses, but rather of the spirit, which would take me to knowledge of the last layer of your being, eternally destined for the mastery of love and death. . . . Back and forth I went from the little cabin to your car.

From the present past to the actual present. Your tenderness was rough then, when you decided that during the summer we were not to see each other again, because you wanted nobody to blame you for marking my life forever. You started the car. I begged for us not to leave. I needed to promise you, with all my strength, that I would never forget you. Your sad face had a distant look when you forbade me to write and asked the opposite of what I was offering you: oblivion.

I spent the summer at my aunt and uncle's at a fashionable beach. The recreational activity—swimming, sunbathing, having a snack, eating lunch, going for a walk, going to the movies or dancing—bored me. My behavior was rather strange: nothing appealed to me except what had not yet started.

I did not forget you. Every night I wrote to you and I put the letters carefully away inside a locked drawer, imagining that some day you would read them all one by one. It was a pathetic bit of happiness, I know, to think that my letters were adding up to a pretty thick pile which would keep you busy for many hours, in which you would inexorably be close to me. Everything you were doing that I did not know about made me jealous. Your comings and goings downtown, the people who were around you, your work. That summer you planned to finish up your dissertation, started long before and almost ready by then. You had asked me to help you out with the indexes, to order and classify the cards which were the product of five years of work. That would have permitted me to be with you all day. . . . Where were you with all your papers? Not to know, not to be sure filled me with sadness. If at least I had some news from you! You had not wanted my address. You tore up the paper that I wrote it down on for you and you covered your ears when, on the way home, I said it out loud.

"It is better for time to do its work."

"Does that mean you think time can wipe everything out?"

"It can, if we cooperate."

I was not cooperating. Summer was passing by, that comforted me. I was eager for fall to arrive, time to go back home. I did not know whether my father was going to decide to take me out of school, and prevent me from seeing you as well as having you for a teacher. Registration would be over at the beginning of September, and writing to my parents, I did not dare to ask them what their plans were concerning my "academic future." I was very lucky. Thinking that the three months' separation and the contact with boys would have cooled off my feelings, they registered me at the same school.

A week before classes started I arrived at Palma feeling pretty relaxed. I was expecting to find you. I could not risk phoning you, even less going to your house. I limited myself to walking around, even beneath your balcony, hoping to see you again. I went to the places where you and I had been together and quite often I thought I heard your footsteps. But you never showed up. I kept going back to our places, one by one; I was looking for something more than your footsteps, your scent, or the trace of your eyes upon the walls, the facades, the stones, the asphalt, the olive trees, the almond trees, the countryside, the flowers, upon the seawater or upon the rainwater. . . . I was looking for something more indefinable. It seemed to me that nothing could be what it had been after you had looked at it. Because all things, even the most insignificant, would forever carry your mark.

I did not see you until the first day of school. You were up on stage with the administrators and the other teachers. I watched you from the last row of chairs in the assembly hall. I don't think you noticed my presence, in spite of the efforts I was making to communicate with you. When the racket was over—the sugary voice of the school principal declared the academic year 1964–65 officially open "in the name of the Chief of State"—I thought I could finally see you up close. You left in a hurry with the other teachers, and all of you went to the reception that the school authorities put on every year. We did not meet. At two you had not come out yet. I could not do anything but go back home. The sycamore leaves were almost yellow in the eighteenth-century boulevards, a gust of wind took the first ones leaving the branch ridiculously naked. When it got tired of playing with them, it abandoned them right at my feet. I stepped on them and they crushed under my weight. Fall was starting, and I was just realizing it. The Rambla seemed longer and more inhospitable than ever. I felt imprisoned. The ramparts— because they are ramparts and not walls—of the convents of Santa Magdalena, the Theresas, and the Capuchin nuns were looming above me. Any moment, I thought, the wind will blow them down like leaves. . . .

I crossed the street without looking. A car braked not a foot away: it was your car. You came out looking frightened, saying, "I could have killed you!"

I hugged you so strongly, so furiously, that you staggered. You did not invite me to get into the car; I myself opened the door and got in, despite people's astonished looks. I was seeing you again. Your face seemed more tired, sadder, older. I stared at you. You seemed absent. You asked me where I wanted to go: "Do you want me to take you home?"

I did not answer. You had turned onto Reis Avenue when I said: "I want to be with you for a long time. I have missed you so!"

You parked the car in front of a furniture store. It was lunchtime. The city was almost empty. I needed your touch, your eyes, your hands, your lips. You knew it and with a sweet but firm voice asked me to understand the kind of situation you were in, and to control myself.

"Time has gone by and everything is clearer now. Our

relationship is senseless, it is not good for us to go on. I don't want to hurt you or hurt myself either. There is no point in going on with this love that leads nowhere, has no objective. . . ."

I did not answer although I did not agree with your argument. Because I knew with all certainty that the only objective of our love was simply love itself.

We saw each other only occasionally from that day on. We behaved with painstaking propriety. In class you treated me even more sternly than you treated my schoolmates. One day you even scolded me publicly because instead of turning in my homework I gave you a piece of paper filled with drawings, boats, little flowers, suns. You scolded me because you understood perfectly what I meant, and you had liked it. Your harshness was the mask concealing a weakness close to breaking through. I addressed you constantly, I asked you to repeat your explanations because I could not understand, I gave you a hard time, interrupting your lectures to make haughty remarks . . . and I always used an aggressive tone of voice that bothered you. I wanted you to recognize my presence. I was taking revenge for all you were making me suffer.

Near the end of the school year, when I started going out with that medical student who arrived in Palma from the Basque Country running away from the police, you got upset. You even spied on us. Many afternoons we would casually see you after class, on our way to the seafront. You acted as if you did not see us, but I know that you looked back through your rearview mirror until you lost sight of us. Jealousy was overtaking you, and it embittered you.

The day we ran into each other outside of school, after several months of coldness, you tried to be kind. You asked me, as if you did not much care, how things were going, you expressed an interest in Jaume, about what we were planning on doing, our—you emphasized the plural—projects. You tried to avoid looking me straight in the face. Your eyes were concentrating on the glass of Coca-Cola in front of you, on the crevices in the wooden table, on the pattern of the ceiling. You did not know what to do with your hands. I said your name. You do not know how many times I have pronounced it with an infinite delight, with the same pleasure as the first time, after you had asked me to drop the formal treatment. You were startled.

"What?"

"Nothing."

"Why did you say my name?"

"Because you weren't here. Can you tell me what is the matter with you?"

"The last days of the term are exhausting. I get tired. I don't see anything clearly, and you worry me. I was weak enough to get involved in that affair you no doubt regret now. Now your life has taken on a different course. . . . I feel happy for you. Jaume is a great boy too. . . ."

"You talk as if you were my mother."

"I assure you I would have liked to be."

I came to study in Barcelona. We wrote to each other. Your letters were very beautiful, not quite frank, intentionally optimistic; in them I could quite often find admonitions and pieces of advice. My letters told you about what I was discovering: the city, and people. They were sad, but my sadness, tinged with the ocher and the gray colors of the city, with the clouds and the walls, faded out between the lines of my handwriting and came to nothing. Maybe that is why my melancholy, my longing, and my grief were hardly perceptible once the envelope was closed and the stamp fixed on it. Occasionally, under the stamp, I would write with tiny letters some love words, just to surprise you if you ever decided to take the stamp off because of a low but precise voice telling you the place of the secret. I do not know whether Aladdin's genie, the fairy of the Golden Comet, or Ali Baba the expert ever informed you . . . you never said.

One night I wrote a really long letter to you, a mixture of confidence and confession, where my adolescence definitely came to an end. When I began to write I did not want to address it to you. I tried to invent some new addressee with whom I had no link, but I found it impossible to make such an effort of imagination. And since I insisted on forgetting your name and address, I wrote to the sea with the secret intention that the waves would take my message to your door. . . . I definitely spent the whole night with you. Sometimes the pen would move so slowly and delicately across the paper that it felt as if I was silently caressing you. Sometimes I would write with infernal calligraphy, not even separating the words. I explained to you why that specific night I refused to sleep and I stayed awake to write. I did not keep that letter. The wind took it away from my window in a thousand tiny pieces when sunrise started looking in through the shutters after the last streetlights faded out. If I had kept it, I would read a fragment now and copy it down for you, now that so many years have gone by. I remember the night, it was warm and starry. They were throwing a party at the next house. The echo of the orchestra's music came to me diminished, but still audible. The garden was full of lights among the branches of the trees. The dancing couples' silhouettes were outlined against the dance floor. . . . The humid air of the harbor comes to Via Laietana. With some effort the smell of the sea is also perceptible. One of my college friends was imprisoned in the basement of the police station, in a cell. They had arrested him in the morning while we were demonstrating. I was beside him, but they let me go with no problem, they did not even ask for my identification. He was caged up and I was free! I felt like I was a part of it, responsible for the lost roses and the fallen birds, guilty. Amid anguish and fear I probed my hope on paper. I refused to sleep. In spite of the sleepiness that pulled at my eyelids, my will kept them open. I stayed awake for the whole night. I wanted to share from the outside Miquel's empty hours in prison, without his knowing, to offer him my sleep and also a terribly sad scent of tenderness mixed with the music and the memory of you. Synesthesia, that is the name it goes by in the literary rhetoric manuals: tenderness was musical notes, the music was my feelings and, as always, the memory of you pervaded everything.

The years went by. May would arrive almost immediately after October. The end of the academic year followed the beginning with hardly a pause in between. Before I knew it, it would already be time for final exams. Blank, void, I did not know a thing about the course material. I had not attended class at all. In the morning, around eleven, I would go down to the university to take a walk in the garden or to sit down at a bench in the cloister. I would usually find some people from Majorca, who used to get together Sunday evenings for nostalgic suppers— *sobrasada*, Majorcan sausage, and pastries. . . . Theirs was a rather poor world, and it bored me; but I was comforted by the fact that often someone would mention your name—you had been a teacher to many of them.

Five years, the classes were of little interest, not even monotonous, just neutral. Lectures at the university, at the Athenaeum, at the colleges . . . colloquiums on sex, contraceptives, political parties, the 1967 referendum . . . (a prestigious professor analyzed the students' situation—fat, arrogant, vain, he imported his clothes from London; his wife took notes in the first row: she had so much difficulty following his line of thought. A Spanish scientist, neither exported nor exportable, refuted the theory of relativity with uncanny arguments. A middle-aged couple, at a round-table discussion, pointed out the living evidence of their love: five short, bad-mannered children squirming on their chairs and making trouble in the audience. And like those, a thousand more).

Exhibits. *Nova Cançó* festivals. (Raimon, with his shirtsleeves rolled up, a glorious morning at the Chemical Institute of Sarrià—Foix's and Gertrudis's Sarrià. Performance of the *Setze Jutges*; a still Catholic, and sentimental, Guillermina; a believing, childish Serrat. . . .) Books read on the recommendation of others: Freud, Marx, Joyce, Faulkner, and then later Vargas, Cortázar, García Márquez, Donoso, Lezama. . . . Movies I did not know your opinion about. Sunsets at Montjuïc, at Sitges, Arenys, Blanes. . . . Trips to the Montseny mountains and to the beach. Experimental plays. Poetry readings. Political rallies organized by Comissions Obreres and the Communist Party. Kisses from other lips, contact with other hands. . . . And life moved slowly in a hurry, the days were a long chill. I tried to cut you out of my memory—I wanted new branches for a new spring—and I could not do it. I could not uproot you.

We did not always meet during vacation. You traveled a lot those summers. You attended international mathematics congresses in Moscow, Paris, Tokyo, from which you would send me postcards: Red Square, the Eiffel Tower, the Royal Palace. . . . The text was so brief that the letters seemed to dance in the white space: "Greetings from Moscow, Paris, Tokyo. . . ." In this last city you met a Jewish scholar, a Nobel Prize nominee, a relative of Ben Gurion, extremely rich, it seemed, who made you dishonest propositions. . . . One day he showed up in Palma with the intention of taking you back with him. He wanted you to work with him at his university in the United States. He offered you as much money as you wanted, along with his disinterested support. In Palma everybody talked about it, because the scholar told the newspapers about his proposals. People said that you were making a fool of yourself letting such a good chance escape. And I wonder why you did not leave. But maybe I wonder because I think I can guess your motives.

A few months after getting my degree in mathematics I went to your house to invite you to my wedding. I was marrying one of my classmates, a Catalan with whom I had been going out for some months. Toni and I informed you of our wedding by means of an old-fashioned visit, a courtesy visit. Toni knew about our affair—I had told him down to the smallest detail. He thought it a beautiful and morbid story. You made a good impression on him, he found you intelligent, kind, despite the fact that he saw something strange, disturbing, darkly dangerous in your appearance.

The day of the wedding you told me that you liked Toni and that you wished both of us all the happiness in the world, all the happiness you would have liked to give me. You said it with trembling lips, as if a chill were moving up and down your body. I hugged you to thank you and I told you—did you hear me?—that I still loved you. Somebody saw how you covered your face with your hands, somebody saw you cry when in the evening you were going back home from the hotel where we had had dinner.

I do not know whether it will turn out that you ever see this piece of writing, or if you will understand it if Toni does give it to you as I asked him to. Months ago, when you came to Barcelona for a couple of days, I told you I was pregnant. The pregnancy is coming to an end. The doctor says that the baby will come into the world most probably within the next ten days. I am afraid, it scares me. I feel too weak and my strength is faltering. I think perhaps I will not know the girl, because it will be a girl, I am sure, and I will not be able to decide her name if I do not do it now. I want her to be called María, like you, and I also want my body to be thrown into the sea, not buried. I beg you to make sure they scatter my ashes into the depths of the unlimited immensity, in that place where water witnessed our love. I miss you, I miss the sea, our sea. And I leave you, my love, the sea as a token.

Translated by Alberto Moreiras from *Jo pos per testimoni les gavines*, © Carme Riera 1977.

Some Flowers

Honestly, the verdict wasn't just unfair, it was pre-posterous. Not only was the separation granted, but he won the suit and he got custody of the girl because she was already seven years old. Since I was considered guilty, he didn't have to give me a penny and I had to start working as a hotel receptionist. According to the experts, I should still be grateful not to have gone to prison for adultery.

I didn't regret having to live on my own. It had been too many years since I had let myself go, boring myself as well as my husband. I recovered many things I had lost: the pleasure of talking to my friends, of walking around in no hurry, of buying trinkets for myself . . . and of not having to give explanations to anyone. But I missed my daughter.

In spite of judges, trials, and sentences, the girl wanted to live with me, and not with her father. It was very hard, especially at the beginning, to give up her company, to tear myself away from her. Many days, going to work, I saw her from my car as she was waiting for the school bus with my mother-in-law, and I had to make a real effort not to stop and hug her and kiss her. Now that she has grown up and I have her trust she knows very well whose side she is on. I like having a modern daughter, with clear ideas, who is not going to fall into the same traps I fell into, who is not going to be forced into an ornamental, humiliating role, like I was.

It was because of some bouquets of flowers that my husband and I separated. Bouquets of flowers which arrived punctually at our house every day for a month. Bouquets of flowers, roses almost always, white, yellow, red, roses filling up every vase in the dining room, the living room, the studio, the bedrooms. . . . The first few times my husband, who never noticed a thing, to whom nothing mattered, did not even see them. One evening, as he turned his bed light off, he knocked a vase of violets off his bedside table and it fell to the floor. And then he noticed all the flowers in the house. . . . I enjoyed the quiver in his voice; he seemed jealous.

"What are so many flowers doing here? Who sent them?"

"No one, they brought them from the flower shop."

The next day he found a bouquet of fresh, intensely red roses.

He started to get nervous, threatening. I played the game, it amused me. He was upset that an alien presence had slipped into his property by means of some flowers. For the first time, I felt secure, even flattered. I tried to kiss him and then he came up with something I would never have believed of him:

"I'll denounce you for a whore!"

Yes, I realize I was wrong. I thought that by having flowers sent to me—flowers I myself had ordered from the nearest flower shop—I would get his attention, always so absent. I know it was a poor subterfuge, but back then, with my upbringing as an oppressed woman, I didn't know any better. Some days later, when I showed him the bill from the florist, he treated me worse than ever. He took it for an alibi to hide what was perfectly clear to him:

47

the flowers had been paid for by someone who had bought my favors, and the favors of a married woman— he said—are never paid for beforehand. . . . The time had come to think about a separation.

He pointed to the bouquets that were brought to our house punctually for a month as irrefutable evidence of my adultery. And the testimony of the flower shop's owner did not help me: he testified with absolute calm that he could not remember who had ordered those bouquets, he had many occasional customers, he had a bad memory for faces. . . . Meanwhile his eyes, mocking and also a bit frightened, looked at me as if I were out of my mind. Later on I learned that my husband had for many years been one of his best customers, and that he used to send flower baskets to the mistresses of certain brothels he frequented, when he had been pleased and satisfied.

Translated by Alberto Moreiras from *Jo pos per testimoni les gavines*, © Carme Riera 1977.

The Knot, the Void

Don't think I don't want to tell you. It just won't come out. I can't. This weight won't let me. It doesn't go away night or day, not even when I go to bed; I was going to say, when I go to sleep, but you already know I don't go to sleep. This weight, this knot I have inside my stomach is to blame. I used to be a hard-working woman, and everything excited me. You can't imagine how clean my house was! Look at my hands and my fingernails, don't you see they're almost eaten up by bleach and turpentine? I am a hard-working woman. Every year I used to whitewash my house twice. And all by myself, even the rabbit pen and the hen house. Well, not all the walls in the pen, because the one on the right was covered up by climbing plants. A beauty of a honeysuckle. It made the place so pretty even if I do say so myself. My husband liked flowers, and I liked looking at them. My thing was taking care of the house. . . . But now nothing suits me. And honestly, it is this weight, this knot that blocks even my breath. I can't swallow food, you know that. I can't bring anything near my mouth, it's a waste of time anyway. And I know the food is good! Sometimes I go into the kitchen and watch the gals cook. But I can't even get a mouthful down. . . .

Yes, I used to be a big eater, I was fat. Does it surprise you? Well, *very* fat, I weighed 160, and that's a lot for me, because I have small bones, look at these bones. I looked like a spinning top, my husband used to tell me, because I was nervous too, and I was always moving around. I didn't know how to be still! Listen, when we got the TV set I couldn't watch it. I'd much rather be taking a little walk or something, looking at the rabbits, to see if they were all right, if they were growing well. . . . Because, believe me, I really am fond of animals. And in the evening, when my husband stayed up to watch a movie or some show, I said good night and went to bed. The only thing I could stand on the TV were the commercials, because there were so many different ones, and they were amusing. A couple of them I know by heart. Like that one that goes: "Wash with. . . ." Okay, I won't tell you if you don't want to hear it. . . . But since I was always cleaning up I particularly listened to the ones about cleaning stuff, but wait, I didn't always buy what those gentlemen on TV wanted me to. Talk about cleaning, for me it was bleach on the floor and turpentine on doors and furniture. And good ones, not the ones with brand names, but the ones the druggist used to sell retail. It was best for me to buy ten gallons at a time. In the kitchen I used to have a barrel of each—I mean bleach and turpentine—because I needed them so often, it wasn't convenient for me to go fetch them every time. And you see, back then, with so much work, I didn't have any knots in my stomach. Not like now, now I have nothing to do but stand around like a fool . . . or start weeping any minute when people aren't looking because at my age it is embarrassing, I'm not a baby any more. But of course I also have my sorrows, and big ones. I know I am fine here, and that at my age it is natural enough for me to be a widow, even more so because my husband was fifteen years older than I. When he died I was sad. The first days I didn't know what to do with myself, being all alone and not having anyone to order me around, because, believe me, he only spoke to give orders or to scold me.

"Ain't dinner ready yet? Holy whores, this ain't got no salt on it!"

Or: "Haven't you fed the rabbits yet? Look at this woman—she doesn't even know how to think any more! Did you lose your brains?"

A month later I had calmed down; no one bossed me around, no one scoffed at me. The rabbits were doing fine, and I had more time to take care of things. No, it wasn't grief about my husband's death that caused this sickness; it was later, when my nephews brought me here, that I first started having trouble. They said they brought me here because I wasn't well. As an excuse they said that I spent all day cleaning up and putting things away or throwing them out, things that any healthy woman would have kept as a treasure. But listen, what I did throw away wasn't any good, like for instance I wanted to put turpentine on some drawers and I emptied them out and when I saw what was inside I thought I might as well get rid of it. It wasn't anything good, nothing valuable at least: the wedding portrait—I never liked myself in that picture anyway, with that black dress on—and a couple of postcards my husband sent me from Barcelona when he went there with some of his buddies, I think looking for hookers, excuse me. I must confess, just between you and me, I don't read much, so I could barely make out what he said on them. What good was it keeping them?

"Uncle's death has affected you, Aunt Bel," they said. "We'll take you to a rest home."

So you see, it's been a year now. I'm here, I can't complain, I have everything I need, but nothing is really mine. There are many of us here sharing the same roof.

I feel empty, except for this knot filling up the pit of my stomach, all cleaned out, as if I had whitened up my insides the same way I whitewashed the walls for the last time, two days before my nephews gave me a miserable sum for my house so that I could pay for my boarding here. I listened to the noise the moving van made as it maneuvered around out in the street. They took everything, that night I had to sleep on the floor. . . . Now inside me everything is dark, no light coming in through any crevice, no dust, all is empty, no door, no windows. . . . So you see, doctor, nobody should think it strange if any minute now I felt like undoing this knot, like filling it up with a cupful of bleach.

Translated by Eulàlia Benejam Cobb from
Epitelis tendríssims, © Carme Riera 1981.

A Cool Breeze for Wanda

The reason that the Viscount of Bonfoullat chose the
Lluc-Alcari Hotel for the summer was the same that
caused other clients to reject it: it had no air-conditioning.
For the old aristocrat, that was a great advantage, since to
him artificially cooled air was the most evil thing in the
world, conducive to colds, pneumonia, and worse. No one
would have suspected, however, that his aversion for air-
conditioning was related to his now-defunct love life, a life
which had begun exuberantly when he was still almost a
child, under the supervision of his father.

The most gorgeous maids of the household, specially
instructed by the noble gentleman Heribert Bonfoullat i
Gulenberg, had facilitated the young master's apprenticeship. Later on, when his voice started changing, it was the
music teacher's turn: a young lady from a ruined aristocratic German family protected by the Bonfoullats. She
showed her gratitude to the family by striving to please
the young man. Naturally she had the father's approval.
He himself sometimes attended the lessons in order to
check on the progress of his heir. Other times, hidden behind an expensive Chinese screen, he watched the im-
provisations carried out by the teacher and pupil and their

53

attempts to take their instruments to their utmost limits. And such was their fervor that more than once the Viscount, infected by the rhythm, rocked by the sweet cadence, executed the melody himself, without missing a beat.

Aware of his son's talents, he planned to introduce him later on to the aristocratic circle he frequented, recommending him especially to the crème de la crème among the ladies. Thus everything would stay in the family, and he would forestall the possibility of Heribert Jr.'s wasting his time, his virility, and his seed—or even worse, of his bestowing upon some predatory middle-class female the attributes with which God and Nature had endowed him.

That was when the sixth Viscount of Bonfoullat helped his son to discover the talent, which he himself also possessed, of distinguishing at first glance the quality of the female complexion, noting long before touching it whether its fine texture was due to chance (an error of Nature, something which unfortunately was happening more frequently of late) or whether it was caused by seven, eight, fifteen, or twenty generations of ancestors who had dedicated themselves entirely to the contemplative life. This life, according to the father, was the only one worth living, as long as one took care to enliven it periodically with hunting parties, trips to other countries, and erotic or military encounters. The contemplative life, lived quietly in the shade of the family tree, left plenty of time for the hands, lips, tongue, and other mobile parts of the body to abandon themselves with morbid passion to lovemaking. This innate tendency toward Eros was genetically transmitted and strongly influenced the physical appearance of the members of the family. No doubt an alabaster skin, almost transparent in certain ladies, revealing the azure veins where only blue blood coursed, was indisputable proof of origin. After this discovery, the future Viscount of Bonfoullat decided to consecrate himself only to pedigreed beauties and, because he was quite sure of their ancestry, he showed a decided preference for the ones in his family.

That was probably the reason why his overly puritanical married aunt took her daughters on a long voyage around the world. Heribert Jr. never forgave her that insult since, being an only child, those girls were his closest female relatives. As a consolation, the young dandy was invited to spend a few days with his father's lover, Wanda von Laderfoll, also a member of the German branch of the Viscount's family on the Gulenberg side, who possessed a magnificent château near Paris.

Heribert had heard talk of the statuesque Wanda's whims and eccentricities rather than of her beauty, and although he had met her as a child, he did not particularly remember her. When he saw her, he was overwhelmed. Wanda was a beauty, a splendid woman, no longer a girl, with immense violet eyes, steely and hard when they challenged a man, but also capable of the most tender glances in the world—eyes that could give life, condemn to death, or do both at the same time with an ancient Provençal skill. Heribert languished with desire as he imagined Wanda and his father engaged in voluptuous games. It was no use his wearing out cars in reckless races, terrorizing the woods with his hunts, or practicing calisthenics to exhaustion: Wanda obsessed him. Not for a second could he stop desiring her. He made up his mind to have her for his own, or die. He would appeal to his father's oft-proven generosity, he would challenge him to a duel, he would kill himself. . . . In fact, everything turned out to be a lot simpler, even easy. The two Heriberts made a deal: if Wanda agreed, the Viscount would cede part of his rights to his son. What is more, he would take strict turns with him. Mad with joy, the young Bonfoullat could not foresee what his stormy love was to cost him, nor could he imagine the fortune he would dissipate in a useless shower of diamonds, tears, and semen.

It all began one fateful summer in Nice, a hot summer

that brought death to the begonias in Wanda's carefully tended garden. Father and son vied with each other in charm and generosity. Wanda was kept busy opening the luxurious packages that arrived from the best stores in Paris, and trying on the expensive dresses that her knights in bondage ordered just for her from the most elegant designers in Europe. Happy and delighted, she in turn tried to please them with a deluge of charming smiles, suggestive glances, feverish words, and exciting gestures.

Each morning she would wish them a pleasant wait as she emerged from her room, wrapped in a long, revealing, cloudlike robe of cream-colored silk, on her way to the bath (she liked to spend long hours relaxing in the warm soapy water). For Wanda would engage in lovemaking only when the heat abated and the September mists appeared. Muggy weather stifled her, and the contact of her body with another gave her dreadful nausea if the temperature was above 65° F.

As soon as fall began, however, Wanda, perhaps stimulated by her long abstinence, would give herself over entirely to amorous games. She lived only to give and receive pleasure. Her voluptuous caresses were so arousing that her lovers found it hard to hold back, as desire spurred them right between the legs. But Wanda was extraordinarily expert in the arts of love. She knew how to lead her lovers, with exquisite delicacy and a courtesan's refinement, down the most pleasurable roads. As if she had been concocting a goose-liver pâté, she knew exactly the precise point at which to add a dusting of fine pepper to the aromatic truffle, in order to attain insuperable ecstasy time after time.

But that fateful summer the heat was unbearable. The Bonfoullats agonized over ways to relieve their desperate state as they watched the thermometer climb. Autumn seemed to them as beautiful, faraway, and impossible as the return of the French monarchy. And Wanda became more alluring every day.

The elder Viscount, discouraged by the forecasts of Europe's most outstanding meteorologists, decided to invite Wanda on a North Sea cruise, in a magnificent yacht which he offered to let her keep if she accepted. He realized how difficult it would be for Wanda to leave her summer house in Nice once she had gotten herself installed there, and the lady, as he expected, refused the offer. She didn't like to travel, and what need had she to complicate her life by going off on a boat?

The future Viscount took a more practical approach than his father. He decided that what he needed to do was to solve the summer problem once and for all. Otherwise it would haunt him for the rest of his life, which he of course could only envision at Wanda's side. He had to find a cooling system for the house. But it had to be mechanical, for fan-waving servants, no matter how skilled and dedicated, would never do, as Wanda would not permit them to witness her amorous diversions.

Now the young Bonfoullat, who was quite a sportsman, had some basic knowledge of mechanics. He tuned the engines of his cars himself, and had even competed in the Monte Carlo Rally, besides being one of its organizers. He knew that a car engine maintained the right temperature thanks to its fan. Except that they already had electric fans at Wanda's. She didn't like them, though, because of their noise, their clumsy motion, and boring rhythm. No, fans were no good either. He had to find another way to make air circulate, to turn hot air into cold. Surely, for the great minds who had invented the gramophone, the telephone, the piston-driven engine, this had to be child's play. . . .

The future Viscount of Bonfoullat told Wanda that he was going away for a few days. "I promise you that when I come back I'll bring you autumn weather," he said, kissing the tips of her rosy fingers as he took his leave, and added, "The first week I want preferential treatment. Tell my father. I expect he'll let me be the one to open the season."

Only the most intimate of Wanda's friends were invited

to witness the inauguration of the cold. It was the twentieth of August, and only 60° F inside the house. Everyone was amazed by the advances of modern technology. Two engineers, a Belgian and an American, were the authors of the miracle, which French workers had labored night and day for a fortnight to install. The contraption consisted of a huge bellows that caused the air to move in a whirlwind and maintained a constant temperature. To keep down the noise, an automatic music box which played the latest melodies had been hooked up to the device. Wanda was very fond of light music.

The future Viscount of Bonfoullat was congratulated by all except his father, who, despite his welcoming embrace, looked at him resentfully when he realized what was bothering him—the idea that the new must succeed the old. It was obvious that his son's car was faster and more practical than his own landau. For a moment he was troubled by the thought that perhaps Heribert was a better lover than himself.

Wanda had the delicacy to treat them both with the same deference. She made love to them strictly by turn, and never gossiped with one about the shortcomings of the other. As far as she was concerned, father and son were perfect. They both fulfilled her. Perhaps—she was a very faithful woman—she felt a certain inclination toward her cousin, to whom she was bound by so many childhood memories. At the same time, however, she had a weakness for her nephew, who had lost his mother at birth. . . . The Viscount of Bonfoullat thought it natural that Wanda should want to celebrate the new season with his son, as a reward for his efforts. After all, Heribert Jr. had made her the gift of unseasonably cool weather.

The new cooling system provided sudden results. A few hours after its inauguration, Wanda, naked but for a fuchsia satin robe, put her delicate hand on the sycamore door handle and opened her nephew's bedroom door. Heribert, fascinated by the apparition whose sculptural forms quivered beneath the soft garment, momentarily forgot the miserable cold that he had just caught and that caused him to sneeze continuously.

Like a wave rocked by the breeze, Wanda advanced toward him. And as if this had been her first time with a man, she undressed with virginal shyness. Slowly, she unbuttoned her robe. Her flesh, which resembled almond paste and whipped egg whites—she hated sunbathing, which was beginning to come into fashion—emerged amidst layers of soft lace. Her breasts, like two miraculously rounded spikenards, had a touch of red on the nipples, a detail that was sure to drive the young Bonfoullat mad, as Wanda well knew.

As she removed the tiny mother-of-pearl buttons from their buttonholes, she exposed a larger field of action to the runny eyes of Heribert, and to his hungry, soft, wet lips: her flat belly, her crotch, covered by a matted blond fuzz, her superb thighs, long legs, fine ankles, and finally her plump little feet with red-painted toenails. With a silent, harmonious, feline gesture, Wanda barely straightened her arms and her robe fell to the floor in a little mound of silk and lace. Then she went toward her lover with her hands outstretched, her head thrown back, her blond, curly locks waving with the rhythm of her steps.

Almost three months of abstinence and anguished waiting, three months wasted in cruel despair, in tortures worse than those of Tantalus, were about to be finally forgotten. Having conquered the heat, winter would be long and full of promise. Just two more steps and as their two bodies met the lover's desire would be sated. Heribert had Wanda in his arms. With all the gentleness called for by the occasion he pushed her toward the bed. The damask coverlet shivered slightly under the impact of their entangled bodies. Hungrily their lips consumed the grapes of their reciprocal kisses, savoring and enjoying their pleasure. Tenderly, the future Viscount ran his tongue over Wanda's body, slowing down in the places where he could penetrate her in his search for even more intimate contact.

He was bothered, however, by the discharge from his nose, which he tried his best to contain. Despite the force of his desire, Heribert realized that it was becoming difficult for him to scale the heights. He felt unsure of himself, fearful that a slip might plunge him into the most profound abyss. With great patience Wanda then undertook the delicate task of helping him to climb, pushing him along with her own hands as she encouraged him tenderly to forsake his fear of heights. But it was useless. Feverish and headachy, the Viscount fell into an exhausted sleep without having achieved what on other occasions he had so easily conquered.

In the morning Wanda sent for her cousin, asking him to visit her in her suite. But the Viscount could not accede: he was in bed with a fever, under a stack of blankets. Worried, Wanda went to see him. And observing that what he needed was warmth, she decided to keep him company. Quickly she undid the ribbons of her yellow robe, adorned with bands of fine needlework, and got into his bed. Heribert did his best to welcome her, but failed. A terrible chill had invaded his bones and was spreading over his skin, making him shiver. He couldn't even appreciate the warmth of Wanda's body, which lay on top of him in an attempt to bring him relief. Hurt and discouraged— Heribert had never failed her—and concerned by the seriousness of the situation, she sent for the doctor.

She spent the afternoon in her boudoir. She felt frustrated, and betrayed in a way. What use now was the cold weather? Why? For whom? She looked in the mirror. Her long blond hair was gathered in a bun. She felt tired. She had spent an anxious night listening to the nephew's sneezes, and in the morning she had run here and there after her cousin. She tried to hide the circles under her eyes with some rice powder, painted her eyelids, and put on lipstick, which she also touched to her nipples. She felt dressed, and better for it. Yes, definitely better. . . .

But whom would she regale with her hungry flesh? Thanks to the cold air she had recovered her desire—for naught as it turned out. She was still for a moment. Then she opened her red robe and looked at her naked body. It seemed to her that the mirror returned her image with an enticing notion. She took a few steps and heard a sweet melody, which she had heard before without paying attention, and which she now found pleasing. She sketched a dance step, stretched out her hands, surrendered her body. She did not have a partner, but that didn't matter. The breeze from the bellows moved in her arms, circled her waist, penetrated her underarms. It slid over her skin, stopped at her crotch, penetrated its moistness, blew into her vagina as it stimulated her clitoris with a sweet motion. And Wanda, who had known mad happiness in the arms of her many lovers, now felt a new sensation, different and intense. The compass turned, red and round like a rose, and the music moved its petals in the deep cleft. Wanda had discovered Time expanded, the heartbeat of the sea, the morning breeze that banishes the clouds, the afternoon's light step. An instant of pleasure could last for centuries.

With loving solicitude Wanda watched over her cousin as he perished from pneumonia, and wept abundantly at his grave. After the first few days of mourning, Heribert Jr., heir of the title which his father had borne with so much honor, reminded Wanda of her promise. His cold was better, although he felt very sad, for in a way it was he who had caused his father's death. Only Wanda's love could reconcile him to life.

She agreed, but the result was a failure. The new Viscount was suffering from temporary impotence, as the doctor diagnosed after a careful analysis of the symptoms. Wanda did not seem unduly worried by the fate of her ex-lover. Still, she decided to help him. In order to excite him, she invited him to watch her make love to the bellows' breeze.

For her, who was usually so reserved, that was a high favor indeed. Bonfoullat couldn't get over how Wanda gave herself to her new lover with the pagan fervor of a Vestal. She advanced with priestly gestures, as if she were carrying out a religious rite, her hands outstretched toward the cold-air outlet. Her body close to it, she started a frantic, somnambulistic dance. Her breath became heavier and ragged, her sighs more frequent. Bonfoullat, tense, red, ready to burst, went to her, but Wanda pushed him away. Prone on the floor, she cared only for the pleasure that filled her, and tried to eternalize her orgasm. Heribert's semen fouled the floor, the walls, and even the ceiling. It was a huge wad—the summer's reserve—and it left him exhausted.

In the days that followed Wanda and the Viscount pursued the same amusements. Wanda spent her time naked, locked in her boudoir, in lustful dances and frantic orgasms. Heribert, no matter how hard he tried, was not able to possess her. Troubled and disconcerted, excited to a frenzy by the continuous spectacle before him, he scattered his semen everywhere, heedless of the large puddle that formed on the floor and of the spatters that besmirched the rich upholstery and draperies.

Despite his youth, Bonfoullat fell seriously ill. The doctors recommended total rest, for his potency was in danger. Toward the end of October, the weeping Viscount said farewell to Wanda. He was on his way to a Swiss sanatorium. He knew that he had lost her forever.

Months later he received a letter from his aunt's accountant in Nice, announcing her death. They had found her naked, her arms clasping the only bellows that was still functioning.

Translated by Eulàlia Benejam Cobb from
Epitelis tendríssims, © Carme Riera 1981.

Miss Angels Ruscadell Investigates the Horrible Death of Marianna Servera

The door was open. As I came up I heard the sound of footsteps inside the house. I assumed they knew I was there and I waited, not daring to go in, hoping that someone would come out. I had rung the bell twice. "Hello!" I shouted, but nobody answered. Suddenly a shutter opened.

"You've got to yell louder. He's as deaf as a post."

I stomped on the tiles of the entrance hall with the heels of my sandals.

"Hello. I don't want to intrude. . . ."

The room was neat. Dark portraits of ancient faces hung on the whitewashed walls. I walked in.

"Mr. Binimelis!"

"Who is it? I'm coming, I'm coming!"

In the slit between the curtain and the floor I could see a pair of feet coming toward me, dragging their heels.

"Perhaps I'm bothering you. . . ."

"Talk louder. I can't hear you. What do you want? Did the agency send you?"

"The agency? No."

"I don't have any money. I don't want to buy or sell anything."

"No, no, I haven't come for anything like that. I'm a

historian and I wanted to talk with you about one of your ancestors, the priest Binimelis."

That time he understood me and pointed to a portrait. The tiny, birdlike eyes stared at us out of the red, full-cheeked, doubled-chinned face of the man who had been a member of the Inquisition. The painting dated from Ciutat, 1696.

"At that time he was about fifty. He must have already been suffering from gout."

"Did he die of apoplexy?"

He did not answer me.

"And what put the bug in your ear about my uncle?"

"The trial of Marianna Servera, sir."

His laughter resounded through the house. It seemed to shake the roof, and I felt frightened. I would never have imagined that the thought of a poor woman burned at the stake could make anybody laugh.

"I'm working on the Inquisition in Majorca, and since I'm spending a few days in Lluc-Alcari and they told me you lived here. . . ."

"That's a fine business. I've done my own investigating too, you know!"

"How fortunate! Then my interest won't surprise you. I'm doing a thesis on the last trials, and I'd like to know whether you have any documents or papers that mention your uncle's role."

"Sure I've got papers! A whole archive even! Would you like to see it? And I know all about it. I don't know if the papers will be any use to you, but . . . my ancestor and I have much in common, and I think that you. . . ."

"I'd be very thankful if you could show me what you have saved. If it's not convenient right now I can come back some other day."

"Tomorrow, tomorrow evening. How about nine o'clock?"

He was waiting for me seated on a low rush chair, enjoying the evening coolness in the little garden, one of the

few in Deià where there were hardly any plants. A cat
slept curled at his feet. Then he ushered me into the
house, and led me to a small room lined with books.

"As you can see I like to read, or rather I used to. Now I
can scarcely see, and my eyes get tired if I have to focus. I
prefer other amusements."

He seemed to be waiting for me to say something, but I
didn't, because I didn't know what to say. He went on.

"May I call you by your first name? You're so
young. . . . If you're carrying a tape recorder, get rid of it.
I don't want anybody stealing my voice."

His hands, like wilted claws with long, black fingernails,
felt my purse. It made me sick to see them.

"No, I didn't bring a recorder. Just paper and pen. . . ."

"Do you like wine? Would you like some nice wine from
the sacristy?"

He went out and returned with a dusty bottle.

"It's been waiting for us for seventy years!"

He uncorked it, filled two glasses, picked one up and
raised it: "To my uncle Miquel Binimelis, may he rest in
peace!"

I sipped the wine. It was too sweet, cloying, a bit rancid.

"Yesterday after you left I thought about what you
would ask me. I looked at the materials I have and since I
couldn't sleep—when you get old you don't sleep much,
you know—I wrote these lines. I think they'll help you."

"Thanks very much. May I look at the archives?"

"If you think you need to later on . . . but start by reading this."

He handed me some sheets and made me sit beside him
on a dirty armchair with torn upholstery.

Marianna Servera was the daughter of the owners of Son Casals.
At the time of her trial in 1691 she was twenty-four, so she must
have been born in 1667. I haven't been able to confirm that date,
since the parish records were destroyed in 1835, when the
rioting crowds burned down the church. She was the eldest of
six, and as a child she went to the nuns' school, where they

taught her catechism and arithmetic. She inherited from her mother the beauty that was to be her downfall. Her hair reached down to her breasts, which were high, white, and well shaped. Two breasts like two quinces among the flowers, two little buttons that stood up under her bodice.

I looked up at the old man. He was watching me with amusement. It bothered me that he had noticed my surprise, but I decided to go on.

Marianna learned to work at home and in the fields. At fifteen, she decided to become a nun, but her family didn't like it. Her parents thought that she wanted to trade her hard country life for an easier one. Besides, the story of Sister Tomaseta, who is today the patroness of the next village, Valldemossa, was quite popular among the peasant girls nearby. They all wanted to go into the convent. It was a fad. And there were many boys after Marianna, and lots of men who courted her. This made the parents think that she could marry well. Marianna's thighs were soft; greedy fingers seemed to melt in her buttocks, where they would have stayed ad infinitum had they not guessed that they had not yet reached their destination.

Marianna's parents did not let her become a nun in the Convent of Santa Clara, so one night she tried to run away. She left at dawn with her little bundle, and headed for Ciutat, but unfortunately a neighbor recognized her, made her climb into his cart, and took her back to Son Casals. Her father locked her up in the attic and starved her. They say he would only give her two slices of bread every other day, and a jug of water. Marianna cried and prayed all the time, asking God to help her. As you can see, Marianna was on her way to becoming a saint.

One fine day the village priest, who was my uncle, Miquel Binimelis, took an interest in Marianna. He talked with her parents and advised them, after seeing the girl, to let her out of the chamber where they had imprisoned her. He gave his word of honor that Marianna would never run away or disobey them again.

Marianna, looking wan, saw once again the light of day. Her dark, brilliant eyes had lost their lively look, and she couldn't stand the sunlight. Her eyelids fluttering, she would quickly fall asleep. Her once-fresh mouth, the fleshy lips accustomed to biting greedily into ripened fruits in thankfulness to Our Lord for

His mercies, hung limp and graceless. Her other charms, except for the most secret ones, had also suffered. Her legs were skin and bones. Only the flower between her legs had kept its curls intact. It was an exuberant, perfumed bush which, because it was planted on good ground, had outlasted her captivity, even if no sun had warmed it and no rain watered it. Soon, however, with the help of my uncle (may he rest in peace) Marianna became her old self again. . . .

I looked up from the papers. I couldn't stand to read any more. I wanted to tell the old man to stop making fun of me, that I wasn't interested in his erotic frenzies. I was only looking for information about a trial. But he was looking at me sarcastically, and I didn't dare say anything.

"Go on. Nothing of what I have written is useless, and if later on you want me to show you the archives. . . ."

At this point in the story, I have to make the following observation: if only my uncle had not been moved by Christian charity! If only he had let Marianna alone in the attic of Son Casals! Perhaps now we in this village would have our own saint, or at least a blessed patron like the people in Valldemossa, and we wouldn't have to be ashamed that one of our neighbors was burned at the stake. But the ways of the Lord are strange sometimes!

Father Binimelis persuaded the owners of Son Casals to let their daughter pursue the religious life, without entering a convent. All they had to do was give her a little toolshed some distance away, where she would plant a little garden, tend the farm's goats, and lead a quiet hermit's life without being seen by anyone. Marianna's parents agreed.

Uncle Binimelis often visited his spiritual daughter and counseled her in religious matters. With her new life Marianna's beauty returned, and her body was once more firm and plump. Her breasts seemed to be bursting out of her bodice, and under her peasant skirt her generous thighs strained against her knickers. Her face regained its color, and her greedy mouth with its beatific smile once more was able to bite into the fruits that Our Lord in His infinite mercy bestowed upon her.

Marianna's beauty tempted the Devil. Neither the prayers and sacrifices of the unhappy girl, nor the good advice of Father Binimelis were of any help. At night Lucifer himself would come to Marianna's room and lie down beside her on the straw where she slept. With his tail he would tickle her breasts until her nipples grew hard and red as two little embers. With his burning tongue he caressed her lips and licked her ears. Although the first few times Marianna was able to get rid of the Devil by making the sign of the cross and sprinkling holy water on his tail, which shrank up like an accordion, soon she capitulated to his siege. My uncle, who almost killed himself trying to help her, begged, pleaded, and did penance in vain.

According to the wisdom of moralists, the temptations of the flesh are far more powerful when they are inspired by Satan himself. His turgid torch knows no stopping inside a woman, and produces a pleasure as intense as the desire to prolong it. Trembling and feverish, Marianna thought only of the arrival of the infernal monster, when she would be ridden by that diabolical body and flung in a frantic gallop toward perdition. Sometimes the visit lasted hours, others just a few minutes. Marianna was left trembling, naked on her straw pallet, her thighs dripping with the juices that leaked out of her vagina, and wishing only to be penetrated again.

Once my ancestor, the Reverend Binimelis, found her naked, her legs shamelessly open, waiting for Lucifer. When she saw my uncle she called to him like a madwoman, and offered herself to him. Uncle Miquel tried to advise her and make her see the magnitude of her sin. But she insisted and, rising, threw herself into his arms. With expert hands she felt for his genitals while she whispered wild obscenities. She had confused the priest with Satan. She was obviously possessed.

After making the sign of the cross a few times, Uncle Miquel returned in a panic to town, and decided not to resume his visits to Marianna. In his fright, he hesitated to tell the Holy Office of the terrible event. Perhaps he held off reporting her in order to avoid a scandal, but matters got much more complicated because of the Fiend.

One evening Marianna showed up in town. Naked, covered only by her hair, which had grown all the way down to her buttocks, she went screaming and uttering dreadful blasphemies to the rectory: "Come back, Lucifer, take me. I'm yours and no one else's. Put out the fire, Lucifer, I beg you!" Her cries woke up the townspeople. My ancestor opened the window to shush her, but it was useless. While he was putting on his vestments and looking for the aspergillum in order to exorcise her, his housekeeper, a feisty woman who had only been in the rectory a month, threw a bucket of cold water on Marianna. That calmed her down, but it was my uncle's exorcism that cured her. Once she was freed of her demons, Marianna burst into tears of remorse, and kneeling at the priest's feet could only kiss his hands in gratitude. Exhausted, she spent the night in town. The next morning Father Binimelis decided to harness the mule to the cart and go to Ciutat. The scandal was already out.

The old man, half-asleep, was leaning his head against the wing of his chair. His lips, sticky with syrup, were parted. The bottle was almost empty. I could have left quietly, but I decided not to. I felt a strange fascination for the story.

You can imagine the rest. It's well known. Marianna went to the Holy Office's prisons in the convent of Santo Domingo. The trial began quickly, which was unusual. Father Binimelis's testimony played a key part in it. In a desperate attempt to save herself, Marianna, doubtlessly under the influence of Satan, accused my uncle of having raped her one night in her shed, disguised in a horrible mask. Not until she was put under torture did she stop insisting that her confessor, dressed up as the Devil, had seduced her. For an entire year he had come to her at any time of the day or night and had forced her to commit carnal deeds with him. At first she had refused, but later she gave in, and finally she wanted him all the time. The rack brought her to her senses and she saw clearly that it was Satan who had possessed her. She was sure of that. Besides, the informers were able to find, among the footprints of the herd that Marianna kept near her hut, the mark of a he-goat.

Having confessed, Marianna was convicted and burned at the stake, for being possessed by the Devil, on March 7, 1691, before the crowd that had gathered below Bellver castle. All the people of Deià went to see her, so that their faith would not be in doubt. They say that among the loudest voices was that of the housekeeper: "Death to the lying witch. Put a flaming torch in the place of her sin! Let her burn!" Uncle Miquel pardoned her before she went to the scaffold. Thanks to his intercession before the Holy Office, Marianna was decapitated before being burned, to make her death easier.

My ancestor returned to his rectory in Deià, took care of the church and built a new cemetery. He suffered an intense attack of hypochondria a few weeks after Marianna's death. In some papers I have kept he even blames himself for the poor unfortunate's death. If he hadn't advised her parents to let her become a hermit the Devil would not have had it so easy. Of course the same thing had happened to Sister Tomaseta, the patron saint of Valldemossa, and she resisted. The Enemy can attack young virgins from anywhere. Don't they tell how he used to come out of the laundry drain to visit the Blessed Tomasa?

Thanks to his housekeeper's care, Na Francina, the priest slowly got better. He died ten years later of gout, as you know. Because of his role in the trial he was made a member of the Inquisition, a charge which he carried out with pride, watching out for the Catholic faith.

I left the papers on the table. The old man was nodding with his mouth open. I went to the bookshelves, which were filled with old tomes with extravagant titles, *Erotika Biblion*, *Memoirs of a Maiden*, *Christ Never Was*, *Manual of the Perfect Fornicator*. . . . I didn't dare pick any up. Mr. Binimelis was watching me with his mocking little eyes which, with their slightly perverted gaze, reminded me of the priest's in the portrait. He smiled.

"Did you like it, Marianna?"

"What? What do you mean? My name is Angels."

"Don't fool with me, Marianna. I am Miquel Binimelis!"

He tried to get up. I ran to the door. I could hear his panting and his dragging footsteps.

"Marianna, Marianna!"

His deafening cries filled the house. I ran out into the street. I was afraid. In the dark, I saw two shadows approaching, and then I recognized them. They were Charles Flower and a Catalan boy who were staying in my hotel. They seemed a little drunk. I asked them to walk with me. My car was parked on the road and I had to pass the Binimelis house again.

"But you were going in the opposite direction. . . ."

"Maybe she likes whiskey, like us. . . ."

It seemed crazy to have to tell them what had happened. I walked along with them. I could no longer hear the old man's voice. Suddenly the shutters clattered open, "Hey, young lady! Sorry I didn't tell you yesterday that the man is crazy, out of his mind. Sometimes the agency sends him—I mean, he has women over. . . . You know how it is. But I heard everything and I would have come down if I'd had to. His brother, Don Tomeu, he's the one who could help you. He's the one who's got the archive. Don Miquel, poor man, he's only got dirty books, dirty filthy books."

Helena Valentí

Helena Valentí

Helena Valentí *Barcelona, 1940*

Creative works   *L'amor adult*. Barcelona: 62, 1977. Short stories.

La solitud d'Anna. Barcelona: 62, 1981. Novel.

La dona errant. Barcelona: Laia, 1986. Novel.

That life can sometimes be a balancing act is no surprise.
But Helena Valentí's image of Maria in "Children" walking the tightrope of a tense relationship is one that strikes
a chord as it underlines the various related opposing
forces in this and other works. Man-woman, dream-reality
develop into man-woman-friend-other; dream-reality-
mist-clarity, while the protagonist constantly tries to keep
her balance with increasingly difficult footwork.

  Whether this footwork is worth the trouble becomes the
inevitable question. Most of the author's protagonists are
female, many of them trying to live with a man, but constantly depleting their psychic energy explaining, arguing,
trying to communicate without success.

  Valentí's feminism is not didactic or moralizing. She
wants to show us alternatives to the norm, creating protagonists whose problems are existential questions, and in
that sense universal. Perhaps the particular situations and

the decisions that have to be made exist because the character is female in a patriarchal system, but basic choices between security and freedom form the bottom line.

Valentí writes about situations, ideas, and new possibilities rather than about characters or psychology. The male bonding she describes in "The Other" is much more everyday than in the hallucinatory Borges story on the same theme, "La intrusa." The exclusion of women from the masculine world, and some of the difficulties of female bonding result in the solitude which gives title to her first novel.

Writing as a way to give strength to people is very important to Helena Valentí. Just as she has received strength and inspiration from certain authors like Doris Lessing, she wants to continue that chain, breaking the isolation of women from each other, fighting against the solitude she has seen and described. She has been called pessimistic, and she does not mind that—it is so subjective, a matter of points of view. But she does not want to be depressing, for that would be debilitating—just the opposite of one of her *raisons d'écrire*.

Translating works into Catalan, and sometimes Castilian, has often paid Valentí's bills, and also had an effect on her style. She writes carefully, with a precision and an economy of language that sometimes approach starkness. When she was working on one of Doris Lessing's books, she almost felt overwhelmed by the power of the other writer, and had to rethink her own writing. Translation has taught her to work the language; unfortunately, it also keeps her from writing as much as she would like.

Translated by Inma Minoves-Myers from
L'amor adult, © Helena Valentí 1977.

Children

The purring of the engines muddled Maria's thoughts while she yielded to the sway of the misty surroundings, which were as vague as her own emotions; the triangular formation of a group of seagulls flying over the stern was her only precise point of reference with the external world. She had gone through passport control somewhat absentmindedly, passively letting the officer turn the pages of the document in silence; he was trying to discover why this foreigner, who wasn't even coming from an old colony of the Empire, dared to go through the immigration controls with such indifference. When he found the official seal that allowed her to enter the island without restrictions, he could no longer resist and he raised his eyes, asking for an explanation: "I am married to a subject of Her Majesty." She had to make an effort to loosen her lips.

The ship had sailed almost empty and the landing was quick and simple, allowing her to remain in her foggy state of mind. But when she went into the station to wait for the train to London, she was taken by surprise by the style, so remarkably English, of the red, compact coaches and their perfectly finished door and window frames; inside, she noticed the waiting room with the velvety curtains and chairs, and the distant, dispassionate look of the passengers, in solitary and concentrated communication with their own souls.

The train followed the gentle curves of the landscape of Kent, made up of nooks and corners of superimposed levels, which sometimes ran along without touching and other times converged in irregular lines, forming perfect spaces for the tiny and huddled world of squirrels, moles, badgers, and small rabbits. Immense tree branches bowing to earth offered homes to owls and the teddy bear who escaped from the children's room, in a house around the corner.

And this is how the English continue to live their lives, with the look of disconcerted children who couldn't find the hiding place of the teddy bear or tinker toy man. From then on, never again capable of being surprised, they are resigned to inexplicable losses and discoveries.

Loud voices in Italian and the banging of opening and closing doors could be heard from the corridor. A woman stuck her head through the compartment door asking in broken English if there was seating space. She brought in two children and left. A few minutes later, she returned and told the children that she was in the compartment next door, and gave them some rolls. Shortly after that, the conductor came in with a somewhat heavyset Italian man who was the father of the children. He seemed surprised by the fact that his family was already so well settled. Then he sat humbly on a suitcase in the corridor, serving as a link between the compartments where his family was scattered.

When everybody got off at Victoria Station, Maria counted six children walking next to the big *mamma* and the round father, all loaded with packages and suitcases, like a forest of thick oak trees. Through its branches she saw Marc waiting for her, and while he kissed her, she noticed out of the corner of her eye that the *mamma* of the six children was pregnant.

Maria felt taller than the people gathered by the train; she felt like the rare specimen in a flock, with brighter feathers and turned slightly away from all the others. She was not somebody's *mamma*, daughter, or anxious wife wanting to end a lonely trip. No one, not even Marc, knew where she was coming from, nor that her stop was only a passing concession. The air of admiration with which Marc surrounded her filled her with sweetness, and she let herself be drawn by the affectionate thread that gently steered her toward the exit.

That somewhat tangled thread was wrapping her up little by little like sweet pink cotton candy. Entangled in questions that she had decided not to answer, she went from lies to truth, and she started laughing as she leaned back against the seat cushion in the taxi. The bright light from a streetlamp hurt her eyes, which she closed, dazzled, as she said in a soft voice: "Let me be, I'll explain everything later." She began to climb the stairs that led to the tightrope; she held her arms out so she would not fall and found that the rope was too slack, or maybe it was lack of practice, too many days had gone by since she had walked it.

Standing in front of the closet, she hung up the dresses from her suitcase; she took care so that they would hang straight; she smoothed the wrinkles and the odd folds that they had picked up during the trip. She also looked over the dresses that she had not taken with her, making an effort to keep herself as busy as possible so that she wouldn't hear the noise Marc was making in the kitchen preparing supper.

Once again, she had to get used to keeping her balance on the tightrope, she thought. On the floor, to one side, were Marc's dirty socks and buttonless shirts; the bed was

very poorly made. Worse than that, though, were certain
new decorations, enterprises of his or of a friend of his
(they had never managed to share the same friends); for
example, that wire twisted in the shape of a flower, nailed
to the wall, and the red velvet fabric on the armchair. She
sat on it, and could not deny that it was a good idea, for it
softened the impact of the broken springs thrusting
against her legs. Velvet, however, picked up dust easily.

"Do you like it?" he asked, watching her happily. "I
found it in the market in Brixton. One shilling."

"Yes, it's fine," and he moved toward her. The sweetness was surrounding her once more. Her eyes collided
with the wire flower, flower or butterfly, she thought;
something was irritating her.

"Can you tell what it is?"

"A butterfly."

"No. It's a woman. Mel made it."

Aha. The irritation was taking over. She felt the danger
of losing her balance; she had always been jealous of Mel
and this awakened strong possessive feelings about her
husband. She made an effort to go on, pressing the tips of
her toes against the tightrope; she got up and went toward the kitchen.

They ate supper in silence. She tried very hard to say
something. She could only think of things that she realized were worrying her. The strangeness of the possessive
instinct. She tried to remember a funny anecdote in an
effort to keep the lines of communication open. She still
needed fresh air, and the intimacy of closed rooms horrified her. Finally she found a solution.

"Have you watched much TV?"

"No. I almost took it back to the store."

On the BBC's second channel they were showing a film
about childbirth. When she saw that, Maria burst out
laughing.

"Here we go again. Adorable England."

Marc looked at her without understanding; he had

never thought that being English was any different from being anything else.

"And afterward they will discuss the well-being of the mother and child."

In fact, the film was being watched by a group of men and women seated around a semicircular table.

They continued to watch the program. The woman was lying in a hospital bed, covered with a white sheet; her feet were held up by some loops, and very heavy socks went up to her knees. Near her head there was a bottle with a tube connected to her arm. Three people in white tunics and face masks were examining her lower abdomen. They had steel or iron instruments in their hands. One of them came close to her and started poking inside of her with the instruments. He went away. Another one followed him; he inserted a hook into her. The third put his instrument on her belly. Everything was done in silence, as if no one was even breathing.

The one with the hook started pulling. The head was coming out; they saw a pair of tiny eyelids squeezed tightly shut and the cord twisted around the baby's belly. The program was in black and white.

"Gray and sordid," thought Maria.

The people gathered around the semicircular table started to discuss the case, gesticulating with animation.

Maria and Marc watched the program from the bed, with the light off. They had not closed the curtains and Maria was observing the outline of the city against the sky. At that moment she saw a flashing light coming through the air toward her. She looked at it attentively because she thought it was coming straight toward the bed, then she distinguished the metallic fish shape of an airplane. She closed her eyes and tensed her body. Slowly the noise arrived and the windowpanes shook lightly.

Maria's dream that night.

Maria lived in a house with a long hallway where an old

man walked; he had a very big head and stooped shoulders. She looked at his face: it was broad, with bags under his eyes and very heavy eyelids. His large mouth was surrounded by tired wrinkles. The man's skin was soft, loose, and flaccid. Maria knew the man was her lover and she was having a nightmare.

She started to fight against her anxiety, making an effort to remember happy and light moments. She was telling herself that she was happy, so all the rest must be a mistake. Finally, she remembered that she was married to Marc.

"I'm hopeless," she thought about her double life, as if she were incapable of accepting a single thread: a simple and normal life.

"This has to stop." She wanted to free herself of the weight on her stomach and she decided she would leave the old man. "At the end of the summer I'll leave him forever."

Then she felt sorry for him.

She was still anxious when she woke up. She looked at Marc sleeping and she felt a deep tenderness, suppressing her desire to touch him. Then she understood that the old man of the dream was compassion, the price his love was forcing her to pay.

She fell asleep again. Suddenly, she saw Marc's green eyes as if they were a cat's clear gaze. She felt afraid.

Later she realized that she had Marc in her arms and that she was holding him against her breast. But his glance was escaping upward, away from her. She felt scared again and the dream softly faded away.

They had been married for five years. They had not wanted children, nor would they ever have any, they said. She didn't talk about it anymore because it was no longer necessary. She knew that he was even more certain than she. He had told her: "You would be a disaster as a mother."

She knew that was absurd, but she never complained about it because she knew that as a wife she was indeed a disaster. She went to extremes, from being very domestic to not being around the house at all, at times even having long escapades in which she fell madly in love with a man who would always end up disappointing her. When she came back she would tell Marc:

"This time it was a KGB agent."

"An impotent sadist."

"A frustrated writer who took his revenge on women."

Marc had never shown any signs of jealousy and she guessed that those adventures had become a necessity for the two of them. She even thought that if one day she didn't return, he would not make the effort to go after her.

"Perhaps that's what he wants and he hasn't realized it yet."

Maria knew that she preferred fear to compassion. Fear was light, and even though she didn't understand what she was afraid of, she was sure that fear made her strong and gave her a push to leave, knowing she would never return. The image of the adventuresome woman traveling with a few suitcases had always attracted her.

Two groups of people were gathered in a medium-sized room that had an open stage in the dark to one side. There were two doors—one open to the street and the other open, through a curtain, into a bar where draft beer was sold. On one side there was a group of young women; on the other, a mixed group of girls and women, and a few men. The women in the first group were wearing jeans or long skirts, their hair was uncombed and they had a wild look. The people in the other group were well dressed; they were of modest appearance and rather severe.

An enormous picture of a woman shouting hung on

the wall behind the first group. A woman's voice was asking, "When we come home from work, who makes supper?"

"Before leaving the house, who makes the beds?"

"And who puts the children to bed? How many meetings in your factories have you had to miss because your husbands refused to put the children to bed, those children who are their sons and daughters, even though you wouldn't think so?" A man all alone in a corner looked up with hostility.

The young woman shut up. The women in the first group kept quiet, letting the ones in the second group talk. Finally, one of them said, "Yes, women's oppression is unquestionable, but men don't have an easy time either."

"That's their problem," snapped one from the first group. Her face turned red as she continued, "They know very well what their problem is, and we will not stop them from fighting. But, they do stop us and they make fun of our fight. Let them be, just keep them off our backs."

She spoke blindly, passionately, her eyes burning with rancor, unaware of anything but her smoldering rage. Maria felt an electric charge going through her, and she thought, "Our hate toward men is the hate that we have toward our feelings of compassion."

Another poster from the movement nailed on the opposite wall caught her attention. In it there were two superimposed photographs: the one in the background showed the attractive, naked young man from Botticelli's *Primavera*; in the foreground was the wrinkled face of an old woman. She remembered the discussion when she tried to oppose the idea of the poster. She had been the only one in the whole group who spoke against it, without very convincing arguments (let's leave art out of it). At that time, she had not understood why the idea seemed revolting to her. Now, of course, she did. The idea of contrasting a young beauty with the face of an old woman was a cry for compassion for the weak one.

84

One of the other women was talking about the same thing:

"It seems to me that the problem is children. You say that men are capable of taking care of young children, perhaps so. But it is us who bring them into the world, and the person they need is either their mother or another woman. When a young child gets sick, who stays home from work? The woman does, it's never the man."

"Why not? Why don't we force them to?"

"Why should we? To us, it feels natural."

The woman who was speaking looked robust; she dressed well, in the style of a blue-collar worker with a good salary. Maria pictured her as a union leader, defending the rights of a female co-worker having to be absent from her factory job because her son was ill.

The discussion continued about what was and was not natural. The women who argued in favor of natural instincts lacked convincing arguments, and it was apparent that the discussion tilted in the other direction. At any rate, the real discussion had stopped with the worker's definitive answer, grounded in common sense. The arguments against natural instincts were subtle and elaborate, but who believed them? Maria thought that what they were essentially defending, without admitting it, was the right of women to go against their own instincts. They were attacking the imposition of women's most spontaneous and profound feelings which had been converted into duties, burdens.

Maria didn't stop thinking.

"The woman who expresses hate against men is doing other women a favor. Hate is the first step in our own search."

"Isn't it counterproductive to accept such a destructive feeling as a first step toward our search for identity?"

"It's the other side of the coin—compassion, which men have exploited and now we must bury and grind into the ground."

85

"What about love?"

"Love of what, of whom? Let's not accept love in the abstract, let's talk about love for something concrete. When we say love, what do we mean?"

"Sexuality."

"Then . . . let's call it the love of life. And everyone has to live life their own way—however they can."

Saturday, Maria's period began and she needed to start her birth control pills again. The day before, she had gone to the pharmacy to get them, but now she couldn't find them. Immediately she yelled at Marc: "I can't find my pills. Come and help me find them."

As soon as she said that and saw Marc starting to look for them, Maria went directly to the kitchen, opened the trash can and found the box. She knew very well that the day before, after coming back from the pharmacy, she had thrown them away as if by instinct.

Maria had often said two things since her youth. One, that she would not have any children. The other, that she would not be the one to take birth control precautions.

"I've done my part deciding I don't want to have children. I want the man to be aware that I don't accept the total responsibility by myself."

But over the last year, she decided that if she wanted to continue her escapades, she would have to deal with it. For Maria, that decision meant the dissolution and death of a dream.

Spring had come to the city, or at least to the edges of the city. One could sense its presence behind the foul-smelling smoke, rising like a gigantic bird with its wings spread over the smog of the city. The tree branches in the parks were trying to dress themselves in green again. It was a depressing sight; Maria had always thought that in the city the only bearable season of the year was winter, and maybe fall, with its reds and yellows.

The sun was warm and the people uselessly repeated the ritual of taking to the grassy parks, dressed in their summer clothes, unable to free themselves of the aggressively murky air. Those who were best able to pretend that they were resting were sleeping off the drowsiness of the mandatory pints of beer consumed during the free hour they had for lunch. Some formed teams, defensively swinging croquet mallets. There were groups of tourists around, many from Barcelona, with billfolds full of sterling pounds, not enough to sightsee beyond what they had already seen in travel agency pamphlets.

Meanwhile the men with mallets rushed to take new positions. A drunken Irishman was insulting those who looked the most English. The young men looked desperate.

Maria felt tired. In the last women's meeting they had been merciless with her because she was showing signs of weakness. They had discussed whether or not men should be accepted in the new communities. The official thesis was—Maria knew it and had often defended it—that for the time being they shouldn't. That afternoon Maria had opposed it. The discussion had taken a false turn because what Maria was really defending was her need to have a man by her side within view. She left the meeting more exhausted than ever. On her way out, she saw Lois, who told her that she was leaving the movement because she was going to work in a neighborhood of Caribbean people. Maria understood that Lois was being swayed by her own compassion. She had been one of the first organizers of the feminist movement in London. The idea of the Botticelli poster with the old woman had been hers, and now she was deciding to go to work for others. Maria felt betrayed and suspected that Lois had never really considered herself one of them. She had always worked for others. Moreover, Maria knew that Lois had been living with a Jamaican man for more than a year.

Beginning in the afternoon, Maria yearned to spend

the summer in France, in the country. She imagined herself renting an uninhabited farmhouse, a long and roomy
one, low to the ground, in the bottom of a valley. Next to
it, there would be cows, chickens, and a haystack.

She was looking at the "Holidays" section of the *Times*,
where they advertised houses for rent in the Dordogne,
near Cahors. She remembered the early morning smells
of animals and manure in Cahors. She also remembered
the cathedral with its rustic gothic style.

When Marc arrived and said that he thought they
should spend the summer separately, Maria didn't dare
complain. She continued to look at the ads, suddenly wondering whether she would feel like going alone. At once
she realized that for the last few days she had not been
balanced on the tightrope; she had fallen on the worst
side, the side of the weakest.

"Don't you want to know why?"

Maria felt surprised. No, she didn't, she found it very
natural. Maybe he wanted to be alone to work on something.

"I want to spend some time alone with Doris."

(Naked thighs with boots up to the knees. Curly hair,
with bangs over naive eyes. Thick lips, half-opened.)

"What! Are you crazy? She's like a young animal!"

She felt thin and helpless inside her big sweater, which
reached halfway down her legs, over a pair of shapeless
jeans. She tried to remember how she looked, she felt that
she had not looked at herself in the mirror for a long
time. I never go to the beauty shop or buy myself clothes
because I don't want to spend frivolously like these silly
women . . . who don't do anything but think about themselves, she thought.

She bit her lips. Really, Maria, and what do you do all
day but think about yourself? The only difference is that
you have decided to play a different role. Why don't you
want to spend money? Are you sorry he works so hard?
Why are you so considerate toward him? What are you

protecting him from, and why, when you don't even know whether he wants to be protected or not?

Maria's dream that night.

A delivery: she is giving birth to a son. She felt a heaviness in her belly that was slipping out, as if a hand were pulling at the weight that suffocated her. The baby was coming out and she twisted her body in a very familiar way. All of a sudden, she realized that she and Marc had made love. Marc got up very serene, ready to leave. She was left alone between the sheets. She, the mother; Marc, the child.

The next day Marc told her that it wasn't such a bad idea to spend the summer together in France after all. She looked at him; again she felt herself on the tightrope with her arms extended to keep her balance. She felt very sure of herself and looked straight ahead. Without looking Marc in the face, she said no.

Maria had realized that compassion can become just as abject a weapon as sexuality, short skirts, Doris's boots.

"It'll be good for you to spend some time with a woman like Doris," she couldn't help saying. She flip-flopped and fell to the other side, that of rancor.

They spent the summer apart. She traveled through Italy and he settled down with Doris in a small town on the coast of Devon.

She wrote a few postcards to him. In the post office of Siena, she found a very loving letter from him saying that Doris was beginning to feel possessive and that he had decided to shorten the stay. The experience had been very helpful and now more than ever he wanted to live with her again. It was a love letter. Maria answered with another. She too felt tired of her freedom and didn't want to leave him ever again.

She waited a few days to mail the letter, until she realized that if she didn't want Marc to get tired of her, she would have to keep on escaping, playing the role of the independent and tough woman.

She mailed him the letter.

At the end of the summer Maria was pregnant by a German. He had been her only lover during the summer. A distant relationship, without illusions.

Maria wrote to Marc that they wouldn't be able to live together again because she was expecting someone else's child.

Marc showed up unexpectedly at the hotel where she was staying. He had come to get her. He didn't talk about an abortion and she was grateful for it. They spent a few days of great tenderness together. Then one day she disappeared without saying a word.

Translated by Inma Minoves-Myers from
L'amor adult, © Helena Valentí 1977.

The Other

She finished coiling the rope and put it in the boat. Daring to go to sea by herself filled her with satisfaction, because her love for it had become a potential source of conflict in her marriage. To her, a day without sailing was a wasted day, but he didn't care much for it: "The sea is mystery and madness. I need to concentrate, I daydream enough just looking at the sky," he said.

A short cut took her past the foreigners' house. Besides, this was a good way to become friends with those women she couldn't help but admire. What attracted her to them was their happy and determined nature; they were people who had stripped away superfluous details, above all, romantic fantasies. And yet they were loving; very loving toward women, even her, who had different life-styles and temperaments. What she admired most, though, was that they lived so happily without men. They were free and daring; men hung around them when they went to town, and from time to time, one of them would get carried away. And even that they handled with refreshing honesty, she thought, as if regret and a need for intimacy were illnesses to which they were immune.

Lluís had assured her that two of the women in the group were lovers.

"The one who drives the motorcycle, who always wears a skirt, and the one with long hair. It's a pity because she is very beautiful."

It was probably true, she thought, but they had the ability to maintain the group equilibrium. When they were all together, it was impossible to discern any preferences.

She liked going in that house, whose walls were covered with posters aggressively alluding to the struggle for women's emancipation: the one of the pregnant man ("What would you do if it happened to you?"), the one with the Palestinian women fighters, the one with the young woman saying to the boy: "Some of my best friends are men, but would you want your daughter to marry one?"

They had told her what they did in their country, Germany. They had told her of the women who abandoned their children's fathers and who preferred to live in houses inhabited only by women. Of the medical centers where women explored their bodies.

"Here, look," they gave her sort of a plastic hook with a little mirror on one end. "It's to look inside yourself. Try it."

"Hey," noticing her surprised look, "don't you use tampons? Well . . ."

In a room all alone she looked at herself. At the beginning she only saw a dark cavity, but little by little she started to discover herself through the channels and ways of her womb.

"It's urgent that we become liberated from doctors; we have to become the masters of our own bodies."

She had just learned that she was pregnant again. It was her second pregnancy, but the first time away from the city and her family doctor. It was hard for her to remember from the last time what she was supposed to do. It had been two years since her first pregnancy and much to her surprise she was discovering that she had forgotten everything about it. Could it be that she hadn't really learned anything in the first place?

Now she was thinking that she would have to do the exercises and find out once more what to expect. She would have to go to the city. It was useless to try to talk to the women in the village—they had always considered her a distant person. They would be astonished to know of her ignorance. She had not dared to ask if there was a midwife in town. The idea that a woman might help her intimidated her, as if no woman could forgive her ignorance and cowardice. Lluis would tell her: "Don't worry. The most important thing is that you feel well, I'll make sure that I find you a hospital."

But she complained. She said she wanted to know exactly what was happening to her, to lose her fear, to be the one making the decisions. He had answered, "You women when you get together . . ."

He was referring to her visits to the German women's house. And he had been the one who had encouraged her to get to know them.

"Learn from them," he had said. "Learn to go about a bit more on your own."

She realized that Lluis was right. From time to time, during those four years of marriage, a great weakness accompanied by feelings of insecurity would come over her, to the point that sometimes she was not able to go out alone. These were crises in which she lost her equilibrium and her life seemed to sink into dependence on her husband. At times like this he got very irritated; not knowing how to free himself from the weight that had fallen on him, he even hated her.

"Look, call someone. No matter who it is, it's all right with me; even an old boyfriend would be okay."

"Haven't you noticed the effect you have on men? Have some fun, sweetheart."

"Didn't you say you wanted to study English again?"

She thought she didn't have the right to feel hurt, that Lluis was only saying this because he was concerned about her sudden weakness.

He should find a way to help me, though, she thought.

She had always been very careful not to cheat him of his personal time, not only in reference to his work—he was a graphic artist and worked at home—but also his leisure time.

At the beginning of their marriage, she thought Lluis would be interested in setting up the house, finding furniture, deciding on colors, creating inexpensive recipes, finding a better baker, and doing all the things that make daily life comfortable. Her husband's indifference was so inexplicable that it took her a whole year to give up hope.

She finally lost interest too, and started looking for a job. She found one teaching a few classes in a school far away from where they lived. After a few months he complained.

"At least find a job closer to home. You have to take a little care of the house, love."

It wasn't necessary to get another job because she was pregnant with the first child.

Of all the adventure of the first birth, the only thing she remembered was that she had spent many months going to prenatal classes and yet when the time came to give birth, the doctor suggested she be given a drug intravenously to facilitate her contractions. She tried to explain to him that it was not necessary, but Lluis intervened: "Let me decide. Let's accept the doctor's advice."

They tied up her arm and in that position, all her preparation was useless.

It was an easy delivery—they had put her to sleep at the last minute.

She'd planned to breast-feed the baby, but she soon discovered that she didn't feel like it. But on this matter Lluis proved to be very traditional. In order not to let him down, she sometimes made believe she was breast-feeding, even though she had very little milk and what there was didn't always come on schedule. It pleased him especially when they had guests or friends in the house. Her recently acquired maternal image filled him with satisfaction.

In the sky, the reddish, round moon began to turn silver. She observed it with a certain irritation: Here we go again. But then the moon's milky, engrossing light filled her with elation, taking her away from the daily urgencies of domestic life. On moonlit nights she did not want to go home. She wanted to suggest to Lluis that they sleep up in the mountains, as they had sometimes four years earlier.

She followed the path that took her straight home. From far away, she saw Pau's curly and blond hair under the palm of a stranger's hand. She tried to remember if they were expecting anyone. But there was no doubt that the man who was caressing her son was a stranger.

She hurried up. Pau called out to her happily, without leaving the stranger's side. She felt the stare of very insistent, intense blue eyes. Something made her try to act normal, as if finding a stranger in the house holding her son's hand were a common event.

"Pau, have you eaten supper?"

The child was no longer paying attention to her. The stranger answered yes, that Pau was ready to be taken to bed. "Don't reprimand him for not being in bed, he was waiting to say good night to his mother."

He said it in a tone that assumed that the woman should feel flattered, yet she couldn't help but feel the need to apologize.

"The nights when the moon is out it's hard for me to come home."

But Pau and the stranger were already doing something else. They had picked up a moth and the man was showing the child how to hold it up without damaging the design of its wings. With moth in hand, the child ran to show it to his mother. She and Pau were amused, but she heard the stranger getting up to go. She turned around and saw him standing, rigid.

Then Lluis appeared, very happy to introduce the two. He was Peter Hanz, an old friend. She already knew something about him; he belonged to a family of German refugees in Barcelona. He was back after a long stay in South America.

Having regained her status as woman of the house, she held out her hand. "I have been wanting to meet you for a long time. Lluis has told me about you."

While she made supper for the three of them, she asked Lluis why the guest bed had been moved to Pau's bedroom.

"Is he going to sleep with Pau?"

"I thought you would, if you don't mind. I thought for a few days Peter might want it to be like before. Peter and I shared the same room during all of our school years. Besides, we have some projects to do together."

Peter had come back from South America with plans that promised fast monetary returns. He was proposing that Lluis work with him on some of them. She was bothered by her husband's enthusiasm. After all, they had always striven for a comfortable but unostentatious lifestyle. What had come over him?

Days and weeks went by. The three adults and the child lived in harmony. Two men, a woman, and a child. Or a married couple with a child and a friend. Or three men and a woman.

Every day when the weather was nice, she went out with Pau. Peter had gotten into the habit of waiting for her at the beach. He would help her bring the boat back to shore, clean the inside, and bring her drinking water.

"What do you do at sea?" he asked one day. She assumed the question didn't need to be answered, because she wouldn't know how to answer. She would have said that they spent the time absolutely motionless. Or rocking themselves in the stillness of the sea.

Since Peter Hanz's arrival, Lluis clung to his wife as he hadn't in years. Inside the house, the situation was very often that of a couple of lovers with two strange men. However, the woman felt that Lluis's sudden renewed enthusiasm for her came from something outside the two of them. Whenever he was overly affectionate, she felt an awkward and grudging responsibility to reciprocate.

One day Peter took some pictures of her and Pau. When the photos arrived a few days later they surprised her. There were images of her alone, of her with the child, of the child alone. She had a hard time recognizing herself: that somber look toward the bedroom, the line that began at the upper neck, followed the chest and the breast with the double fold of a sudden decline and then a soft rise. Her straight hair next to Pau's curls. And above all, what surprised her most was the air of security, of a pregnant and serene woman, that he had captured. Just then she realized that she had not worried any more about going to Barcelona to see the doctor.

"You have to introduce them to me. Remember that I'm German too." That evening Peter did not come to the beach and she had taken advantage of this by going to the women's house.

"Maybe it would be better if I introduced myself with the child." He said it as if it were a spontaneous thought but she knew that he had been thinking about it for a few days.

She imagined him going in with an eager look, squeezing the child's hand in his.

"It's me. The man."

" . . ."

"Hurry up, bring the teapot, the bottle of wine. Come out to welcome the man with the child."

The matter took on a strange twist when Lluis intervened.

"I met them first. . . ."

The visit of the two men to the German women's house was followed by a tumultuous period of comings and goings, disappearances, furtive runs, and glances between Lluis and Peter. She often had the sensation that there was a constant murmur around the house, even though in appearance they continued with their established habits. The only change was that coming back from the beach, the three of them would stop at that house. Peter told them things about the South American countries. The theme of the conversations was the life-style of the Indians. The women listened to him, captivated. She herself began to realize that Peter knew something important, something unknown to her. Peter had become the traveler who brought necklaces of mysterious stones. He evoked a different reality, a reality in which material objects, the posters on the walls, conclusive statements, remained in a corner like useless pieces of furniture. On the other hand, the smallest details, like vaguely sketched air currents, took on a concrete and tangible weight.

One night, when they returned home after one of those conversations, Lluis looked like a helpless child to her. She saw a bewildered look in his eyes and sat on the arm of his chair to hug him. She thought: it was she who was discovering Peter's secret, the secret of his old friend.

The room they were in was dark, only the window was bright with moonlight. In a corner of the glass panels the profile of a face appeared. She went to have a closer look, but it quickly disappeared. Suddenly the air in the room seemed heavy.

"Didn't you see him?"

"Who?"

"Peter, at the window."

"No, I wasn't looking."

But Peter was looking. The difference between the two friends was precisely that, that one looked and the other didn't.

She suggested to Lluis that they go to eat in the village and have Peter take care of the boy. The friend accepted happily—he liked nothing better than to be alone with Pau, he said.

The couple came home late, light and happy. In the restaurant they had met a loud and funny group of acquaintances. Lluis felt comfortable right away and he was one of the ones who made the most noise. She felt carefree, in a good mood.

At home they found a note from Peter: "We're at Ingrid's."

"Well, well, he is no longer at the German women's house, now he's at Ingrid's," she said laughing. She was happy that the evening could continue without the presence of the friend. But then she saw Lluis looking gloomily out the window.

"Ingrid, of course. The one who has the nicest legs," he said. The wife, paralyzed for a moment, made a special effort and suggested that they go over. He quickly agreed but she decided it was better that he go alone. She said she wasn't feeling good and she preferred to stay home.

Alone in the room she turned on the light in the mirror. Her eyebrows furrowed in a crease. Her eyes were dilated and bright.

"Who has Peter fallen in love with?"

"Oh, her, naturally." The question had not been precise enough, they meant something else. Finally, one of the women told her. "Peter has loved Lluis for years."

"You mean he's jealous of her, not him?" That was true, they knew, but there was something else.

"Maybe he is jealous of both?"

"He loves Lluis, but now that his friend has a woman, he wants one too."

"Ménage à trois?" The remark was trivial, but it posed a possibility. The quest had to follow a certain formula.

"Does Lluis love Peter?"

"He admires him. He is in love with his wife."

"Lluis takes and accepts things unconsciously. He doesn't know how lucky he is, or the sacrifices she makes."

"You mean to say that he is insensitive?"

"Or naive."

"They say that a woman who feels herself loved gives herself over completely to the one who loves her. For Lluis that is natural; for Peter it's a conflict."

"Peter can't take it. He can't stand love from women."

"Then what is the conflict? Why this anger?"

"He is jealous of the ease in which his friend lives."

"And of something else. Of something coming from her, that makes her exceptional."

It wasn't easy. The point was to explain Peter's jealousy, but what was there to be envied in Lluis's natural manner?

"Lluis is happy."

"You mean his happiness is enviable," they looked at each other for a moment, "worthy, perhaps?"

"Yes. She is worthy. That's it, we've found the answer."

"Her outings to sea, alone. A certain self-sufficiency that she has. Like a strength, a self-realization."

"The strength of women is the great paranoia of men."

"Peter sees it and he's afraid. And we don't inspire fear," they said laughing. "Especially Ingrid," they added, nudging her gently on the shoulder.

There was a moment of silence. Then one of them said what was left to say.

"We're afraid too, like Peter."

The next day, she got up early with the intention of spending the whole day at the beach. Peter came up to her in the kitchen while she was preparing lunch.

"May I come with you?"

What was the force of that man who, when absent, felt as present as a swarm of dark bumblebees, and whose presence, when he returned, cleansed her with a human and tender touch? He was looking at her from the helm, she was at the bow of the boat with the child between her legs. She had suggested that the four go sailing but Lluis was exhausted from the night before and it was impossible to get him up.

At the beach they went swimming and ate lunch. Pau made them look for snails but when he saw the little creatures come out of their shells he got scared.

Peter started to talk to her about himself. He spoke with irony, as if he were talking about another person, a naive, inexperienced person. She paid attention because she had already learned that with him everything was done consciously, voluntarily, purposefully. He was telling her that he had the problem of falling in love too often. Women were his downfall, he said. Now he was in love with Ingrid. The week before he had been in love with Greta, the lesbian.

"When will you fall in love with me?" she asked smiling.

"Never. You scare me." He became serious and added, "No woman has ever rejected me."

Suddenly she realized that fear had been the dominant theme since Peter arrived. The fear of shadows in the nocturnal light. Of comings and goings that became apparitions. Of a hissing in her ear and pounding waves that seemed to say things. She thought of the fear provoked by the pictures of her with Pau, of the power of Peter's glance, and of herself, the night she spent looking at herself in the mirror. It was fear of the other, of the effect that we have on others, and that others have on us. Of the power that Peter had over Lluis and among the entranced German women. And of her own power over Lluis and Peter.

The sad, bewildered tone in which he had said "No woman has ever rejected me." She remembered that heavy sensation of someone's love falling over you, Lluis's irritation about her weakness, her desire to run away when faced with Lluis's detachment.

The dialogue resumed with a lighter tone.

"It's the women that we must feel sorry for," she said with a smile.

"Not at all!" With a severe look, "You women like it when we make love to you and then you don't need us anymore."

She had the feeling that he was saying it with conscious fury, like the person who pounds on the table or slaps someone's face.

"Not even you believe that," she said to him.

"Now they don't even want us to support their children."

She thought about Lluis and herself. But she didn't say anything. She had the feeling that her own case was not relevant. Her marital existence seemed deprived of significance, as if it were nothing more than the skillful touch of a tradition. Supposedly for killing fear, perhaps marriage was really the fear of fear. And she felt outside the world, exiled from the country of new men and women, of the new sensibilities.

She tried to remember who she knew in Barcelona who had not married, who might live alone. Above all, women. Yes, there were a few. And also, those who had separated from their husbands to live a fuller, if riskier, life. They were women alone, really alone, without true friends like the German women. There was a difference. In Barcelona, women alone gave up their children. She had a hard time remembering anyone who had left her husband and was living alone with a child. She remembered one, Mariona, who lived enslaved by her own insecurity. The emancipation of women in Barcelona was a new thing for which they always ended up paying—it became a crime they had to pay a certain price for. And men took advantage of the situation. Barcelona had changed some also, but for the time being, progress had stopped for women. In this country, men still had the upper hand, they had the power. She smiled. It was a different power from that of Peter, it was the power of one who takes advantage of the situation. Peter had the real power of one who faces genuine women, like the Germans. And it was he who really felt vulnerable.

The next few days Peter wasn't around the house much. He spent long stretches of time with Ingrid. He spoke of going to live in Germany. He spoke with determination, as if possessed by a secret will. Lluis had become more reclusive and had resumed life as it was before Peter's arrival. The married couple had regained the confident air of a man and a woman who have found each other and don't want to search any longer.

Ingrid was the toughest of the group. She worked for German television and she was ambitious and conscious of her career. Everybody respected her. She was petite and dark-haired, with a slight body and delicate hands. She had a smile that burst out and disappeared immediately; her manner was serious for the most part. She spent most of the time listening, without speaking.

One morning Peter came home with a defeated look.

"They're leaving tomorrow."

That night there was a farewell supper at their house. Ingrid was very lively. Of the men present, probably more than one had made love with her. She treated them all tenderly, and she generously fell into the role of hostess. As if she were thanking them for all the good times they had had. It was the first time in that house that she felt uncomfortable not being a man.

After Ingrid left, Peter settled himself in a hut in the yard and announced that he would plant a vegetable garden.

He started to prepare the plot of land. Pau helped him, or thought he did.

Seeing that Peter loved Pau's company, she decided to leave them alone and go sailing by herself.

One night Peter was teaching Pau how to throw rocks. The mother heard him say to the child: "You must learn to be a man. Little girls don't know how to throw rocks."

A few days later, when she came home in the evening, she found that the two men had a pair of scissors and were cutting Pau's curls away. They were curls that he had had since birth, which gave him a soft and golden aura. Often, the people in town had taken him for a girl, and she had felt a secret joy.

She stopped to look at the group from a distance. Two men and a boy. And a woman.

Maria-Antònia Oliver

Maria-Antònia Oliver, photo by Pilar Aymerich

Maria-Antònia Oliver   *Majorca, 1946*

Creative works   *Cròniques d'un mig estiu*. Barcelona: Club Editor, 1970. Novel.

Cròniques de la molt anomenada ciutat de Montcarrà. Barcelona: 62, 1972. Novel.

Coordenades espai-temps per guardar-hi les ensaïmades. Barcelona: Pòrtic, 1975. With drawings by Josep Maur Serra. Novella, reprinted in the collection *Figues d'un altre paner*.

El vaixell d'iràs i no tornaràs. Barcelona: Laia, 1976. Novel.

Figues d'un altre paner. Palma de Mallorca: Moll, 1979. Stories. With a prologue by the author.

Punt d'arròs. Barcelona: Galba, 1979. Novel.

Vegetal i Muller qui cerca espill. Barcelona: La llar del llibre, 1982. Two television screenplays.

Crineres de foc. Barcelona: Laia, 1985. Novel.

Estudi en lila. Barcelona: Magrana, 1985. Novel. Translated into English by Kathleen McNerney as *Study in Lilac* (Seattle: Seal Press, 1987).

Though one finds subtle points of contact between some of Maria-Antònia Oliver's work and Gabriel García Márquez's masterpiece *One Hundred Years of Solitude*, she does not need a Latin American brand of magic realism. She has her own Mediterranean island version, and she delves with mastery into the rich source of the Majorcan "rondalles," popular songs and sayings full of mythical creatures and fantastic narrations.

Cròniques de la molt anomenada ciutat de Montcarrà (Chronicles of the Oft-Named City of Montcarrà, 1972) serves as an example of the relationship to García Márquez's novel, which cannot be called influence. Oliver's work is in the form of a family chronicle which predicts social destruction, using the rondalles as a basis. There is a linear progression in the fragmented narration, showing us three generations of linked families as concentric circles. Complete with adventures in America, incestuous relationships, and the transformation of a tranquil though sometimes stifling Majorca into a tourist haven, the novel ends with a vision of its destruction by the creatures from the rondalles.

Oliver says that she would accept the fact of having been influenced by García Márquez, if indeed she had been. But her novel was in its final revision when she read *One Hundred Years of Solitude*. She liked it so much that as a form of tribute she changed to Macondo the name of the South American town one of her characters visits.

The similarity has to be sought, rather, in the parallel experiences of the two novelists. Tourists represent for Majorca what the banana companies mean to Macondo—a seeming prosperity based on exploitation which creates first a dependency and finally destruction. The final wind that sweeps away Macondo is water, naturally, in Oliver's Montcarrà. Oliver's ballads perform the same function as García Márquez's grandfather—a great source of fantastic tales and inspiration.

Much of Oliver's work reveals a binary structure which

allows her to present us with different levels of interpretation, while she distances herself from her characters and gives them life at the same time. Recently, this tendency has been underscored by her modus operandi of working on two books simultaneously. Her two 1985 novels, *Crineres de foc* and *Estudi en lila*, are so different in style and theme that they do not seem to be written by the same person. But structurally, both reveal a bipolarity, which serves as a contrast in one case and a reinforcement in the other.

Of course these two novels also have in common with most of Oliver's work her preoccupations as a feminist. *Crineres de foc* shows the parallel struggles for independence and self-identification of a woman and a community; *Estudi en lila*, a detective novel, and "Broken Threads" both deal forcefully with the problem of violence against women. In *Vegetal*, Oliver deals with the problem of older women in society and their feelings of uselessness, the limited choices open to them, and the stagnation and frustration that inevitably result from a lack of meaningful personal development.

Translated by Nathaniel B. Smith from *Vegetal
i Muller qui cerca espill*, © Maria-Antònia Oliver 1982.

Vegetal

ACT III

Marta has put up all the clocks and now is hanging mirrors
in the spots where she has already driven nails. She also places
some on the few remaining pieces of furniture, trying to achieve a
series of reflected and repeated images. She even wants to put
some mirrors on the ceiling, but once she is perched at the top of a
ladder, she finds this position too awkward for hammering nails.
Maybe she could use the nail that the lamp hangs from . . . but
she abandons the idea. She also puts up calendars from various
years with thumbtacks, each one open to a different month. She
decides to take the picture off some of them and leave only the
months. . . .

While all this commotion is going on, she talks continuously to
the plants, judges the effect some produce in the mirrors, loops
others around the clocks, mixes calendars' leaves with plants'
leaves. . . .

She is wearing a long dress, lightweight and somewhat transparent, and she is barefoot.

MARTA

I wish you could see yourselves all the time in a mirror
without having to move, without having to make any
effort. . . . So, now you're proud of yourselves, aren't you?
[*she listens carefully to some leaves*] Of course, I was too . . .

111

and I'm getting like that again. . . . [*listens*] Yes, gorgeous,
and do you know what? I liked to put on makeup, get my
hair done, dress elegantly . . . always elegant, I was. . . .
And when we were courting, John also liked me that
way . . . but once we were married, and especially after the
child came, he used to say:

JOHN [*elegantly dressed in a silk dressing robe, with a calendar in his
hand*] Marta, don't you think a married lady should be
dressed more . . . more seriously? You look less like a
mother than a girl looking for a fiance. . . .

MARTA [*to John, laughing*] So, you were jealous, my friend? Or
maybe you didn't find me ladylike enough? [*to the plant,
again*] And of course, if he didn't like the way I was any
more. . . . Whom should a woman please, if not her husband? So, little by little, I changed my wardrobe. . . . I
never lacked money to buy clothes, no . . . and those he
bought me to please himself were much more expensive
than the ones I liked. . . . [*listens and turns to another plant*]
No, don't think that: I got used to it soon, it even began to
seem natural not to put on a lot of makeup. John was
right, about that. . . . In our group of friends, it wasn't
taken well, the way I dressed up. Often I got indirect remarks, but I went on just the same, because I thought
John liked it, until I finally understood he didn't, of
course. . . . [*listens*] Look, don't distract me, or I'll never
finish. . . . [*stops*] Yes, maybe I will hang one on the ceiling . . . but how? If you all could help me. . . . [*pauses*]
How's this for a balancing act? Imagine, if I got dizzy, up
here. . . . And don't laugh! I know I'm ridiculous, but I'm
doing it for you; what good to me is a mirror on the ceiling?

JOHN [*holding the ladder so she won't fall, says to her*] Marta,
wouldn't you like us to put a mirror on the bedroom ceiling?

MARTA Why would you want to do that, John?

JOHN You mean you don't know why people put mirrors on
bedroom ceilings? You're so innocent. . . .

MARTA   The one in the closet isn't enough?

JOHN   For what I'm after, no.

MARTA   [*to the plants, without coming down from the ladder; John has already disappeared*] And when he told me why he wanted it, I almost died of embarrassment, I swear. . . . [*listens*] You're innocent too, you baby. Well, he wanted to see us while we were making love. . . . [*listens*] No! I completely refused. . . . It must have been the first time he couldn't do what he wanted, because I always ended up giving in to everything . . . but not to that! I told him, if he wanted to do things like that, to go find professionals. . . . [*listens*] No, don't think so. . . . Well, I couldn't be sure, because men, you know, have a different way of thinking from women, but I think he was always faithful to me. . . . [*listens*] Obviously: I've always been an honorable woman. . . .

It's another day. There are still more plants. Marta is in the solarium, surrounded by plants, clocks, calendars, and mirrors. She is sitting on a heap of cushions and is reading The Years *by Virginia Woolf aloud to the plants. Occasionally she stops reading and makes comments to the plants about the text.*

MARTA   [*reads*] "It was an uncertain day, with passing shadows and darting rays of bright sunshine. The funeral started at walking pace. Delia, getting into the second carriage with Milly and Edward, noticed that the houses opposite had their blinds drawn in sympathy, but a servant peeped. The others, she noticed, did not seem to see her; they were thinking of their mother. When they got into the main road the pace quickened, for the drive to the cemetery was a long one. Through the slit of the blind, Delia noticed dogs playing; a beggar singing; men raising their hats as the hearse passed them. . . ." It's funny, you can see that that happens to lots of people, when they lose someone they love a lot. . . . When John died, I didn't feel a thing. And at the funeral, I noticed a lot of everyday things and couldn't think about him. . . . [*listens*] Of course I loved him! What a question. He was my husband, wasn't he? All

113

right, let's go on. . . . What, you don't like it? ". . . But by
the time their own carriage passed, the hats were on
again. The men walked briskly and unconcernedly. . . ."
[*listens*] Well, I don't find it sad, I think it's very beautiful—
OK, OK, I'll read that part again, but all this going forward and back, I think it's really stupid. . . . [*looks back a
few pages*] ". . . And the walloping Oxford bells, turning
over and over like slow porpoises in a sea of oil, con-
templatively intoned their musical incantations. The fine
rain, the gentle rain, poured equally over the mitred and
the bareheaded with an impartiality which suggested that
the god of rain, if there were a god, was thinking Let it
not be restricted . . ."*

[*The doorbell rings and breaks the spell. Too bad, and when everyone was so happy! Marta gets up reluctantly and slowly goes
to the door, dragging her feet so much that before she gets there,
the bell rings again.*]

MARTA   What a pest, eh, little ones? Who can it be? When I
wanted people to come to the house because I felt lonely,
no one ever came; and now that I don't want them, they
come—OK, OK, I'm coming—What a hurry they're in!
[*pauses*] Oh, Charles! Son!

CHARLES   Hi, Mom!

[*Julia has come too, and Marta doesn't know what to say to her.
Charles must have told her about Marta's reaction the other day
and Marta isn't sure how to act in front of the girl. She is so overcome that she hasn't let them in yet.*]

CHARLES   Are you going to let us wait all afternoon on the landing,
Mom? [*he says this without any trace of reproach, gently*]

MARTA   Forgive me, son. . . . I was so surprised to see you . . . to
see both of you.

JULIA   Good afternoon. . . . I'm very glad to meet you.

MARTA   Good afternoon, dear. Come in, come in. . . .

[*Marta leads them into the living room. There is a moment of in-
decision on the part of all three of them. Marta worries about her*

*Virginia Woolf, *The Years* (New York: Harcourt, Brace, 1937), pp. 84, 48.

*son's reaction to the changes of decor. There is surprise in
Charles's eyes and Julia does not succeed in hiding her shock.
Rapid glances of interrogation pass between the two.*]

CHARLES   Oh, how nice, Mom. . . . It's much more pleasant like this.

MARTA   Do you like it? I was so worried to think that you might
not. . . .

CHARLES   A little heavy on the plants, maybe. . . .

[*Julia has perceived a shadow pass over Marta's face and hastens
to intervene. She wants to gain the woman's goodwill on one
hand, and on the other she feels a natural solidarity with her.*]

JULIA   I wouldn't say so. . . . These plants are beautiful, so exuberant, so well cared for.

MARTA   Don't touch it!

JULIA   No; I just wanted to see it up close. . . .

CHARLES   Of course, they're pretty. . . . And then, they give you
pleasure, Mom. . . . Now that you've taken out all the
other furniture, why don't you change the sofa and arm
chairs?

MARTA   Yes, I was thinking of it. . . . One of these days. Watch out,
son, please!

[*Charles looks down at his feet; the cuff of his pants was touching
a plant, making Marta nervous.*]

CHARLES   Oh, sorry, Mom. . . . I'm just not used to them. . . .

MARTA   No harm done, don't worry, son. . . .

JULIA   What a beauty! Did you notice this one, Charles?

CHARLES   Yes, very nice. . . . Where did you get so many clocks,
Mom? Are you collecting them?

MARTA   Oh, from here and there. . . . At flea markets, antique
stores. . . . But sit down, both of you, sit down. . . . A little
whiskey?

CHARLES   For me, maybe so . . . with ice. How about you, Julia?

MARTA   Maybe you'd rather have a glass of anisette?

JULIA   No, whiskey is fine.

MARTA   I'll go get some ice. . . .

JULIA   Would you like me to help you?

MARTA   No, thanks, I'll just be a moment. . . .

[*Marta goes out, and the two young people look at each other.*

Julia makes signs to Charles to indicate that there are at least seven calendars and that none are of the same year. He is worried. He walks carefully through the room, looks into the bedroom and has Julia look in; they are even more surprised to see there the same verdant environment.]

CHARLES We'll talk about it later. . . . [*he speaks in a low tone, as if to forestall the flood of questions that are in her expression*]

MARTA [*with a tray*] Now I've got everything in the kitchen; glasses, bottles, so there's more room here for the plants. . . . But why don't you have a seat?

CHARLES There are so many new things here. . . . It's fun to look at them. . . .

JULIA So many plants must give you a lot of work. . . .

MARTA I don't have anything else to do . . . and it's not that much work. . . . A labor of love. . . .

JULIA This one is very pretty. . . . What kind of plant is it?

MARTA You like plants?

JULIA Yes, they're nice to have around. . . .

MARTA Liking them is not the same as loving them. . . . Don't you know?

JULIA Yes, I suppose so. . . .

CHARLES Hey, I'm here too. . . .

[*The two women laugh. A kind of complicity has been established between them, nourished by Julia, who actually couldn't care less about plants. But she feels an immense curiosity about Marta and a great desire to understand her.*]

MARTA Are you going to have supper with me?

JULIA Sure, of course—if it's no bother for you, I mean. . . .

CHARLES Julia, we were . . .

JULIA We'll do it another day, Charles—don't you think?

CHARLES Well, all right.

MARTA Oh, good! You're a good girl, Julia. . . . I'm going to start getting things ready. . . .

JULIA We'll help you. . . .

MARTA No, dear. . . . Look at the clocks . . . and the mirrors; some are really pretty. . . .

CHARLES We'll look at them later; now we'll help you.

116

MARTA   No, son, no. . . .

JULIA   Yes, yes. . . .

[*And despite Marta's protests, they follow her to the kitchen. It doesn't seem the same kitchen as before: now everything is green and it's hard to turn around in it. To open the cupboards you'd need to move the hanging plants; to get food ready, you'd have to find a nonexistent space on the counters. The table and chairs no longer can be used for sitting down to eat. Even on the ledge of the exhaust fan there's a small flower pot.*

    The two young people are so overwhelmed that they don't know whether to go in or go back to the living room; Marta, who realizes this, is taken aback, and feels the need to defend herself.]

MARTA   I have them in here to water them. . . . In the living room, it gets water all over. . . .

CHARLES   So why don't you put them in the solarium?

MARTA   [*with a smile half of excuse and half teasing*] There too.

JULIA   [*answering Charles*] What makes you think she has to be accountable to you?

MARTA   Don't worry, it doesn't bother me. . . .

CHARLES   Well, what shall we make for supper?

MARTA   Look in the refrigerator. . . . I'll move some pots away from here. . . .

[*When Marta has gone out, carrying pots, and as Julia is opening the refrigerator, Charles, curious, draws near and asks her:*]

CHARLES   Why do you have to keep trying to get on her good side?

JULIA   Don't you see she's beaten down? She's hanging onto whatever you say. . . . And she's afraid of you. . . .

CHARLES   Afraid? Why?

JULIA   I don't know . . . but she is.

CHARLES   Frankly, I'm worried about her. . . .

MARTA   [*enters*] Well? Did you find anything you like?

JULIA   We can have bread with tomatoes, and make omelettes, with a little ham. . . .

MARTA   Yes, I know, there's not much; but it's because, just for me. . . . Look, Julia, don't you think . . . [*pauses*]

JULIA   Yes, what?

MARTA   You haven't seen the whole apartment yet. . . . Would you like to? It's quite big. . . . Charles' room is still the way it was when he left home. . . .

[*There is a look of fear on Charles's face. He suspects that his mother is preparing the way to propose that they move in with her.*]

JULIA Yes, I'd like to see it. Charles, you can make the omelettes, can't you?

[*Marta can't avoid registering an expression of surprise, but seeing that Charles begins to beat the eggs, as if it were the most natural thing in the world, she leads Julia out of the kitchen. While she is showing her the apartment, she doesn't stop talking, and Julia feels trapped. She doesn't say a word.*]

MARTA Listen, dear . . . I . . . Do your parents know that you're living with my son without being married? And what do they say about it? I'm sure they must be horrified. . . . I can see you're a good girl, and not what I thought at all. . . . That's why I don't understand. . . . Would it be such a big problem, to get married?

[*Charles, in the kitchen, beats the eggs violently; from time to time he looks out in the hallway and listens. But Marta is speaking too low, in a confidential tone, and he can't make out what she's saying.*]

MARTA . . . See how big it is? Two families could live here comfortably, without getting in each other's way. . . . If you wanted to, you could convince Charles. . . .

[*Charles has finished making the omelettes. He's restless and, as he's about to cut the bread, he calls the two women to help him. When Julia hears him, she considers herself saved. On the other hand, Marta makes a gesture of annoyance at the interruption.*]

CHARLES [*off*] Hey, the omelettes are ready—Are you going to come help me with the bread?

JULIA OK, we're on our way. . . .

[*Now they are all in the kitchen. Marta is cutting ham and the two young people are spreading a fresh tomato on the bread.*]

MARTA I was telling Julia, well, this apartment is so big, and I get lost in it. . . . Son, why don't you both come and live here?

JULIA   But, we'd have to get married first, I suppose, wouldn't we?

MARTA   No, not really, though I'd prefer it that way, of course. . . . But no one would need to know you weren't married, would they?

    [*They all have stopped what they were doing. An unbearable tension fills the room, and only Marta doesn't seem to realize it.*]

CHARLES Mom, last time I came we had an argument about that. . . . Why don't we just leave things the way they are, and be friends, like always?

MARTA   [*to Julia*] You'll understand me better. I'm very lonely. I've tried to think what I can do, work in an office or a shop, or help at the church, or at the neighborhood association . . . but I don't know how to do anything, I'm only good for keeping house, no one ever taught me anything else. . . . Do you know why I have so many plants? Because they keep me company. They're my friends, we talk to each other, and we get along fine. . . . All my life has been like theirs . . . put on a shelf like a rag doll, to look nice, to keep people company . . . and nothing else. That's why we get along so well, because we're the same, but if I'm not careful I'll turn into a plant for real, a fuchsia, or ivy, or a *ficus*, who can tell? But if you were living here . . .

CHARLES Mom, that wouldn't be a solution, and you know it. . . . And besides, you can't make us . . .

MARTA   Why can't I? Haven't I been living for you ever since you were born? Haven't I sacrificed everything for you?

CHARLES That's the problem, Mother. . . . You should have started thinking of yourself a long time ago. . . .

MARTA   But I didn't, and you should be grateful to me for it. . . .

CHARLES I am, Mother, but we can't come to live here. We'll help you find a job, if you want . . . and to find friends, and activities . . . but we won't come and live here. . . .

MARTA   Julia, dear, why don't you put some sense into his head?

JULIA   I . . . well . . . I . . . think Charles is right. . . .

MARTA   Of course, of course. . . . You have no right to interfere in this, you hussy!

119

CHARLES	Mother—
MARTA	Yes, *hussy.* Son, this Julia, she thinks she's something special, but she's not worth ten cents—I'm sure she's the one who made you lose your senses—and now she wants you only for herself. . . . Oh my God . . . [*pauses*] All right, out of here, both of you, out, I said!
CHARLES	Calm down, Mother.
MARTA	Out, I said!
CHARLES	We won't come back, Mom.
MARTA	Of course, you won't come back—And if you do, I won't open the door—Out! [*Charles and Julia go down the steps in a state of consternation.*]
CHARLES	She's crazy . . . she's crazy. . . .
JULIA	No: she's lonely.
ACT IV	*In the house there is no one, now. In the living room no furniture remains. Only plants, plants and more plants. Some cushions, both small and large, serve as seats on the floor. Everywhere, repeated to the point of excess, are clocks, mirrors, calendars, all mixed in with the plants. There's no furniture in the bedroom either—only a mattress, perhaps on a platform, or else on the floor. It is the only piece of furniture on which there are still not any plants.* *Marta has gone out in a last attempt to integrate herself into daily life and flee the allure of the plants. She will visit the priest, the neighborhood association, look for a job . . . but she will always be thinking of her home and longing for the plants that await her there.* *Now she is with the rector, who treats her paternally, but in fact, her case interests him as much as any of the others that come through the rectory; that is, not much. He repeats the usual clichés of the office of a rich parish such as this.*
RECTOR	. . . At your age, my daughter . . . it often happens . . .
MARTA	But I'm still young . . . and I want to live. . . .
RECTOR	Yes, of course, but you have to be careful, my daughter. . . . There are some people who don't believe in the

	Devil, but I assure you that he exists and is constantly working against weak souls like yours, whatever their age. . . .
MARTA	I don't understand, Father.
RECTOR	But you do. . . . You don't accept the life that it is your lot to live. . . . And you are beginning to rebel against the will of God. . . . You know that can be dangerous. . . .
MARTA	Maybe what I want is to be useful . . . not to be like a plant and just be around for decoration. . . .
RECTOR	You have too much imagination, my daughter. . . . The business about plants and decorations is literature; in this life you have to keep your feet on the ground!
MARTA	But Father, that's precisely what I want: to keep my feet on the ground!
RECTOR	Look, Marta. . . . What you need to do is forget the idea of living with your son. Young people have to make their own lives—without forsaking the law of God and men, of course. . . . Now you have something to work on: to get your son and this girl to marry each other. . . .
MARTA	What about me?
RECTOR	Don't be egotistical, my daughter. . . . You are only thinking about yourself. . . .
MARTA	All my life I have thought only about others. . . . I don't believe it's a sin if I want to think about myself, now. . . . My son, who is a good boy, Father, the other day told me it was time to start worrying about myself and let others be.
RECTOR	The young. . . . And, my daughter, do you think that a woman of your age should listen to the advice of a young man who doesn't yet have any experience in life?
MARTA	. . . He told me I should do what I felt like, live my own life now that I can. . . .
RECTOR	Those are dangerous fantasies! What do you mean, live your own life, Marta? You've already lived it, with your husband and son. . . . Such a fine family, you made others jealous. . . . The memory of it should be enough, my daughter, to fill all the hours of your old age. . . .
MARTA	But I'm not old yet!

[*And she longs for the clocks, the calendars, the time that has remained stopped among the plants at home, which are now alone, waiting for her to return and keep them company.*

Now we see all Marta's favorite objects, sometimes panoramically, sometimes in the detail of a leaf, a sheet of paper, a clock hand showing the hour, another hand showing another hour. And we also see Marta leaving the priest's office, disappointed and indignant.]

MARTA [*off*] My life! I should have gone to see a younger priest, one of those more modern ones who understands things. . . . This guy is an antique, a fossil, my kid would say. . . . My life, he says! Such a fine family, we made others jealous, he says! What does he know about it? So everything's fine, because I always shut up, because if I didn't. . . . I don't want to live on memories!
[*Once again the plants, clocks, calendars, mirrors. . . .*]

[*And then: Marta sitting at a table, in front of a young man from the neighborhood association. The atmosphere—so different from the priest's imposing office!—is one of disorder, full of dust, with posters on the walls, unstable chairs, papers. . . .*

Marta strikes a discordant note, discreetly and elegantly dressed, with expensive clothing; she fit in better in the rector's office.

At home, hanging from a wall clock, is the loose-fitting dress she has been wearing lately. But it's not something to go out in the street in.]

YOUNG MAN . . . Prepare the newsletter, send it to the members, organize parties, campaign for green spaces, seek solutions for all the neighborhood's problems, things like that. . . . You aren't a member of the Association, are you?

MARTA No, no—but I'll join right now. . . . But . . . I'd like to do more. . . . I already explained, I have lots of free time, I can help. . . .

YOUNG MAN Yes, of course. . . . We need help. . . . What do you have experience in?

MARTA	A little bit of everything. . . . What needs to be done?
YOUNG MAN	Well, typing things, going around to houses in the neighborhood to sign up more members, organizing activities. . . . And in that kind of thing, you—
MARTA	Actually, it's true, I don't know how to type . . . and going around to houses . . . frankly, I'd be ashamed. . . . And about those activities, what would that be?
YOUNG MAN	That would mean organizing things for the neighborhood: popular celebrations, classes for children . . . and also senior citizens. . . . There's a committee in charge of all that. . . . We want the neighborhood to have its own character, and people to feel at home in it. . . .
MARTA	Oof! For people to feel at home in it would take a lot of changes. . . .
YOUNG MAN	Of course, yes . . . and what would you change?
MARTA	Cars . . . I'd prohibit so many cars from going by . . . if I could, of course. . . . You can't imagine the noise they make, those cars. . . . It's a madhouse. . . .
YOUNG MAN	Yes, we've already taken some action on that question. . . . It's part of the Association's campaign: traffic, green spaces, the market place. . . .
MARTA	The market place?
	[*The young man has a lot of work. He is pleasant enough with Marta, but doesn't have the desire or time to have a long chat with her. And, besides, she doesn't fit into this atmosphere.*]
YOUNG MAN	Yes, the market place, it's in terrible shape—too small for the neighborhood, dirty—and inconvenient for the housewives. . . .
MARTA	Yes, now that you mention it, that's for sure. And just imagine how many times I've gone there. It's that we get used to things, and then we don't even realize how bad they are and that we could improve them. . . .
YOUNG MAN	Yes, Ma'am . . . if you'd be interested in working on that committee . . .
MARTA	What committee?
YOUNG MAN	The one for, let's say, improving the neighborhood. . . .

MARTA	Do you think I'd be of use on it?
YOUNG MAN	You're the one who has to say. . . . But you can't lose anything by trying. . . .
MARTA	I don't know, I don't know. . . . What other jobs that need to be done do you think I could help with?
YOUNG MAN	Gosh, what can I say? From sweeping out our headquarters to sticking on stamps . . . as much work as you like. . . .
MARTA	Yes, yes, I see. . . .
YOUNG MAN	The best thing would be for you to come some day when we have a general meeting. . . . That way, you'd get a better idea what a neighborhood association is and would be able to see how you can help out. . . .
MARTA	Yes, maybe so. . . . You're right, yes . . . and when is that meeting?
YOUNG MAN	Leave me your name and address and we'll let you know.
MARTA	Fine, OK. . . .
	[*She writes her name and address on a sheet of paper. During the conversation her attitude has been changing. First she was interested, enthusiastic, but slowly she has been backing off, without really knowing why. In fact, she doesn't like to have anything to do with this kind of thing: she is making a last attempt not to remain shut in at home with her fantasies. But she misses her plants, and thinks about them, and sees them as she leaves the neighborhood association.*]
MARTA	[*off*] I don't know if it's because that guy doesn't think I can help them or if I don't really feel like it. . . . What would I do in that place? I'd have to be with people, talk. . . . I can't even stand to think about it, but I have to make an effort. . . .
	[*She takes the newspaper out of her purse and looks for some ads she had already marked. She'll make the effort and go ask for a job. . . .*]
MARTA	[*off*] I have to find something satisfying, I must be good for something. . . .
	[*She again sees her clocks, her mirrors, her plants, which are waiting for her at home.*]

[*But now she's in an office, sitting in front of a man with his back to us. She's nervous, insecure.*]

MAN   Have you ever worked in an office before?

MARTA   No, no sir. . . .

MAN   What is your age, if it's not indiscreet?

MARTA   I'm fifty and a widow.

MAN   You seem much younger. . . .

MARTA   Thank you. . . .

MAN   So, you've never worked before. . . . Do you type?

MARTA   No, no . . . but I can learn. . . .

MAN   How about filing? I suppose not. . . .

MARTA   I suppose I could learn that too. . . .

MAN   Do you know any foreign languages?

MARTA   No, no sir . . . and that must be the most difficult to learn, isn't it?

MAN   The problem, Madam, is that we aren't looking for an apprentice, you know. So, I don't see how you could be useful to us. . . .

MARTA   Oh, I think I'd fit in somewhere.

MAN   Cleaning ladies we already have, Madam. . . . Still, if some day we need you, we'll be sure to let you know. . . .

MARTA   Yes, of course . . . thank you . . . thank you. . . .

[*And now she is waiting in another office. It might be better not even to try . . . and to return to her plants.*]

MARTA   [*off*] But I don't want it to be my fault. . . . Here they aren't looking for anything in particular, just a certain sense of culture and distinction. . . . How I'd love to go home and drop all this. . . . My poor plants, all alone . . . but I don't want it to be my fault . . . no one can say I haven't tried. . . .

[*A door opens and a voice tells her to come in. Marta gets up reluctantly and enters the office, where a woman, also seen from the back, invites her with a gesture to sit.*]

MARTA   I came because of the ad. . . .

WOMAN   Yes, I thought so. . . .

MARTA   What kind of work is it? Why didn't the ad say?

WOMAN	Oh, it's an easy job, very pleasant. And what's more, you won't have a fixed schedule; you'll be able to work in your spare time. . . .
MARTA	All I have is spare time. . . .
WOMAN	All the better for you; that way you'll earn more. . . .
MARTA	But what would I have to do?
WOMAN	It's a serious job, I don't want you to think it's not . . . and we need serious people. . . .
MARTA	That I am, serious. . . .
WOMAN	Yes, I can tell, but you might not like it. . . .
MARTA	If you don't tell me . . .
WOMAN	What have you worked at, up till now?
MARTA	Nothing . . . that is, I mean, I've only managed the house. . . . Now I'm a widow, you know. And my son has . . . gotten married, yes, and now I don't have so much work at home. . . .
WOMAN	Are you used to dealing with people?
MARTA	Yes. . . . That is, when my husband was alive, we had an active social life. . . .
WOMAN	So you have many friends. . . . That's excellent, because friends are possible clients. . . .
MARTA	But what kind of job is it? You still haven't told me. . . .
WOMAN	It's a job selling cleaning products, one of the best brands. . . .
MARTA	You mean selling things from door to door?
WOMAN	Yes. . . . It has to do with presenting a new product, a whole range of products. . . .
MARTA	And you mean for me to go to the houses of our friends?
WOMAN	That's always easier than going to the houses of people you don't know. . . .
MARTA	It seems to me—
WOMAN	The commission is high—and since you say you have lots of free time . . .
MARTA	I think I've made a mistake. . . . All day long, back and forth, bothering people at home. . . .
WOMAN	It's not bothering them, Madam, it's making it easier for them to buy what they need, it saves them a trip to the

store—but if it doesn't interest you, there are more people looking for work than we need. . . .

MARTA   What I don't understand is why you mislead people. . . .

WOMAN   Mislead?

MARTA   Yes, the ad sounded like another type of work. . . .

WOMAN   If it doesn't interest you, let's drop it. . . . I don't have time to waste explaining things. . . .

[*So they drop it. Now Marta returns to her apartment and her own environment and explains all the day's adventures to the plants and other objects.*

She changes her clothes, waters the plants, caresses the faces of the clocks and the days shown on the calendars. She makes plans for the future.]

MARTA   I'm tired. . . . It's like they all cheated me. . . . The rector—if you knew all the stupid things the rector told me. Then I went to the neighborhood association. . . . There was a nice young man, that's true, but it's not for me . . . I couldn't get along there. . . . And then I went to look at the ads . . . and nothing, nothing at all. Of course, since I don't know how to do anything, I'm not good for anything. . . . And then that woman who wanted to send me out selling soap and who knows what else door to door— What did she think I am? I'm tired . . . sick of it all . . . and it wasn't my fault, no, I tried. [*listens to a plant speaking to her*] Yes, you're right, I was afraid of all of you. . . . I was afraid of being shut in with you, of becoming like you for real . . . and I tried to escape, but I'm not afraid, now. . . . What makes me afraid is everything outside this house . . . as if everyone were against me. [*listens*] Yes, I know, you love me . . . and I love you too, a lot. . . . You could even say you're all I love. [*listens*] Of course, Charles too, despite everything, but it's different . . . [*a long pause*] . . . There's another possibility, though. Travel, a long trip around the whole world, for many years. . . . To start over, as if I were a young girl. . . . To forget everything I've been up to now, everything I've done, to forget about you, too, and see the world. . . . The idea doesn't displease me, no. But I like to think that I'll never go back out in the street, that you will feed me and some day I'll be a plant for real . . . and that day I'll really have my feet on the ground! I'm tired, very tired. . . .

[*And she enters the bedroom; the plants have already invaded the bed, and Marta gently moves them to make room for herself.*]

MARTA Ah, you rascals! Maybe you too want to throw me out of the house? Come on, come on, leave me a little room, I have the right to rest too, don't I? Would you be angry with me if I went away? A long, long trip—to unknown lands, far away . . . a change of air. . . . I always wanted to, but John couldn't see his way clear to do it. . . .

JOHN Wasn't going to Paris enough? What do you want, to leave everything in the air now? What about work, the business?

MARTA . . . We didn't even go to Paris. . . . But, if I went away, what would happen to you, poor little things? I don't know, I don't know, we'll see. . . . Now I'm very tired, I'll think about it tomorrow . . . or another day . . . I'm very tired. . . .

Previously unpublished story, translated by John Dagenais with the permission of the author.

Broken Threads

It was almost like starting from nothing. But the important thing was to begin and it didn't matter how.

I had the option of letting it be, of trying to forget it, and perhaps that would be the easiest. Of course it would. Or maybe not?

I knew that I could eventually erase it all, as if it hadn't happened, as if that evening I had gone to bed early, as if they didn't exist. But I was afraid that one day, unexpectedly, in the most banal of circumstances, everything would come out, make itself felt insolently and insistently. And then I would find myself up to my knees in mud with no way to get out. Now I had the strength that hatred gave me, the powerful desire for vengeance was on my side. Later on, I would only have desperation and impotence.

And, furthermore, letting it go would cost me just as much time and effort as carrying out my plan. And in a situation like mine, I knew, knowing myself as I do, that immobility would be more difficult for me than action.

They had deceived me, they had tricked me, they had abused me. They had cast me aside like a dirty rag, no longer useful, and had disappeared without worrying about the consequences. And I had to face it all, alone.

I could not let things go; I could not just try to erase it; I could not leave them to their own devices; the consequences affected all four of us and we had to settle accounts together. It was a matter of principle.

And so I got to work.

I worked systematically. I kept all feelings out of it and saved them for the right moment.

It wasn't clear-cut. It could be fatal if it wasn't stopped in time.

"The loss of blood can be quite rapid," said the doctor, half-intrigued, half-amused.

And afterward there was the danger of infection. And above all, it hurt. But that didn't matter in the least.

"And it is irreversible, of course, at least as far as today's techniques are concerned. . . ."

So much the better. And if it hadn't been irreversible, I would make sure myself that it was.

But I did have to take some precautions.

The third night I realized that if I didn't ask the waiter I could spend weeks and weeks going to the pub for nothing.

The truth was that now that I had gotten started, I was ready to take my time. I was capable of waiting and waiting the days and months it would take to find him. I had nothing better to do: just find him. And after finding him, to follow the thread to the other two.

"Sure . . . he comes here a lot," I persisted with the waiter, "with a bunch of guys and girls."

The waiter looked at me mockingly. It was easy to see he wasn't interested in my questions. I mean that my questions didn't interest him in the least; but *I* did. And I thought that maybe I could get to him that way.

And so I started staring at him with big moist eyes, playing the kitten.

"Lady, if you don't even know his name . . ."

"And how would it help if you knew it? Are you trying to tell me you know the name of everybody that comes in here? Do you know what my name is, for example?"

"There's no need to, honey . . . just looking at you is enough."

And how he looked at me! I had to make an effort not to burst out laughing and to keep playing my role.

"You're really that interested in that guy?" he asked. "Maybe I'd do just as well, eh?"

Idiot. When men are on the make they lose their sense of the ridiculous. Someday I'd give him a mirror as a present.

"For what I want him for, no, man, you won't do . . . sorry," and I gave him a bewitching smile.

"And what is it you want him for, if I may ask?"

"No, you may not. . . . But I can tell you don't want to help me. . . ."

What if I offered him money? I felt silly just thinking about it. And anyway, maybe it was the truth that he didn't know him. I tried a different strategy, as a last resort.

"He owes me money . . . a bundle."

"Do you run around giving money to people you don't know?"

"He made me feel sorry for him, see . . . and now, the bastard has disappeared right off the map. We'd agreed to meet here and . . ."

"I'd like to help you. . . . I like you. . . ."

I listened hopefully.

"But you don't make it very easy for me. . . ."

What did he want, the bastard? I'd already described the guy and his crowd. I didn't know anything else. What did he think? That if I knew more I'd be getting drunk with a waiter, leaning indolently on the edge of the bar?

"And you don't offer much in return."

There it was. He wanted something in exchange. Of course. Nobody gives something for nothing. But that meant he had something to give me.

"What do you want?"

I put my purse on the table. Very obviously.

"No. It's not money I want. I want company. Understanding. Love. Understand?"

I would definitely have to give him a mirror. I didn't know whether to get really pissed off or to break out laughing. Ugly, scrawny, sweaty. . . . I wasn't prepared to pay the price he was asking. Even if I knew for sure that that price would put me on the track of the blond guy. I could still pick and choose the men I wanted. I still wanted to choose them.

My face must have given away what I was thinking because the dude looked at me, perplexed, realizing that all his ideas, all his fantasies were going wrong.

"I don't believe the only reason you're looking for him is because he owes you money. . . ."

I'd had enough. And I felt really stupid. So I got down off the stool and without saying anything else headed for the door.

But before going out, I looked over the whole place. I was somehow sure that I would see him.

And if I saw him, what would I do? What would I do when I found him?

He was blond. And tall. And he stood out from the crowd not just because of his height but also because he was good-looking. Or maybe because he had a familiar face and way of standing, like people you think that you know for a moment because they resemble somebody else you know or have a fashionable style.

My eyes were drawn to him without thinking about it. And while my friends went on talking and laughing, I tried distractedly to imagine him naked.

Maybe he could figure out what I was thinking about.

You would think he would. But the whole evening he only looked my way two or three times, without really seeing me. He ran his eyes over me with the indifference of someone who isn't looking at anything.

Between the table where my friends and I were sitting and the table where he and his friends were there was a dense shadow. But luckily one of the spotlights lit his face up enough for me to see him.

And then he went off with his crowd. I hadn't seen him again until two weeks later. With two others. I had recognized him, but he hadn't recognized me.

Then I lost him again.

I left the pub. I felt tired.

Maybe I had chosen the most difficult of all possible ways: looking for a needle in a haystack. I mean trying to find, in such a big city, a man with no name, without knowing his job. I thought I knew his age . . . maybe. A man I had only seen two times under very different circumstances and with whom I had scarcely exchanged more than a few words.

And through him, whom I couldn't find, I thought I would find the other two. Whom I had only seen once and with whom I had exchanged even fewer words. All I knew was that one of them was named Pere.

"Dammit, don't rush me, Pere!"

I was worn out and I had just begun. I couldn't give up so soon.

In the taxi I went over it in my mind. The car, maybe. A red Renault 14 with Palma plates. And that's all. A car whose license number I didn't know, a man named Pere, and another man I'd seen once in the pub.

But the next day, halfway through the morning I left work on some silly pretext.

The girl who waited on me looked at me with a dumb face when I asked her how many cars of that model and color had Palma plates.

"If I had the number of the plate, I wouldn't have come here, Miss," I told her.

"Why are you looking for this car?"

I hate answers that are questions. Especially that particular question.

"He ran me off the road and didn't even stop. The driver must have been drunk. Or he was out of his mind. Luckily nothing happened to me, only a few scratches on my car, but he could have killed me."

"Didn't you report it to the police?" the girl said with complete indifference.

She looked like she didn't believe a word I was saying.

What good would it have done to report it to the police? Look, inspector, or sergeant—what rank did cops have?—Look, sir, it was a red Renault 14. . . . No, I didn't have time to get the number, but I'm sure about the PM for Palma. Yes, I'm sure. Yes, one of them was named Pere, but I don't know if he was the owner. Another was a good-looking blond I saw at the Pub Clau on the Born a while ago. Were they friends? Not exactly. Half an hour more or less. Yes, I came directly to the station to report it, don't you see how bruised I am?

But I hadn't gone there, to the police station. What good would it have done? File it away and that's that.

"What good would it have done to report it to the police?" I said, and the girl looked at me without interest. All her attention was focused on the file she was using on her nails.

"Well, I don't really think it will do you any good to have come here, Ma'am. I'd have to wait several days to find out how many cars are that color . . . and I'd have to ask permission from headquarters to give you the list. . . ."

It was too much work for her, obviously. Too much getting involved. And all in all, what good would it do me to know all the cars that were that color?

I went back to work with my tail between my legs. How stupid! No, I don't mean the girl at the police station. *I* was the stupid one. Why would she, or anyone else give me the name and address of all the owners of red R-14's with Palma plates, supposing, of course, they even had the information on who they were?

The traffic cops, of course! But what reason could I give them? What reason that would not get me involved? That wouldn't tie my hands and keep me from settling accounts with those three thugs?

My plan was not complicated, but it was absolutely essential not to make them suspicious if I wanted to carry it out successfully and make a clean getaway.

And so, nothing to do with the traffic cops; no way. I had to do it on my own.

I quit my job in order to dedicate myself completely to the search.

They were full days, days of an obsessive intensity. I gave myself so completely to the task that there were moments in which I even came to forget the objective. The search turned into an end in itself, and the motive that had driven me got diluted among the cars and the faces of men.

Now those days are like a thick fog moving out onto the horizon and dissolving into the air, because the tranquillity that has come over me is like a sun which rises splendidly and drives away the shadows. I wouldn't even know how to count, nor does it matter, the days I spent walking, my eyes tired from so much looking, my feet swollen. All I have left are the confused sensations. I checked, obsessively, all the cars. Those that were parked and those that in a dizzying way drove by. I wandered through all the neighborhoods, I went systematically down every street, I went into all the parking garages and stayed there until the closed atmosphere suffocated me, until the beams of the ceilings seemed to touch the ground and I felt that they were about to crush me. And when I saw a red spot among the dead rows of parked cars, my heart gave a jump, and when a red splotch stood out among the crowd which went down the street, my legs began to tremble.

Sometimes, when a red car disappeared on the other side of a stoplight, I had asked myself what I would do if it were the one I was looking for. How would I follow it? What good would it do me to find it? If I found it parked in the street I could wait. If it were parked in a garage, the same. But if it were going down the street and I was on foot. . . . Trying to reason things out was useless. The chase had become the reason for my existence. A reason beyond reason; I couldn't stop myself.

I alternated between red cars and men's faces. I looked at the men who passed by me. I went into bars, I waited at the exits of movie theaters, I went into department stores. And I looked at the men. Often with a shameless insistence that earned me, naturally, more than one bit of uninspired vulgarity. Why is it that men, when you stare at them, seem to turn into imbeciles?

But I hadn't had enough. I went into banks, and I looked at the men who worked there and at those who were customers. And I went up into offices and if someone stopped me I invented the name of some nonexistent friend; and while they went looking for her and didn't find her I looked at the workers. I went to public offices and private firms; I waited at the exits to suburban factories, I went into the workshops in the city and into the slums in the old quarter.

And I returned home exhausted, discouraged, obsessed. I may have been stupid, but even if that search lasted a lifetime, I couldn't abandon it; because without those three men my life had no meaning.

At home, with insomnia for my only companion, I rifled through telephone books searching for a ghost.

Sometimes, obsession gave way to a flash of lucidity and then I tried to organize the task. But the sensible organization that I proposed was impossible. I would have to remember details that could put me on the right track: if they were businessmen or if they had hands covered with calluses, in what setting would I find their faces? And I realized, in despair, that I could scarcely remember even their faces. The details and their faces got mixed up in my memory with a thousand details and a thousand faces which were good for nothing, not even for keeping me company. How many men's faces had I looked at? I had stared at so many that *their* faces melted into the memories. If I saw them I would not recognize them.

And maybe they had never existed: neither he, nor the other two, or the car, nor the evening I met them.

But the next day, early, I left the house and began my pilgrimage all over again. A sidewalk, all the parked cars, all the bars, all the shops, all the men's faces. Then another sidewalk. And then another street and another, and another. . . .

I don't know how many days I spent that way. I don't remember having taken a shower in all that time. Until I finally realized that I had to go back to keep watch at the pub. And then I realized that I had lost the few friends and acquaintances I had to the absurd obsession that filled all the folds of my brain, all the emotions, and all the feelings, all the minutes of my days.

I got to know who were the habitués of the bar and who weren't. I witnessed three changes of waiters. I let everyone think I was looking for a living there, though when someone made me an offer I refused it. I got to know all the other bars on that street and their habits, because, to be more subtle, I sometimes sat at an outdoor table at some place near the pub, watching the door until closing time, until all the customers had gone.

And when the lights went out, when on the sidewalk there was only some summer dawdler, when the windows went dark, I stayed on, with my insomnia, sitting a long time, senseless, empty inside and out, with a loneliness so overwhelming I couldn't feel anything.

At home, already well into the night, I lost myself once again among the rows of incomprehensible names in telephone books—like a last act of faith in an impossible miracle.

And when day came, out onto the street again, stopping at lights without crossing when they turned green, waiting for the stream of cars to pass, hoping that maybe at the next change the red Renault 14 would come. . . . And more suffocating parking garages and swimming pools churning with all sorts of people and markets gaudy with fruits and greens. In my memory there remains no recollection of having eaten that whole time, but I must have eaten something.

Theaters and open-air concerts without even looking at the performance, only searching among the avalanche of people for one of the three faces. And the sensation of hot sand burning my feet at some beach crammed with people. The sweat trickling down my neck and armpits. And a whirl of men's faces swallowed in the dirty foam of the waves.

And in the evening or at night, once more to the pub to wait without letting myself give in to despair, more obsessed with each passing day.

He was coming up the street, with a group. Like the first night, he stood out from the others.

Sitting at a sidewalk table, I felt my legs wilting beneath me. If I had been standing I would have fallen to the ground. I grabbed the arms of the chair without realizing it, my thoughts in turmoil, an unbearable noise in the walls of my brain.

One thought stood out from the others, luminous, insolent: what would he be like, naked?

This time I would not take long to find out. I could not afford to take long.

But what if he recognized me?

He passed right by without noticing that there was

someone sitting there: me. . . . Me, with my legs cut out from under me. He went into the pub with his friends. A few moments later, when I had calmed down, I went in too.

The two times I had seen him, and the third that night, had been in dim light. Now, the brightness of the ceiling lamp made him seem more mature, and stouter. But just as blond and good-looking. I felt unsure of my body, un-cared-for after so many days of thinking only of finding him.

In the bedroom he turned on the night-table lights and turned out the one overhead. On each table there was a photograph: beside the man a woman who looked a lot like him; beside the woman, another man. Joy and disgust made me stagger. He was one of the other two.

"Is that your house?" I asked, pointing to the photos.

"No, it's my sister's."

"But you live here?"

"No, I'm from Arta. . . . I only come here every once in a while, but I have the keys to their apartment."

I had them!

"And where are they?"

He got undressed, and his body was a temptation that made me shiver.

"On vacation. It's August, sweetie. . . ."

He came up to me, naked, and began to unbutton my dress, wrinkled and dirty from I don't know how many days of wearing it night and day. I felt ashamed and un-dressed hurriedly.

He caressed one of my nipples and I felt it as if it were not mine. I would have liked to have been able to enjoy—without taking sides, without another job to do—that body and that tenderness so unusual, so unexpected.

But I had to wait. Now I had found the thread and I had to wait because if I got too impatient, the thread that tied him to the other two could break. And I would have liked to be able to take advantage of that pleasure, while I waited. But I could not: I had my head too full of things and he, although he was an expert, was not able to empty it for me.

"Do you come to Palma often?" I asked in a moment.

"What? What did you say?"

"Does your brother-in-law know that you bring women to his house?"

"What, honey? Honey . . . don't talk, don't talk. . . . Don't you like it?"

It seemed impossible that I was so lucid. To be so much outside myself and, at the same time to be able to fake a pleasure that I didn't feel.

He, on the other hand, was after the total pleasure. And I, coldly, among groans that came out of a throat that was not mine, thought over my plan. When would they return, the sister and the brother-in-law? Where could I find *him* again when the moment came?

But had the moment come now or not? Should I settle the score with him now or was it better to have all three located and within reach? How to ask him about the third partner in crime without arousing suspicions?

"When do your sister and your brother-in-law get back from vacation?"

He continued his delirious movement upon my body. He was skillful at the art of sex, done tranquilly and without hurry.

"Dammit, don't rush me, Pere!"

"Are you coming? Are you coming?" he asked with a trembling voice.

I was thinking. I was thinking too much to be able to feel even a touch of pleasure. I was struggling between common sense and desire, between the sensible idea of remaining unknown and the desire to announce who I was.

And suddenly I felt tired, full of disgust. And I told him imperiously, "Come, come!"

Like an electric discharge, his beautiful body shook violently on mine. After some deep breaths, a sigh of satisfaction—his eyes closed, his breathing became regular. A smile on his lips. He was handsome in this state of repose. What a shame.

I decided to wait.

"Albert, will we see each other again?"

Without opening his eyes he told me slowly his address and telephone number in Arta. And then I went away stealthily, in order not to wake him.

That night I looked up the specific information in the telephone book. And a shower took away from me all the disgust of so many days and all the dirtiness of that encounter.

"Good morning, Mrs. Puignal. I'm from the Quest Company, and—"

"Oh, yes! They've already called . . . come in, come in." She opened the door the rest of the way to let me come in.

The house, seen in daylight, was completely different. Above all, the suffocating air of an apartment closed up for vacation was gone. The woman was talkative and told me without letting me get a word in edgewise about the marvelous trip she and her husband had taken. And how, a week after they had gotten back, she had still not finished putting the mountain of things they had bought in order.

"Sixty kilos of excess baggage! Imagine, a fortune. . . ."

But her husband was so kind that he had allowed her all her caprices, and she began to show me the silly baubles they had spent their money on.

Time was passing and it seemed that the woman had forgotten the reason for my visit. Until, a long hour later, she said, "Oh, excuse me. I'm wasting your time." And she offered me a whiskey and put herself at my disposal for the interview.

"Your husband's current employment?"

"He works for Surgrass, Inc. He's an assistant manager,

but soon he'll be a director, or vice-president. . . . I don't know for sure how those things work, myself. You'll have to ask him."

And she told me that he was very hard-working and a very good man. And that he had made it all on his own, and that it was a shame that they had no children but he didn't want to adopt any because like father like son and how are you going to know how a child of unknown parents will turn out?

Now I had the address of the company, the work schedule, the couple's habits, his interests. . . . And it was getting late. He would be arriving soon. If he found me at his home and recognized me everything could fall apart.

He did come. But nothing fell apart. On the contrary, my plans advanced in some way through his presence.

He looked at me hard, with a strange look.

"I think I've seen you somewhere, Miss. . . ."

"Ju . . . lia," my legs giving way. "Do you think so?"

But I understood immediately, and, it goes without saying, with great relief, that the strange look he gave me was not one of recognition, or, at least, not the sort of recognition I feared, and that the phrase was part of a whole style of relating to women he didn't know.

His wife understood too. All the friendliness, all the confidence that had driven her to tell me even intimate things, turned into sullenness. And haste. Haste for me to go, so that I would not figure out that her praise of her husband was a lie.

"Don't worry, honey," he told her without taking his hungry eyes off me. "If we eat a little late tonight it doesn't matter. . . . Let Miss Julia finish her work. Everyone has a right to make a living, isn't that right, honey?"

"I think I have enough with what your wife has given me already. If I find I'm missing some information when I'm preparing the report, I'll call her."

And I headed for the door. The man accompanied me

solicitously. He had a sparkle in his eyes which promised something when he gave me his hand.

The card said: Pere Puignal, Management. Surgrass, Inc. Majorca Avenue. . . . One corner of the card was cut off.

"Dammit, Pere, don't rush me!"

I had already been there once during the days of my obsessive search. If by chance the assistant manager had come out at the moment I was there asking for a nonexistent friend whose name I didn't even remember now, it would have saved me a lot of time. Or if I hadn't been so impatient and had waited on one of the benches in the hall until quitting time. . . . I wouldn't have found Albert, but I would have found Pere, and it didn't matter which one I started with. But maybe the thread would have broken with Pere himself. . . . In any case, it was not the time to be thinking about how things might have gone, but about how they had gone, and above all, how they would go.

I gave the card to the doorman and a few seconds later Pere received me in an ostentatious office, decorated with the same bad taste as his house. His arms open and smiling.

"The rounded corner on the card is a sign so I can tell whether to see the person or not," he told me with a mischievous voice.

It was easy: a few moments of pretending that I was interested in some professional information for my report, some penetrating glances, a smile and a low neckline well dowsed with perfume . . . and we had agreed to meet that same evening.

He confessed to me that he liked expensive whores.

"Yes, honey . . . I know you're not one, a whore," he told me as if he were doing me a great favor.

He was a boor, one of those men from whom neither the most exotic hotel room, nor the most luxurious office, nor the most refined profession could ever take away the overwhelming vulgarity that seeped through his pores.

He asked me paternally if I did it often, going with men . . . without charging.

"I like girls like that, like you . . . 'liberated' it's called, isn't it? But the truth is that you're the first one like that. . . ."

And he fondled me uneasily. Upset, suffocated, as if ashamed, insecure with the novelty of it all.

The champagne flowed in rivers. The best, he had said. He was ostentatious, ridiculous; the champagne was a heavy *semi-sec*, lukewarm. But he gulped it down with pleasure.

He undressed rapidly and wrapped himself up in the mauve silk sheets. He told me to wait: he wanted me to do some special things. I don't mind doing them, but only when *I* want to. He was another one who should be given a mirror.

And I wasn't even completely undressed when he did his thing on the silk. And he felt so satisfied, his virility so obvious, that I couldn't keep from laughing.

"What are you laughing at?"

"And what about me?"

He looked at me surprised, without understanding my contemptuous attitude. Certainly expensive whores were very happy to get paid for so little work. And of course his wife, now that she had all the clothes she wanted, didn't ask for anything more. So he didn't understand why I didn't admire him and why I was asking him troublesome questions. And it wasn't because I wanted that moron to make love to me, but because I enjoyed making fun of his pretensions, knocking him off the pedestal where he alone had placed himself.

"Don't you know that girls like me, 'liberated' you know, want to feel some pleasure too? Or maybe you think that

144

just from looking at you I've had an orgasm? I bet you don't even know what a female orgasm is. . . . Huh? Do you know how a woman has one?"

He kept looking at me and covered his sex with his hand, although it was already covered by the silk sheet.

"The sexual prowess of a man isn't based on the pleasure he can feel, but on the pleasure he can make the couple feel. Didn't you know that?"

The phrase had just come out. I had never thought about it just that way, perhaps because I had never found myself in this sort of situation before. But the phrase had come out just right.

And I felt a cruel satisfaction seeing him stretched out there, overcome with shame. I really got into it. It almost would have been enough in itself, but I had promised to keep feelings and emotions out of it, until the last.

He was almost crying.

"Don't worry, honey. . . . You'll see how in a little bit I'll be ready again, and then—"

"Do you think I need it for something, your little flap of flesh, you jerk?"

I pulled the sheet off him. I looked at his withered *bon-bon* and began to empty my glass of champagne on it, a little stream that trickled happily from my raised glass onto his private male parts.

When I had emptied it I went to the table and filled it again. I opened my purse and dropped the pill into the champagne.

"Here, drink a little more. . . ." I smiled at him.

"You're not mad anymore?" He was disconcerted.

I lay down at his side, patient, docile. He touched my thighs with one hand and with the other he drained the glass into his mouth.

His hand stopped dead between my thighs as the empty glass rolled onto the floor. Then I pulled on my clothes. I wiped the glasses and the bottle with a towel, I put on my gloves and went back to the bed.

The blood almost made me ill and the disgust nearly kept me from finishing the job. But I finished it. And he slept like a baby.

Outside the hotel I looked for a booth to call the clinic from. It was a warm night.

The thread had broken.

Eight days of waiting, of searching again all the faces that entered, of storing up eyes and mouths and noses of men, resting only in the middle of the night when I was sure that no visitors would go to the clinic. Pretending I was waiting for the bus, walking up and down the sidewalk, sitting hours and hours in my car, always wondering whether he had alerted the other two or if he had kept his secret.

One day, just for a change, I went into the clinic. I had coffee in the bar inside from which I could easily watch the stairs and the elevators. It was much more comfortable to watch from inside. I could stay there for several hours. Like some friend of a sick person who was trying to relieve herself of the unbearable tedium of the hospital room.

But his wife came in and I realized that that observation point wasn't safe for me. That she might see me and recognize me was no risk: I was sure her husband hadn't told her that he had taken me to a luxurious place and that I had baptized his balls with champagne. But Albert might come by and put two and two together, if he hadn't already. And it wasn't Albert I was looking for now: it was the third member of the trio.

And it was all for nothing. The wait, the precautions: neither Albert nor the other one came. The day they let Pere go home I felt cheated. The thread had broken.

But now that I had found two of them I couldn't be satisfied without finding the third. I wanted to do a good job.

I had to find out what relation there was between the two brothers-in-law and the third one, where they were coming from, or who the red car belonged to, or which of the two was the missing one's friend. And I couldn't ask either Albert or Pere.

I had before me an impregnable mountain. And at its top, another cloud. Where were they coming from that night? Where were they coming from? Were they just friends, or were they business partners? Did they belong to some club? Or political party? Perhaps the third was also from Arta and had come down with Albert to go bar hopping and they had taken Pere along with them to go on a binge or so that he could take them to the liveliest haunts in the city. . . . Maybe they were coming from a soccer match . . . but no, the games never end that late. . . . Who knows; maybe the third man was a chance companion, a guy they scarcely knew and then I would never be able to find him through them.

I began to lose myself in conjectures, hypotheses. None of them showed me a way out that seemed reasonable or workable.

I could hire a detective. But what would I tell him? Look for an individual like this and like that who on such and such a day at such and such an hour was with those two in a red car. Well, maybe so. But what would assure me of the detective's discretion when he put the "accidents" together?

I had to find him myself, as I had done with the other two. The first had led me to the second rather easily, but the first had been difficult to find. And to find the third now seemed to be as difficult or more than finding the first: the thread had broken. I had broken it myself because I hadn't been able to wait. If I hadn't been in such a hurry, I could have stayed in contact with Pere and, in time, I could have found the third, who didn't even have a name.

I could spend my life looking for men.

I didn't care. I was ready to do it. I had nothing better to do.

I don't know if it was by premonition or simply because

it was the easiest way—although not the safest: I set up my watch in front of Pere's house.

In my surprise I almost left without paying, leaving the pastry and the coffee half-finished: Mrs. Puignal was leaving her house with another woman, one I had seen at the clinic but had not tied to them.

It could be, of course, just that, a friendship formed there, two sorrows which join together and keep one another company and all that. Or it could be that the thread had not been broken. . . . Hope brought me alive again, after days of drowsiness in front of Pere's house.

I paid the rude waiter quickly and followed the two women.

They went tirelessly from one shop to another. What stamina! And they chattered without stopping. But I didn't dare approach them in order to listen to their conversation. Back and forth all morning!

Until lunchtime. They went into a restaurant and sat at a table with three place settings. I sat down in a corner and saw that, as time passed, they looked more and more impatiently at the door. They ate the first course alone, and the second. As dessert was being served, my third man sat down, excusing himself, before the empty plate.

Now I had to work quickly. The three threads were tied together.

I left the restaurant and waited outside. The man and the two women separated on the street and I followed the man, naturally. To an office building nearby. The red Renault 14 was parked right in front. I waited a while, and when I had calculated that he would already be at work, I went in to talk to the doorman.

"Does the red Renault 14 belong to anyone in these offices?"

"What's it to you?"

"Listen, I just broke out a headlight on his car when I

was trying to get my car out. If it belongs to anyone in this building, I'll talk to him to arrange the insurance papers."

"Leave your name and telephone number on the windshield."

"Do you think I go around the world leaving personal information on the windshields of cars? If you won't tell me I'll go up floor by floor and when I find the owner I'll tell him just how well you've looked out for his interests, and the report won't be so rosy, I assure you."

The man left his little booth reluctantly, looked in the street and coming back in he told me that the car belonged to John Varell.

"Which company?"

"Plywood Products."

"What floor?"

"Fifth. Number four."

"Thanks. I'll nominate you for the amiability prize."

I went up to the fifth floor, I went in to all the doors except number four and when I thought enough time had passed, I went down again. I didn't speak to the doorman going out.

I went into a bar and asked for the telephone book. There were only a few Varells and it wasn't difficult to figure out which address belonged to mine.

"Mr. Varell of Plywood Products?"

On the third call the maid said "yes" but that he was at the office. Would I like to leave a message? No, it wasn't necessary. I'd call again. . . .

I jotted down the address. I had no time to lose. If Varell had been warned by Pere, if the doorman told him about the altercation he'd had with me and the lie about the headlight, if the maid told him a woman had called asking for him, the man could slip through my hands.

Things were moving too quickly.

I called Albert.

"I'm coming to Arta, on business. . . . Good, OK."

We'd have dinner together . . . and then. . . .

By the time I got to the highway Albert would already have asked for the apartment of some friend to spend the night with me there. And before meeting him at the restaurant, I had already found out about the emergency services in the town.

It was a shame. But the blood no longer made me ill.

The place was an apartment on Cala Ratjada, without a phone and with no booth nearby. I took his car into town; I called from a booth next to the lot where I had left my car and the ambulance probably still hadn't picked him up by the time I was back on the highway and headed for Palma like a woman possessed.

The red car was parked a few blocks beyond the building where John lived. I broke open the door and spent what remained of the night inside.

The excitement kept me from feeling tired. And the brightness of the streetlamp made it impossible to remain hidden. I had to crouch down between the front and back seats and wait.

I wasn't thinking. I was like an automaton which moved through a series of programmed actions. But programmed by me, as if I were on another side of my body, very far from there. The light of the lamp hurt my eyes and made everything look red. Two bloody plastic bags, one tossed in a trash can in Palma, far from the luxury hotel, the other under a highway bridge close to Manacor.

Soon day broke. I heard people walking down the sidewalk but no step paused beside the red car. My bones were stiff, my mind blank. I began to look impatiently at my watch and it seemed that the hands had gotten stuck. At ten no one had gotten in. What time did that guy go to work? What if he wasn't going today? What if Albert had called him? But of course Albert was in no condition to call anyone, poor thing.

At ten thirty someone got in the car and started it up. I
held my breath. What if instead of the man it was his wife?
What the devil was I doing in that situation? How did I
get into this mess? But I shouldn't think about it, I
shouldn't ask questions, now. I had to act and that was
that, feelings and doubts aside.

The driver coughed and I knew it was a man. I sat up
and with the noise I made, John tried to turn around. But
I didn't let him.

"Watch where you're going; you could kill us, and if
you don't kill both of us, I'll kill you."

"Who are you? What do you want? What are you doing
here?"

His voice trembled. Especially when he felt the touch of
metal on the back of his neck.

"Can't you guess?"

He couldn't guess.

"Didn't Pere tell you what happened to him?"

He hadn't told him anything. Only that they'd operated
on his prostate. How about Albert? Didn't he know what
had happened to Albert? He didn't know.

"Head for Bellver. And don't try anything foolish. I
don't have anything to lose anymore and in a bit I'll tell you
why. But you can still save your life if you're a good boy."

As we headed toward the mountains, I reminded him
of a few things. And when I told him about my meetings
with the other two, his surprise turned to terror.

"I was just there—I didn't want to—"

"Well, for someone who didn't want to, you certainly
managed to take advantage of the situation. And now, on
one little spin through the mountains, we'll take advantage of the situation in order to satisfy my curiosity. . . .
Turn right. . . ."

He was too nervous to drive safely. I made him stop on
a shady side road and we looked like a car sheltering a
pair of lovers.

"Albert and you are relatives?"

"No." And he tried to turn around to look at me.

"Don't turn around or I'll shoot you. And you and Pere?"

"No."

"What's the connection among you then?"

"Albert and I were friends in school. . . ."

"Is Albert married?"

"No. And if you think you'll be able to do to me . . ."

I gave him a blow on the back of the neck and he fell over, stunned. I could have finished knocking him unconscious and gotten to work, but I was curious and wanted to satisfy myself. I waited until he came to again.

"Where were you coming from that night?"

He opened his eyes and didn't answer.

"Where were you coming from, I said?"

"From celebrating at my bachelor's party," he said with a thin voice.

"Well, I'll be damned!" I burst out laughing, "What a group!"

And this time I really clobbered him with the iron bar. He fell unconscious against the steering wheel and I had to move him to the other seat. With the movement, a thin thread of blood ran out of his ear. But the pulse was still beating.

I undid his pants and cut it with a single stroke.

Without taking off my gloves, I drove down from the mountains very carefully, without running even a single light.

John was still unconscious when I left the car in the parking lot of the same clinic they had taken Pere to.

I called from the booth on the corner and threw the plastic bag with the scraps of skin in it into the trash can next to it. I waited a few moments until I saw some people in white looking for the red car. Later they brought a stretcher and when they took him into the emergency room I looked for a mail box to mail the three identical letters that I had written long ago.

Dear Pere, John, and Albert:

When you left me lying in that doorway, raped three times, I decided that I had to settle up with you, no matter what. It was not just revenge. I also wanted to make sure that you could never rape another woman, the three of you at once or individually.

It would have been easier, once I found you, to make you disappear from the map. But if I had killed you, I would have spared you the obligation of remembering me for the rest of your lives, and I would have taken upon myself the burden of having you in mind forever.

Once I was the loser even though I hadn't entered voluntarily in the game. Now I've made the rules and, naturally, I've won.

Until never,

Isabel-Clara Simó

Isabel-Clara Simó

Isabel-Clara Simó *Valencia, 1943*

Creative works   *Es quan miro que hi veig clar*. Barcelona: Selecta, 1979. Short stories, winner of the Víctor Català prize.

Júlia. Barcelona: Magrana, 1983. Novel.

Idols. Barcelona: Magrana, 1985. Novel.

Bresca. Barcelona: Laia, 1985. Short stories.

T'estimo, Marta. Barcelona: Magrana, 1986. Novel.

Isabel-Clara Simó directed the literary-artistic-sociopolitical journal *Canigó* for ten years, contributing many of the articles herself and editing the others. Until the publication closed in 1983, she described herself as a journalist, although she also translates, teaches philosophy, takes care of her family, and writes short stories and novels. Like Pablo Neruda and for the same reason, Simó makes a deliberate and successful effort to write accessible literature—stories and novels that can be read and enjoyed by working people—in a style at once simple and elegant. She attributes to her work as a journalist some of the qualities others have seen in her creative writing, such as being able to express ideas in clear, brief language, aiming

157

for a rapid but panoramic vision. It is an agile language, sometimes brilliantly simple and always balanced . . . an everyday language for everyday anecdotes.

Simó's preoccupation with the triple level of oppression suffered by workers, women, and Catalan-speaking people forms the basis of her first novel *Júlia* and some of her stories. The novel is historical, based on the struggles of laborers in turn-of-the-century Valencia. The sudden entry into the upper class of a former factory worker underlines the protagonist's own strength of character as well as the political turbulence both within and without the household as a result of the whim of an old man who breaks the unspoken rules of class rigidity.

Children's literature is of great interest to Isabel-Clara Simó. She has written a few stories about and for children herself, which have not been published. She believes that the function of literature for children is too often to teach them to fit into society, to inculcate conservative and often alienating values. She feels it is a mistake to depict children always as sweet angels, with attentive and loving parents, and few problems.

The alienation suffered by Lena as an adult in "A Crumb of Nothing" is seen against flashbacks of her stifling childhood and adolescence. In this short story, Simó captures the perpetuation of this solitude—Lena as a mother is unable to communicate with her sons. The narrative is juxtaposed with a discourse about the structure and interrelationships of mathematical sets and subsets. "Melodrama in Alcoi" is a classical story of jealousy with a bizarre twist.

Isabel-Clara Simó's use of Valencianisms and working-class speech in her dialogues lends veracity and gives some of her stories a very colloquial flavor. Her own speech is peppered with expressions and usages from her birthplace, and she revindicates her right to speech variants in opposition to the standard Catalan of Barcelona.

Translated by Spurgeon B. Baldwin from *Es quan miro que hi veig clar*, © Isabel-Clara Simó 1979.

A Crumb of Nothing

PART I   He caressed her breasts with his lips, gently, scarcely touching them. Lena's nipples grew firm, and she put her hand behind the boy's neck, and caressed him as well, running her fingers through his hair, which the clippers in their fury had left in reddish patches, so short, so closely cropped.

They hugged each other tight and made love a second time. But so ineptly that Lluis was embarrassed and hid his face between the breasts—Ah, Lena's breasts! / you shouldn't have such full breasts at age fifteen / I'm going to have to lose weight: I attract too much attention / with those breasts you can't wear your gym shirt tucked tight inside your belt, you have to wear it over your shorts— and she sat up a little and took his face in her hands and kissed his eyes with the silent intensity of someone who is trying to console when she sees no reason for consoling.

"I will always love you."

It was a splendid afternoon, and they had by mutual consent initiated each other into the rites of love, in an enchanted daze, each obviously blinded by the beauty of the other, filled with love and pleasure. They were amazed at

159

having discovered that each muscle, each pore, each hidden corner of the other was beautiful, tender, dense, and humid; and they didn't feel, even in the deepest hiding place in their hearts, the slightest pang of regret, since it was physically impossible for them to feel guilty. In spite of all that and many other things, a sudden sadness fell upon them. And they found themselves, without realizing it, and both at the same time, looking—she leaning her head, hair uncombed, on his shoulder—at the light which shone dimly through the slits in the blinds. He turned his head. His gaze went from the balcony to Lena's eyes. They looked at each other sadly, and were surprised at their sadness.

"Don't you think it's getting late?"

And she said it as if looking for a reason for their languor. But he said, "It's just six."

And she said no more, for the boy hadn't looked at his watch. He modestly put on his pants—half-sitting, half-lying down—to get up. He wrapped the sheet around her in a paternal gesture and led her to the balcony and pulled the cord. He was able to wrap it around the nail, which was wobbling in a hole that was too big and which some prudent person had driven into the unpainted window frame. The blinds squeaked and rolled up. And they squinted in the last rays of sunset. Affectionately, Lena cuddled up to Lluis's chest, covered with puerile fuzz, and murmured, "It's cold."

"Get dressed." And then he kept quiet, so she could dress without being embarrassed by his looking at her.

"Don't you think they have noticed, Lluis?"

"Who?"

"Miss Ursula always takes roll. She's the music teacher."

"Don't you girls ever miss class?"

"Yes. But next day you have to bring a note from home."

"Well, tomorrow tell them that your mother sent you

160

on an errand. They always believe that. If you say you
didn't feel well, they don't believe you."

"How about you?"

"I have it better. At home they know I miss gym a lot.
They know I don't like it at all."

"Why?"

"Why what?"

"Why don't you like it? Your body . . ."

"What's wrong with my body?"

"Nothing. I mean . . . well, you're really well built."

And she couldn't help blushing. Just as he couldn't
help looking down. He saw a slim body, supple, firm, and
young. And he didn't see anything unusual.

"Me, I want to be a writer."

To-toto-to-to-to-to-toto-toto-tototo-toto.

"Magdalena, the news is on and you still don't have
supper on the table!"

"I'm coming, I'm coming. Lena, girl, help me!"

And the clink-clink of setting the table. The soup that
burns your tongue and you have to blow on it.

"Lena, don't slurp your soup!"

Yesterday, Sunday the twentieth of December, 1942,
was a historic date for Spain. In the National Palace of
Cintra, the head of the Portuguese government, Oliveira
Salazar, and the Spanish secretary of state, Lieutenant
General and Count of Jordana, declared that Spain and
Portugal formed from that moment on a solid block of
mutual friendship and external peace.

"Would you mind telling me what's going on? I'm talking to you, and you are on the moon."

"She," Alex butted in, "has a dumb look on her face: do
you think she's in love?"

. . . the Allies think Italy is the Achilles' heel of the
Axis . . .

"Shut up, Alex," his mother ordered him.

Father kept on eating, without looking up.

. . . the American landing in Africa . . .

"Lena's in love! Lena's in love!"

. . . the strange reasons for the Anglo-Saxons landing on the Atlantic coast, when . . .

"Imbecile!"

(That which pertains, on the other hand, to the reflexive abstraction which characterizes logico-mathematical thought is to be obtained not from objects, but rather from the actions which can influence them and, essentially, from the more general coordinations of those actions, such as gathering, arranging, putting in proper relationship, and so on. So then it is precisely these general coordinations which we find in the set and, first of all: a) the possibility of a return to the point of departure [the inverse operation of the set] and also b) the possibility of achieving the same goal along different paths and without the arrival point being modified by the path taken [associativity of the set]. With regard to the nature of the compositions [gatherings, etc.] it can be independent of the order [commutative or Abelian sets] or it can depend on a necessary order.)

PART II

Zap! Lena squashed the bug between her thumb and index finger. She pulled two more dead leaves off the lily, and felt the stem. She looked at it thoughtfully, with her head held back. Maybe it should go a little more in the corner. It's too breezy here on the sixth floor. She sprayed it with insecticide, and cultivated the dirt. Then she turned to the geraniums and smiled. They also need love, the poor things. Her geraniums were delighted to see her. And she watered them, taking care not to let the water drip down below, because you have to pay a fine if your water drips down in the morning. The dahlia was wide open, and she couldn't resist caressing it. But she got dirt on it, because even her fingernails were dirty. Suddenly she ran to the patio, to wash her hands under the sink faucet. Pcheeeeeeeeeeeeeeee, the icy water slips through her fingers.

(You pig! You pig! You've wet your bed again! Look at that mattress!)

She turned around, drying her hands with a rag which she grabbed as she passed through the kitchen. She blew on the dahlia and tapped it a little. It seemed to cry. And very carefully she inspected one by one each little clump of earth and went along dusting them off with her apron. I'm sorry, darling, but you're the one who's dirty. . . .

(Nine years old! Almost a grown-up! And the mattress sopping wet! Pig!)

She went along blowing and scraping, tapping on the petals as if they had choked and she was whacking them on the back.

(I'm going to put the sheet here in front of the door, so everybody who comes in can see it! And when it's dry, you're going to put it on your bed. And if it smells, you'll just have to put up with it!)

She leaned forward on one knee so she could inspect the other side of the pot, and the flower jiggled its head, all puffed up and proud. She moved her knee forward a little more and . . . crash! She turned around and saw that she had knocked over the daisy pot. Broken. And the daisies scattered about, and the ball of dirt broken to bits.

(That girl has wet her bed again! But this time she won't forget it. And if it bothers you, take off and get out of here, because the sheet is going to stay there the whole blessed day. We'll see if she dares to do it again. Pig!)

Now Lena sweeps. Stooping down again, she goes along putting the daisies in her skirt, examining them one by one to see if they've been damaged. She looks all around, with the corners of her apron held up in each hand, but she can't find an empty pot. What about the one with the carnations in it, the ones that never sprouted? But what if they still were to sprout?

(Nyah, nyah, nyah! Lena is a pig! Lena is a pig! I never peed in
my bed, and I'm younger, nyah, nyah, nyah! Hey, what red
cheeks! Did somebody hit you in the face? What for? They
should have hit you where you pee. . . .)

She tries to fit the daisies in the pot with the carnations,
and she picks through it to find the roots. She finds instead a half-wilted little seed. She looks at it, touches it,
puts a little water on it. But she does not throw it away, instead she puts it in a corner of the pot, and continues to
plant daisies and cultivate the dirt.

(Is that thing still there? Magdalena, girl, you should be in bed
by now. Take that sheet away, or I'll lose my supper. And you, go
to bed and don't let it happen again. Look at Alex, who is younger than you and never wets his bed. And stand up straight,
you're making me nervous! I work all day in the house and
never have a moment's peace. . . .)

She picks up the handful of leftover dirt, puts it in her
apron, and marches to the kitchen to throw it in the gar-
bage. Then she returns to the balcony to see how everything looks. She puts the lily further back in the corner, so
that the blossoms touch the wall. The wind blows and she
realizes then that she is cold. She bends over now, because
she thought she saw a dark spot on the dahlia.

(What the heck do I care if they've killed that fellow Calvo
Sotelo? If she doesn't know how to make her bed, let her learn,
and if she can't turn the mattress over, *you* help her: you can
read the paper later. Do you think I am the maid?)

"Mother, where is Xavier?"
She turns around and sees little Jordi with his scarf up
to his nose and his bookbag over his shoulder.
"Are you here already? Is it one already? I haven't even
started to fix dinner. . . ."
"Where is Xavier?"
"Which Xavier?"
"Xavier Xavier. Little Xavier!"

"I don't know. He must be at school."

"No, because I saw big Xavier downstairs and he told me not to mess around because it's getting late."

"Don't say big Xavier. Say Daddy."

"OK, then, Father."

It wasn't a spot. It was the shadow of a leaf. She stood up and wiped her hands on her apron. She went into the dining room and then came back to the balcony, with a yawn.

"What were you doing out there on the balcony? It's very cold out there."

"Cleaning the plants."

"When do we eat?"

"Soon."

"And Xavier? Little Xavier . . .?"

"Your brother must have gotten sidetracked on the way home. Hey, pick up that coat and put it in your room."

(What? Let her do it? My back is killing me, all day long up and down, to keep a decent house on your miserable salary. And if she wets her bed again she can wash the sheets herself: I'm tired of doing it, I'm tired of doing for everybody and nobody doing for me. And that dummy says she was dreaming! You see how she is. She's always dreaming, asleep or awake. You, you will never be a lady!)

Lena goes into the kitchen. She opens the cabinet and gets out some potatoes. She starts to peel them with a little wooden-handled knife. Little Jordi comes back from his room, without his bookbag and his coat.

"When is little Xavier coming?"

"I don't know. What do you want with him?"

"The director says we're the only ones who haven't signed up to go to camp. . . ."

"You know father doesn't want you to go. You can tell him that."

"Let Xavier tell him, he's bigger."

"How late it's getting! You'll see what a bad mood your father will be in. But where are you going, so dirty? Go on, go clean up or you're going to get it."

(Given this, the structure of the set is consequently an instrument of coherence which subjects logic itself to internal regulation or autoregulation. In fact, by its own action, it puts into effect three of the fundamental principles of rationalism: the principle of noncontradiction which is embodied in the reversibility of the transformations, the principle of identity, which is assured by the permanence of the neutral element, and, finally, that principle on which one insists less, but which is equally essential, according to which the point of arrival is independent of the path taken. All displacements in space, for example, form a set [since two successive displacements are still one displacement, since a displacement can be nullified by a reverse displacement, or a "return," and so on]; and we see that the associativity of the set of displacements which corresponds to the conduct of the "turns" is, in this respect, fundamental for the coherence of space, since if the points of arrival are constantly modified by the paths taken, there would be no more space, but rather a perpetual flux comparable to the River of Heraclitus.)

PART III

No, no, it's making me sick. A little bit and no more. If you are not used to it, why drink at all? You ought to do the things you like. Me? Certainly not. No one does what they want to in life. That doesn't mean that . . . but, for example, you love a son. You love him a lot. Yet who wants to go through childbirth? It's one thing to do what you like and another thing to do what you don't like in order to get what you do like. No, it's not that. Of course I remembered you, dear. Now, lately, not so much. I did at first, a lot. We were inseparable then, remember? And now we hardly know each other. We've changed so much! No, you don't look old; on the contrary, I envy you: you look a lot younger than I do. Or maybe it's not that we have changed, it's that a lot of things have changed. But no: we're the same age, we're of the same vintage, as they say. Forty-one. Impossible. Well, you will be next month.

The month after, then. But we have passed forty. We're forty-one, or forty if you will, and we don't need to tell everybody we're younger: it doesn't take any years away. Especially you, with that hairdo and that dress that looks so good on you. Maybe. . . . No, nothing. But it doesn't matter what we say, we'll still be forty. Not me, not at all. I don't worry about myself at all. It's the house, the children . . . I don't have. . . . Yes, you're right, saying there isn't enough time is an excuse. Deep inside it's laziness. And if you let it happen, you'll end up not caring and never trying to look good. You look in the mirror and get discouraged. And if you go to the movies and you see those beautiful women, it's worse. No, he never took me to any striptease. I didn't even know there were any here; I thought it was only in other countries. What? It would be embarrassing, I'm such a dummy, I . . . and your husband didn't . . .? Of course, he got all excited, but for sure he was thinking about those well-built girls. Hey, don't get mad. I don't mean . . . I don't know what I mean, sorry. You know it's been a long time since I've talked so much? I think we two ought to be able to tell each other everything. Without . . . without . . . how do you say it? Ah, yes: without inhibitions. Even though you and I are not at all alike. Yes, I remember well: she was the most unbearable of all. She looked like she was crying. I think I didn't like history because of her. She wanted us to know everything. And for what? Now we don't know beans. I'd like to see how much *you* know about history. Because back then, when she asked you a question you said you didn't feel good. No, it was impossible; as we well knew, you couldn't skip class. When she found us, hiding in the bathroom, I thought I would die. And you, boy were you cool! "Ma'am, Lena has her period and she doesn't feel good." What a stone face! Well, that's right. That was different. As if I was dying. Of course, you're the only one who knew it. I know, I know, you never told anyone. But I told you all about that. No, it's not that. It isn't that I needed to tell somebody . . . I still had him. But I thought it was a betrayal of our friendship. Something so important, so decisive. . . . You told me, I remember well, that I was telling you to show how important I was, to brag. And it wasn't true. You know? It didn't make any sense to brag about that . . . it was too . . . too profound. Yes, it was very important. It still would be today, for a fifteen-year-old girl, even if today there is more freedom. It's hard to believe it happened to me. No. I mean yes. I don't know. I don't know if I remember. But when he left I thought I would die. It's not that I didn't love Xavier. But sometimes I think I got married to . . . to, how should I put it? To not think about Lluis anymore. No, it's not that. To put an end to it. To say "I'm through waiting and waiting." Or rather, so I myself would understand that there was no hope. And Xavier was a good guy. He loved me. Afterward . . . you know what happened afterward. You get used to it. And you get tired. But he shouldn't talk like that. Anyway, it's just . . . let's see: yes, five years. It seems like yesterday. Get a separation, you say? What are you saying, dear! Don't do it. Of course, you don't have any children. But that stuff about nothing holding you together. . . . It's been years, think about it. Sixteen? You don't think that's a lot? Hate, hate . . . what nonsense! Think about how hard it'll be. There's the trial. Such private things will come to light. And the neighborhood: have you thought about your friends, about the neighbors? And furthermore you'll be all alone. Yes, you were always braver than I am. I wouldn't do it, you can be sure. I would put up with anything, but a step like that. . . . Life, after all, is a routine, right? And we have to conform. Besides, everybody will say he was right, you'll see. Yes, yes, I know you're still young, you've got a lot of life left. . . . But, to live your life all over again, what can I say? No, no, a little more, if you wish. OK, OK. But make it sweet. Forty-three, for example. I'm getting dizzy, really. I *am* a dummy, you're right. Xavier . . . Now? Nineteen.

He says I am a cream puff. He means if they touch me I
break, I get all upset over nothing. . . . No, I don't think
so: he doesn't say "fragile." It has no imagination. It's
too . . . prosaic? Yes, prosaic. What he means is a real
dummy. That I come by it naturally. I know: I wasn't then.
If he hadn't taken off to avoid the draft. . . . Why did he
do it? I've asked myself that so many times. Yes: a
postcard. He said that, in spite of everything, he loved me
and that he would always carry me in his heart. . . . Words!
From where? Arles, yes, France. I don't know if he came
back. I never heard anything. I don't know if time ran out,
either. All he had was a father. And an older sister who
took care of the family. No, I never met them. You don't
know. No, you can't know how I loved him. Maybe he
really did kill something deep inside me. But I kept on living, didn't I? Xavier was good to me. To be frank, I don't
know if I can fault him at all: in fact, I live the same life as
when he was alive. I, the house: he, the job. Now when
Xavier was born, little Xavier, then, yes. He made us very
happy. As a child he was so good, so likable! Yes, he still is,
but now he knows it, and he uses it. You know what I
mean? The younger one, Jordi. There's not much to say
for him. A good boy, that's for sure. He was mischievous
when he was little. He's seventeen now. Yes, they are two
years apart. He's a student. He likes books. Sorry, I'm boring you, talking about my children, especially since you
don't. . . . Yes, yes, you're right, we said "without inhibitions." Xavier is a brilliant boy, he makes you like him. A
little bit lacking in seriousness. I mean a rascal. Your husband too? What does he do? But dear, business never is
honest. You don't need to pay any attention to that. I was
thinking something else. That must be why you told me
about the striptease. . . . Yes, he had another woman, and
that's why . . . you know. And you want a separation just
because of that? But . . . I understand, yes, yes. It must be
hard to live together. Fiction? What do you mean? Listen
to what you're saying! Everybody does it. Everybody has

conformed. Of course it's going to kill your father, and
that hurts. It was a long time ago, the war and all that . . .
we all ought to forget. But do you know what a clean life
means? It means a life of poverty. And poverty causes a
bad life. If you had seen my parents! It was Hell. Very
pure, yes, very spiritual, but my mother . . . she lived a bitter life. She would have preferred less purity and more
food on the table. Xavier? A salesman. Well, we got along.
You had to skimp to get to the end of the month. But we
didn't lack anything essential. Yes, the pension is fine. But
since they're in school. . . . Of course, it's not the same.
Things have to run smoother. But since there is one less
mouth. . . . The bad thing is that the younger one has his
mind set on going to college. . . . I don't know why.
There's no future today in a professional career. The
older one is sharper, more realistic. He has his feet on the
ground. Why don't you like that? There's nothing wrong
with being realistic. . . . But you don't do anything without
thinking it over carefully first. Besides, now you're used to
a way of life that. . . . Work? Don't even think about it!
Even if there were jobs to be had, you still wouldn't know
how to do anything. Money, clean or not, is money. Me?
What if after a few years of marriage Lluis had shown up?
I don't know. I don't know what I would have done.
Nothing, I think. What do you expect? I don't know
why. . . . You, listen to me, don't be hasty. You have nice
clothes, and a maid too? See. Money is money. That is,
being well-off. . . .

(The set is then an essential instrument in transformations, but
in rational transformations which do not modify it all at the same
time, and each one of which is jointly subject to one invariable: it
is as if the displacement of a solid in the usual space leaves the
dimensions unchanged, and so on. In itself the structure of the
set is sufficient to reveal the artificial nature of the antithesis on
which E. Meyerson based his epistemology, according to which
all modification is irrational, because of the fact that identity
alone characterized reason.)

PART IV

"What are you doing out there on the balcony, mother? You'll catch pneumonia."

"Hi. I didn't hear you. I'm cleaning the flowers."

"In this weather? Hey, Mom, don't be stubborn. Let's go inside."

"No, no. I'm just finishing. How did you get in without my hearing you?"

"What do you expect to hear in this wind? Thieves could come in, and you with your flowers would never notice."

"No: it's just you—you always come in like that. Why this visit? Is today Sunday?"

"I was passing by. And I wanted to talk to you. But let's go inside, Mom!"

"I'm coming, I'm coming."

"It's our little girl, you know? Montse wants to know if you can babysit her tonight. We have an appointment, you know. Business. We want to make a good impression. We want to take them to a good restaurant. The Guria, for example."

"Where is that?"

"On Casanova Street."

"I've never been there, myself."

"You know what? Some day the three of us will go: Montse, you, and I. Would you like that? You know that Montse cares a lot for you. But about the girl. . . ."

"OK. Bring her over."

"She'll keep you company. She misses her grandmother a lot. . . ."

"Xavier, cut the fiction. Bring the girl over, but without the sweet talk."

"Well! Are we in a bad mood today?"

Lena looks at him then. She feels cold up her spine. She doesn't feel her hands anymore, stuck in the wet dirt of the flowerpot, which she is cultivating. She sees him standing there, smiling solicitously. She sees him a little bit out of focus, as if through the bottom of a glass. She tries

171

to remember what he was like when he was little. His voice, well, a little bit heavier, but the words . . . dripping with honey when he asks for something. Seeing him is different. Bent over, she doesn't dare touch her thighs together because each one is like ice to the other. She tries hard to remember the Xavier who no longer bears any resemblance to this well-dressed gentleman who is looking at her and smiling. Now the smile really *is* . . .

(My little crumb of nothing! My little crumb of nothing! Daddy's little boy, cute boy of this house!

"Don't throw him so high in the air! Don't you have any sense? He might fall—"

"Oh, be quiet, be quiet, don't be such a coward! Daddy's little boy! My little crumb of nothing! My son and heir! You like that, huh? Alex Rovira. Just like his father. Huh, cutie?")

"Why are you looking at me so hard? Hey, let's go inside. I don't have much time, you know."

"How big you are, Xavier! How different . . ."

"Yes, Mom, I'm real big now. Let's go inside, OK?"

"Just a minute. I want to finish the rosebush. It's all wilted. But it's growing real well, not a spot on it. But this wind . . . wilts it."

"What time, do you think?"

"What?"

"The little girl, what time shall we bring her over?"

Maybe he does look like Alex. But with that coat, such an elegant one, and those shoes, so shiny, he doesn't look like anyone. Nobody I know at least.

("Mother, if the baby falls will he die?"

"Be quiet, don't say that."

"But will he die?"

"I don't know. Be quiet."

"And how will he die? Will he break to pieces?"

"I said be quiet."

"I want him to break. . . .")

"Be quiet, stupid! Little girls don't say that. Don't ever say it again. Do you hear me? Do you hear me?"

"You're hurting me! You're hurting me!"

"Don't yell, you'll scare the baby!")

"Mother, don't you hear me?"

"What were you saying?"

"You're on the moon! You . . . you just can't live alone. But you can't come to our house, you know, there's no room, and I'm really sorry about that. We're both sorry. Montse would like it. But when Jordi comes back. . . ."

"I'm fine. Just fine. Move, I want to get the dirt out of that pot."

"What have you heard from the soldier?"

"He's fine."

"What? Talk louder, I can't hear you. . . ."

"I said he's fine. He wrote to me. . . ."

"It's about time. I'm glad. Let's see if the army makes a man out of him. You'll see, soon we'll have him back here. Time flies. When you least expect it. . . ."

("Daddy, what's an 'idiom'?"

"Be quiet now, darling, I want to hear the radio."

"The teacher says I have to look for five of them. . . ."

"I'm not sure. Set phrases, I think."

"Like 'A Dios rogando y con el mazo dando'?"

"No, that's a proverb. And it's in Castilian."

"The teacher wants it in Castilian."

"Well, you give her five in Catalan! And if she doesn't like it, to heck with her. Let her go back where she came from, we didn't ask her to come here."

"Well, what do I put?"

"Let me think. . . ."

"Can I put 'My little crumb of nothing?'"

"My little crumb of nothing? Where did you hear that?"

"You used to say it to Alex, when he was little. . . ."

"Me? Be quiet, be quiet now, they're starting."

"And now, for our Spanish listeners, here's Father Olaso.")

"I'm going, then. But something's wrong with you, mother! What are you doing, so quiet there, with this cold? You're not well. . . ."

"I'm fine, I'm fine. Go on, it's getting late. . . ."

"Yes, that's right, I'm late. A client. From Badalona. He doesn't agree with the bill, and I've got to go see him. He's a jerk: the export business is like Chinese to him. He doesn't know shit. And instead of asking, he just doesn't believe you. . . ."

"I don't know anything about it either."

"You, you're different. You're a woman. Or rather a mother. Like Montse. Mothers don't know anything about it. . . . Hey, beautiful, I'm going. I'll bring the girl over at nine. No: a little bit earlier, nine would be too late."

"OK, OK, get going."

"And don't catch cold. Some other day we'll all go out together. We'll drink to Jordi, how about that? We'll see if the army makes a man out of him, and his feet at least come in contact with the ground. Bye, Mother. How about a kiss?"

"No, no, I'm all dirty. Go on. See you tonight."

Lena's face is soaked with tears, and she has turned away so he can't see her. When she turns back, Xavier is no longer there. Through the balcony door there is just the back of the easy chair and the shining glass, cleaned just today. She looks at the rosebush: it's wilted. Her tears are bothering her, but her hands are too dirty to wipe them away. She looks at the rosebush, which trembles through the tears. . . .

(As an antisocial combination of transformation and conversation, the set, then, is above all an incomparable instrument of constructivity, not only because it is a system of transformations, but also and especially because the latter can be, in a certain way, measured by the differentiation of a set into its subsets, and by the possible steps from one of these to the others. It is as if the set of displacements leaves constants, in addition to the dimensions of the displaced figure [that is, the distances], its angles, its parallelisms, its straight lines, and so on. We can then vary the dimensions, but retaining all the rest, and we get a more general set, of which the set of displacements becomes a subset: this is the resemblance set, which allows us to increase the size of a figure without modifying its form.)

PART V   Dear Mother, you are not going to like this: I have gone AWOL from Sant Climent. As soon as I finish writing this and put it in the mailbox, I'm leaving Perpignan and going to Paris. I've got friends there. From there . . . I don't know. Anyway, I think it's better, more prudent for me not to write to you again. At least not for the first few years. But it was absolutely impossible for me to take this step without writing to you. I want to explain everything. Even though you, I'm sure, will not understand me.

In the first place, I want to tell you I'm not running away out of cowardice. Just the opposite: this is an act of valor. Military life was becoming insufferable. I mean it's not to avoid the discomfort of the service. The discomfort, or the discipline, these things are not important to me. The reason is that I will not conform. I don't even want to conform. If I don't do it now, I never will. I don't want to conform to nonmilitary life, to civilian life, as you have, or Xavier has, or my father himself did in later years. I can't. The comfortable thing would be to take off later, without risks. And I had to avoid that. I know you won't understand me.

But I have a lump in my throat. A lifelong lump. Just think how I'm leaving behind a lot of good friends. A lot of people I love. Even a girl. But I have to write to you, because you're the most important person in my life. The center of everything. You don't understand, right?

Mother: you—and I must be totally frank, for this is farewell—don't know how to love, and you have never loved. You don't even know what it means to love. And, curiously, you have been a very loved person. An injustice, don't you think? I know perfectly well that you have no idea how my father loved you. I saw it many times, when I was still too little to understand anything, how he looked at you. It was a look filled with love, and with pain. He never said anything: he just looked at you, but there was more love in those looks than in all the words in the world.

And you have had yet another love, and you couldn't see it either: mine, Mother. I loved you—and I love you—more than anybody. More than myself. When you looked at me it was like when you looked at my father: it seemed as if you were seeing something else. In your eyes there wasn't even a look. Xavier you did look at. You might even say that him you did love. But I know you well: you just enjoyed him.

Let one thing be perfectly clear: this isn't a letter to reproach you or reveal my jealousy for Xavier (I was quite jealous when I was little; but not now. Now I don't care). On the contrary: I am writing to you precisely because I love you. But you won't understand me. You will say: "What a dreamer! What a dummy!" And maybe you will cry a while. Mother, Mother! Do you know what it is to love a person like you, so indifferent and so marvelous at the same time? I'm not reproaching you, believe me. I remember when you held me on your lap, when I was little, when I was sick. I liked that a lot. I wanted it never to end. But you were in a hurry. What could you do; aren't mothers always in a hurry? You didn't talk: but you rocked me in silence, and I liked to feel your warmth, the softness of your skin, your smell, to feel the silkiness of your blonde hair. . . . And then I looked up and saw your gaze, so distant, so distant! Ah, if I could have said to you: "look at me, look at me!" But I'm sure you don't understand anything I'm saying. You never understood father either. You enjoyed Xavier. He's a scoundrel: you know that as well as I do. I love him, don't get me wrong. But he goes his own way. Soon he'll be rich, if he isn't already. He's likable and good-looking, and you enjoyed him. I think not so much now, since he got married. He is a conformer, something I will never be. That's precisely why I'm running away.

Mother, I'm not a coward. Or maybe I am; you can see that I've had it with Xavier, so satisfied in that wretched country. What I mean is that I am not deserting out of cowardice, but out of principle. Father would have understood me. Or maybe not, who knows? He had changed, in the last years. He had conformed. He no longer looked at you like before. I think he died of sadness. And to think I never even saw you fight. You are a soft person, someone who is present without being present, someone who makes everything nice but at the same time someone who dries everything up with a kind of strange detachment. . . .

Mother, Mother! Why didn't you love me a little bit? Why didn't you ever take notice of me? You could have done me so much good! Or maybe not: maybe I would now be another conformer, one more sheep in the flock. Happiness, or ambition, as in the case of Xavier, dulls our senses. I need you so much, Mother! But don't think this is a reproach: it's not your fault. It's part of your nature: you weren't born to love, you were born to be loved.

I wish you would remember me. Sometimes at least. Or you would look at me with that look you had in a photograph I have. Or, even now, you would love me, at least as you love your flowers.

Good-bye, Mother. We'll never see each other again. Here's a hug from your son. Jordi.

Lena folded the letter just as it had been folded, and put it back in her apron pocket. Mechanically, she wiped away the remains of tears, leaving her cheeks all masked with dirt. She looked at the rosebush and sighed: she couldn't blame the wind, now, with that canvas screen. . . . It was really cold on that balcony. March, dear March. . . . How did that go? The seventh of March!: "It's my birthday. To-day I am . . . let's see: forty-five. Yes: the seventh of March 1927."

She entertained herself for a moment counting the cars that passed by. But there were too many of them, so she tried to do it just with the red ones. But she lost count. "And maybe you will cry a while." "And maybe a while you will cry." "And a while you will cry maybe." "You will cry while a maybe and." "While a you will cry maybe and."

She got up and took hold of the railing. She looked at the people, so small, and the cars, so shiny. She raised her left leg and tried to put it over. It seemed too high. She put it down and tried the right one: yes. She edged her right thigh over the railing, to help the left one along. Now she sits, with her legs outside. A little push, she lets her hands go, and the body falls, falls, falls, falls, falls, falls, falls, falls, falls, falls, falls, falls . . .

f
f
f
f
f
f
f
s
s
s
s
s
s
s
z
z
z
z
z

PAAAAAAAAAAAAAAF!

(One after the other we can change the angles, but preserving
the parallelisms and the straight lines, and so on; we obtain thus
an even more general set, of which the resemblance set becomes
a subset: this set is the adjacent geometry set which intervenes,
for example, when one transforms one rhombus into another.
We will continue with the modification of parallels, always preserving the straight lines: we arrive, then, at the "projective" set
[perspectives, and so on], the precedents for which become subsets contained within it. Finally, we can fail even to preserve the
straight lines themselves, and consider figures which are in a certain way elastic, in which are maintained only the bi-univocal and
bi-continuous correspondences between their points, and we
have the most general set, or the set of the "homeomorphs," pe-
culiar to topology. Thus the different geometries, which seem to
constitute the model for static descriptions, purely figurative and
distributed in disconnected chapters, no longer form, in utilizing
the structure of the set, anything but a vast construction, the

transformations of which permit, through the encasement of the subsets, passage from one substructure to another [without speaking of the general metrics which one can base on topology by deriving from it the particular metrics, either noneuclidean or euclidean, and return in this way to the set of the displacements]. It is this radical change in a figurative geometry of a total system of transformations which F. Klein has been able to develop in his famous Erlangen program, and in it we have a prime example of that which, thanks to the structure of the set, we can call a positive victory for structuralism.)

Translated by Charles Merrill from
Bresca, © Isabel-Clara Simó 1985.

Melodrama in Alcoi

Conxita was very young when I met her, fifteen I think.
I was only twelve. But then I was still a little girl, dreaming of candy, or good grades at school, or that Mother
would call me "princess," or that Father would tickle me
when he got home from work, if he wasn't too tired. Not
Conxita. And not because she was three years older, but
because she seemed to have been born with the roguish-
ness and wisdom of an adult. I couldn't remember even if
you paid me how it was that we became friends, as different as we were. And then I don't know that you would
really call it friendship, because I adored her. I'm not sure
what she thought of me. She was probably playing at
being a mother, like playing with dolls, only for real. I had
pigtails, and wore short socks and I was pale as a sheet of
paper. She, on the other hand, was a beauty. People
turned to look when she walked past. Especially the men.
But she had such a lofty demeanor that they didn't dare
make the sort of remarks that seem to be as natural to
men as it's natural for a woman to blush.

She used to take me to the movies, and if anyone was
sitting in front of me, we traded places, even though we
were the same height. In those days she wanted to be a

nun. She'd been to their boarding school for a couple of years, and had come out of it with a nearly total ignorance. I knew more than she did about almost everything, except life. She had also come out of that school with a piety that was stubborn and fanatic. She used to tell me about the baby Jesus, saying how devoted to him she was. I didn't know how to tell her that I thought all that praise of a baby that neither she nor I nor anyone living had seen was a pile of old wives' tales. One day she showed me a holy card with his picture on it. He looked like a little girl, with soft lips and makeup, and I told her that the baby Jesus couldn't look like that. But she said no, I was right, he didn't, he was "much better looking," as if she had supper with him every day. It was clear she was trying to convert me, but the idea of that exaggerated piety and the notion of wearing a habit gave me the creeps. She wanted to be a nun, but her mother wouldn't let her. Her mother had been a beautiful woman and for many years, ever since Conxita was born, she had led a life of lonely widowhood. I can't explain the type of beauty that Conxita had. She had the face of a rich girl, and everything she wore looked good on her. Her hair was golden, really golden, I mean the color of gold. Not that light straw shade, but the color of old gold, with some red shadows in the background. She wore it curled and short. What I liked in those days was long unwaved hair. But Kim Novak had just made the other style fashionable, and shown the whole world that short hair is as sexy as long. Conxita's nose was short and straight, so straight that it seemed to have been carved or chiseled. And her eyes, depending on how you looked at them, were green and gray, with dark eyelashes. Her complexion was as smooth as a peach, and never shiny. What I didn't like was the gesture she made when she talked. She would raise her eyebrows a little, and with the back of her right hand she would clap the palm of the left. That made her seem older, as if she were saying very important and very adult things. It was the gesture of an adult, and it made her look ugly. Everyone in the class had fallen in love with her, but she was so pretty that no one dared to tell her. And it was humiliating when the boys paid attention to me, since they did it only to get close to her, to Conxita, because I was her best friend.

I also couldn't say for sure when she got over the madness of exaggerated piety, but it must have taken several years. Because what I know with certainty is that when I returned in the summer of the first term I was away, that is, after I had begun the university, she wanted to talk to me in private. She was very nervous and very excited. She told me a hundred times that what she had to say I mustn't repeat to anyone in the world, and that I was the first person to know about it. The secret was that she had fallen in love with a boy, that he was courting her secretly and wanted to marry her. And that he was like this, that, and the other, meaning that he was very handsome and that he was a highway engineer. The catch—because there was a catch, without it there couldn't be a secret—was that he was going to have to move far away, to Mozambique, I think it was, because he had found a very good job, one that paid very well. And so either they had to get married right away, or keep up their romance for two years by mail, without ever seeing each other. The firm in Mozambique would give him a vacation, not the first year, but the second, at Christmas. But he was going there to make money, and the journey was very expensive and he didn't intend to return until the contract was up, and that would be after two whole years.

"But if he loves you, he ought to be able to spend a little and come see you. . . ."

"Even then it would be after—let's see—a year and three months. . . ."

"Why don't you get married before he leaves?"

"I just can't. He's leaving next month. And mother

doesn't even know we're going out. How could I tell her? No, it's impossible."

"Then wait for him. . . ."

"And spend two years writing letters? Don't be silly! That I couldn't stand."

"But you love him?"

"A lot. Look, just thinking about him I tremble all over. . . ."

For two hours that's what I heard. The long and short of it was that she loved him, but didn't want the risky sort of life he was offering. Really what she didn't want was to live in Mozambique. . . .

"You're wrong, Conxita. The cities in Mozambique are as modern as Valencia, and with all the conveniences. Or do you think you'll live in the jungle among savage tribes? They're cities like all cities. And there will be many girls like you and many boys like him. And besides, it's for two years, not your whole life."

It seemed to me that her great love wasn't so great. Maybe I had changed, judging from how it made me furious to see her so calculating. And that secret desire to get married in Alcoi, with a husband to show off in the town. That's what she was really interested in. I found her contradictory and confused. But then all that meant that the business about becoming a nun had left her mind forever. Now that I think about it, I don't understand too well why she told me all those things; because even if I wasn't a little girl any more, our friendship was still the kind between a grown-up and a child. What I mean is, I don't think she was asking me for advice. Maybe it was like thinking out loud, so she could counter my objections. It's something lots of people do: make someone listen to them just to counter arguments that they've already disposed of mentally.

But I have to admit that Conxita was prettier than ever. Sometimes I've thought that the secret of her beauty was in her eyebrows—that is, when she wasn't arching them, while slapping her left palm with her right hand—her eyebrows, unlike her hair and eyes, were very dark, with a shape that was sharp and soft at the same time. It gave her a tone of sensuality. It's true, isn't it, that cats don't have eyebrows? Still, Conxita's eyebrows made her face look like a cat's. Like a little cat's, because it wasn't a sly face, like big cats have.

Later the memories are more confused; I was living my own life and discovering the world. My village friendships were far away, and if I thought about them at all, it was in passing. Memories like these are images that appear for a moment in the mind, and then are shooed away, like flies or smoke, by other thoughts. The images fly away like kites, and you can't catch them, no matter how much you want to.

But I know that the business with the fiance in Mozambique didn't work out. And that she finally married a soldier—a second lieutenant, I think—because the military barracks were right in front of her house, and she got to be friends with one of the soldiers who called out flattering remarks to her as she passed. The idea of marrying a soldier was hard for me to accept, and when she told me, I was appalled and thought she must have wanted to get married pretty bad. And I wondered about his salary, because Conxita had always been dressed well and expensively, and wore dresses made by her own tailor that were the envy of the women who are envious of that sort of thing—they don't mean a thing to me one way or another.

I also learned that she had a baby, and that was for me something even harder to imagine. I must have been eighteen then, and if I had been a little girl when I was fifteen, at eighteen I was still an adolescent, and that business of sex and birth was like something from another galaxy, or from another generation. And then I believe I heard that her husband was sick, and that she had to go to work to support the family. Because she had more babies, four of

them, I think, but I'm not at all sure. And then the last
thing I found out was what was in the papers, and what
the family told me, with so many exaggerated protesta-
tions that I didn't manage to get a very clear picture. It
was a tragedy like in a novel, and it seemed that the person who had been my intimate friend was now nothing to
me, that I didn't know her and had never known her. But
maybe that's a defense that we build to be able to stand
things that happen to people we love or have loved. . . .

"I think the best thing is for you to stay in bed. And
you just tell me what I have to do, like go to the headquarters, or whatever it's called. And your doctor will come.
You can never be sure, and we have to take care of ourselves, because our health . . ."

"My doctor! Isn't he yours, too?"

"He's not mine. Don Ramon has been my doctor all my
life."

"And he charges a thousand *pessetes* a visit, when we've
got the military doctor; you've got as much right to his
care as I have."

"But now we're not talking about me. You're the one
who's sick, and you're the one who has to be visited. . . ."

"But there's nothing wrong with me! I just got dizzy. It's
probably stress. Father always suffered from it. . . ."

"Fine, we'll see when your doctor comes."

"There you go again with 'my doctor'."

"Get in bed and don't make me talk any more!"

"All right, but I don't want you to go anywhere. Call the
doctor on the phone, and he'll write a prescription."

"Everything has to be in writing for you! What a life!"

"I don't know why you're complaining. Before we were
married everything seemed great to you, and then later it
was nothing but complaints!"

"Come on, give me the number before I lose my patience. I didn't sleep all night, little Jordi wouldn't stop
crying and I can't stand any more."

Conxita finally notified the military doctor, then she straightened up the house so that when he came he would find everything in order. Little Jordi, the rascal, was sleeping—he only cried at night. She finished straightening up, put some things on to boil, and still had time to comb her hair. Jacint must have gone to sleep, because he had stopped calling her: first he wanted water, then he needed to go to the bathroom, give me the thermometer I think I have a fever, a little milk might not taste bad. . . . She went into the bathroom, and right there, even though it was so tiny, she changed clothes, because she didn't want Jacint to see her undress, because she was afraid that again she was . . . what bad luck! From just one time! Some women, even on the most unlikely days. . . . Not the pink satin, it would show too much. Maybe the blue crepe—but it would show her belly too, With little Jordi, she showed from the second month, and now, if she was indeed pregnant, she was well into her third. She picked up the checked one, brown and beige; it was hot, but it made her look thin. And she combed her hair and looked in the mirror, deep into her eyes. "I'm ten years older, that's for sure," and she felt her heart break in pieces for having kept all that beauty for that poor fool in the other room, who gave her nothing but work and frowns and, especially, poverty. "I was so well off with Mother. My wish was her command." And she would have started to cry if she hadn't heard the doorbell.

The doctor was unpleasant and impatient. Ugly and haughty in his uniform, he looked as if he had a stomachache and too tight shoes. And he asked a hundred questions. Jacint was scared to death, because if nothing was wrong with him, he'd be in for it.

Afterward the doctor took her to the dining room, and interrogated her as if she were a prisoner or a suspect. About everything. Even about intimate things, and Conxita was on the point of slapping him when he asked her how often they did it. But he just kept writing. And finally he became a little more human and began a sermon about "being strong, bringing honor to the uniform of the husband, because being both of one flesh, as Saint Paul says, the uniform obligated both of them."

Conxita was startled. "But what's wrong with him? Is it serious?" And she felt a burning in her throat and a swelling under her tongue, and then she threw up and was on the verge of fainting. And then, sobbing and cleaning up the mess she had made, she confessed that she was three months pregnant, and what would become of her, with a four-month-old baby and an invalid, and a starvation salary. . . .

I don't know anything about the courtship, because when I was posted in Alcoi he was already married. We became friends right off, because we agreed on everything. It's not that he was unfriendly, as some people are saying, he was just very introverted. In fact he was a very good sort, as good as gold. The wife I met later, after he and I were already good friends. They invited me to dinner, since I was a bachelor then, and I didn't know anyone in Alcoi, and at first we planned for the three of us to go out, then decided that to go out, two couples would be better. And that's how I went to his house. Later I was told that I didn't know what an honor it was, because he never invited anyone to his house, because he kept such a close eye on his wife. It was clear that he didn't trust her much. Women, at least many of them, aren't to be trusted. And he . . . the thing was, he loved her very much. Too much. No woman is worth the suffering that Conxita made him go through. Because jealousy is nothing more than love, too much love, more than any woman deserves. And don't think I am talking about myself, because Immaculada is incapable of deceiving me . . . or so I thought, and I wasn't the only one. During the mess it was remarked many times that what happened to him was very strange. When I met him it must have been a year since his opera-

tion. It was something to do with his spleen, its exact
name I can't remember, but the doctors knew what was
wrong. And they knew it was serious. The operation was
difficult, but Lieutenant Colonel Palamares, who was the
head surgeon, said he had come out of it perfectly well,
and that the danger had passed. That's how I began to
wonder if Conxita . . . who knows? A potion or something.
Because Lieutenant Colonel Palamares said quite clearly
that it couldn't be explained, that clinically he was perfectly healthy. And they brought in a bunch of doctors
from outside. No one understood how, even after the operation, he still had the same disease. Later they said it
had to do with nerves, but that didn't really make sense.
And now, of course, everyone thinks he's crazy. I believe a
man has a right. Especially a soldier. It's a matter of
honor. And Conxita was unfaithful, I'm sure of it. No, it's
not that he actually told me so, he never would have told
anyone, not even me, his best friend—a soldier can't say
that sort of thing and keep his dignity. But the sadness,
the anger, the things that slipped out without his realizing . . . a sort of jealousy. And what happened proved that
she was guilty, I don't have any doubt. I accept and respect the verdict of the military tribunal, but I know him
better than anyone, and I know Jacint wasn't insane. His
only crime was to love a woman, who was his by rights.
The truth is that she was beautiful, Conxita was. Ill-tem-
pered and always complaining about the children, and
about his pay . . . as if it weren't her obligation and her joy
to bring children into the world and to keep the house!
But when women are too pretty they only think about
clothes and parties. . . . The pay was small, that has to be
admitted. But the wives of our other friends got along
with it. And Immaculada has never reproached me about
it. It must have had to do with the mother, Conxita's that
is, who I hear had also been a beauty, and must have infected her daughter with delusions of grandeur. What I
can say is that in that house there was no happiness. And

that Jacint's sickness was very strange. And that Conxita had been unfaithful to him. Three years in the stockade! And even though it's in fact the military prison, because of his health, his days there must be bitter. I respect the verdict of the tribunal, but I think they were too harsh. A man's honor is his wife. And honor is sacred.

"So you won't be getting up today either?"

"What's eating you this morning? You must want something. . . ."

"It's no use trying to talk to you. Isn't it enough that I have four little children and a sick husband?"

"You forgot the third complaint: the miserable salary. Have you forgotten how to tell your rosary of misfortunes?"

"Look Jacint, I'm a good Christian and I know how to be patient, but don't take advantage. . . ."

"Conxita, I've got a fever. And my superiors have ordered me to rest. So don't nag me."

"Me nag you? That's a good one! Do you think I don't have enough to put up with? And if I complain, so what, I do my work. Or haven't you noticed? And the children, don't they look good?"

"You know I'd help you if I weren't so weak."

"I'm glad to hear you say that, because you have to help me. Things just can't go on like this. I want you to be here at home, so I can take care of you. Even though here we have to pay for the medicine, I prefer that to their taking you to the military hospital in Alacant. That would be too much."

"I don't want that either. But if I'm such a burden, and make you cry all the time . . ."

"There is a solution. Here's how you can help me. I've found a job—"

"Absolutely not! Never! My wife doesn't work!"

"It's not what you think, Jacint. Don't get excited, and promise me you'll at least listen. I'm doing it for your own good."

"Forget it! I'd rather go to the hospital."

"What about the children? You think they don't need a father? Because if you go away and this thing takes a long time, as it seems that it will, when you get back they won't recognize you, they won't know who you are. They're so little still! Or hasn't that occurred to you? That's why I want you to show a little understanding. You'll see that the idea isn't so bad. And besides, no one has to know."

"Look, don't try that excuse on me, because of course they'll know. And so forget about—"

"Listen, will you? It will just be for a couple of hours a day. With a typewriter, see—"

"In an office? Absolutely not!"

"But will you listen a minute? Do you know who Mr. Roura is? No, of course you don't. Well, he's a real gentleman—a marquis, in fact. And he's written, I don't know, lots of things. He's well known in Alcoi. I don't know him personally, just by sight. But as a little girl, I went with my mother to his house one day. I remember it as if it were yesterday. He gave me chocolate, fine chocolate, better than anything I'd had before. From France."

"So?"

"So it seems that he is writing his memoirs. But since he's old and has lost a lot of his vision, typing is too hard for him, and he wants some help. No one knows about it yet, but with the scads of money that he has he could have ten secretaries if he wanted. He mentioned it to Gloria. You know, mother's hairdresser, who gives her a manicure every two weeks—"

"That bimbo!"

"Well, yes, she is that. They say she's responsible for the education of I don't know how many boys. But that doesn't have anything to do with this. The point is, Gloria told Mother, and Mother told me."

"Great! You must have complained so much that now the grand lady stabs me in the back by getting my wife to go to work."

"Look, she just mentioned it. She didn't really think I'd be interested. You can believe that. He—Mr. Roura—is in no hurry. And I'm good with a typewriter."

"You mean you can type with more than two fingers?"

"Sure, I learned it at Almi. I had two years of secretarial training. A little French and how to type, and I remember everything. Not shorthand, though, I never had that."

"What about the children?"

"I've got it all figured out. If you're feeling too bad, Eulalia will be delighted to keep them, she's offered a thousand times. At four, after lunch, I'll leave and by six I'll be back. I'll pick up the kids and come home again. After all, Jordi's already grown up, and he's crazy about Eulalia. And little Lluis will do fine. And the baby, since I'm getting him shoes next month. . . ."

"And Eulalia wouldn't charge you anything?"

"Her? She'd pay me! I tell you I know what I'm talking about. And do you know how much I'd make working for Roura?"

"Did your mother know that, too?"

"Yes—3,000 a month. With that we can pay for your medicine, and have money left over. It'll be a distraction for me, and some help for the home. And nobody else has to know."

"Of course they will. Just as Gloria knew he was looking for a secretary, she'll know he's found one."

"No, because I'll ask Mr. Roura not to tell. You don't understand: he's a gentleman, a real gentleman like one in a novel. When he goes to Valencia he's a big wheel, because they know him. He's a great writer. He's famous even in Madrid. He's a marquis, and he knows I'm married, and that it's necessary to be discreet."

The truth is that as for being a beauty . . . I never saw it. For me, her neck is too short. Or it was, poor girl, may she rest in peace. And her walk was pretty common, eh? On the other hand, as for being a good girl, I can vouch for

that, and no one knew her as well as I did. After she got
married, that is, because before, she and her mother
looked down on me. Because I had served in her house,
yes sir, I'm not hiding my past as a maid. That was many
years ago, when her father was still alive, because later
that house went to pot, and nothing was left but pride.
But they really could have married Conxita better, how little foresight they had! I'm the one who found an apartment for them, right underneath mine; it had become
vacant and was the kind of bargain that you won't find
again. And she seemed much more simple to me than
people think. She wasn't happy, that's for sure. Well, she
was at first. I don't believe she was really in love, but she
was so thrilled at being married! And he was good-looking, and he always said nice things to her and treated her
like a lady. But then she began to sort of fade. Bound to,
because she wasn't used to washing clothes and cleaning
house, it had always been done for her. But that wasn't
the only reason. Many's the time I've heard her crying,
"Eulalia, Eulalia, I can't stand it anymore!" And what was I
supposed to tell her? I'm a single woman; I only know
about such things by hearsay. I do know she could have
put up with everything else, and gladly; but it was clear
that in bed she couldn't stand him. Even her mother
didn't know about that.

Poor Jacint, he always thought that mother and daughter were conspiring against him, and in fact they couldn't
stand each other! Conxita, at any rate, didn't like her
mother at all. I think that when she was little, she saw
things a little girl shouldn't see. And maybe that's the reason for the anguish Jacint caused her in bed. And men, you
know, are always in the mood for it! Even when he was sick
he was after her. And since Conxita was so devout she
could say that she didn't want to do certain things, because
the Church didn't permit it. . . . What I don't understand is
why, knowing this, he didn't take precautions. Because
right off they had three children, in three years. And they

argued about it. Not about Conxita's vanity, or their lack of money: about what went on in bed. It seems that he wanted it two or three times a day. Maybe that was because of his sickness. I'm not just guessing about this. One day she came to me crying. She was far along with little Jordi, seven or eight months. She was crying and sobbing in my lap for half an hour. "I can't take it anymore, Eulalia! I can't take it! I'd rather he beat me. It disgusts me! It makes me want to throw up! Can't he see what condition I'm in? Can't he see? He can never get enough! Men are animals, animals!" And she was a brave girl. Three deliveries without so much as a groan. The second one, little Lluis, came out upside down, she was in labor for twelve hours. The midwife told me she had never seen a woman so strong and brave, that she wouldn't even moan. For her, adversities were like tests she had to pass to get to Heaven. That's why, no matter what they say, I'm sure she didn't cheat on her husband. The very idea that she could have done that with Mr. Roura! It's enough to make you die laughing. He was an old queer, that one, quite addicted to vice, they say. When she began to work as his secretary, she told me about it. Not even her mother knew about that. But she had to tell me— how else could she explain why she was leaving the children with me every day? I like to have them. I'm crazy about little kids. It's the only misfortune in being single, you know. She made me swear not to tell anyone, and I kept my word. Of course you have to understand how it was for Jacint: all day long sick in bed, nothing to do but think, as jealous as a Moor! And if he really thought she was cheating on him, what could he do about it? They couldn't get separated, not with three babies. And besides, he was sick—a cross to bear. I figure he lost his head. He was certainly a little insane. But to shoot her twice that way. . . . Poor Conxita, such a good girl!

Conxita raised her eyes and looked at him, astonished. Could Jacint have been right? Because, what else is this supposed to mean: "Conxita, if you wanted, instead of 3,000 it could be 30,000. . . ." But it couldn't be! Why he must be almost seventy. . . . He explained it to her, slowly, with such a low voice that at times she couldn't hear him. A little nervous, but as if he were talking to her about something else. "It's a vice, I know, but I swear I won't touch you. Just that. I know you think it's swinish, but you'll see, you'll take a shower and won't even remember it. I know that you wouldn't sell yourself for money, but thirty thousand every month . . . and it's for my health. You'll find it hard to believe, but I don't know, without it, I feel older than I am." Conxita shook her head no. "Think about it. Remember I'm assuring your children's future. You know that your husband won't be able to support them—I'm sorry—even if he lives so long; excuse me, but I'm talking to you like a father. I could have, I don't know how to put it, professionals. But that's not the same, I want it to be you. Consider that it's just for a few seconds. And then you can take a shower. And a short year from now, you know you'll have a small fortune. Your husband can't provide for the future of your children. Now you've got an opportunity you won't be offered again. I won't touch you. If you like, I'll even close my eyes. I know you're a good girl. But it's that I . . . need you so much!"

Finally, after considering it well, Conxita gave a little nod. And he, delighted, leaped about and clapped his hands, like a satyr. For the sake of my children, Lord, only for them. Forgive me. And it's not a sin, it's a self-sacrifice. He's the one who's sinning, the repugnant old goat! He took her to an enormous bathroom, and waited outside while she undressed. Conxita felt her heart beating like a bucking stallion. She wrapped a towel around herself, and with a thin voice said, "I'm ready, Mr. Roura." When he took the towel off, she closed her eyes and lowered her head in embarrassment. By a strange association of ideas she began to think about a picture she once had of the

child Jesus; and she commended herself to him. The old
man looked at her, without a lot of interest, and gently led
her into the bathtub, gleaming, black as onyx. It was like a
swimming pool, so large that four people would have fit in
it. As she let herself be led into the tub, she folded her
arms over her breasts, her eyes shut tight, her skin in
goose pimples from the touch of the stone. She heard Mr.
Roura get into the tub, completely dressed as he had
promised. Standing up, facing her, one foot on each side
of her recumbent body at the level of her hips. She heard
him unbutton his fly. But she didn't open her eyes. She
was cold and frightened. He took out his dick, cere-
moniously, as if it were something very delicate, aimed it
carefully, and released a stream of urine. With his hand he
aimed the stream at Conxita's face, her hair, her breasts,
her stomach, her private parts. Conxita thought she'd die
of disgust. It smelled so strong it made her sick. It was hot
and sticky like syrup, with an unbreathable odor. She
raised her arms to cover her nose. And then it was over.
"Now take a shower." And he left the bathtub. She turned
on the shower with a single quick motion, without caring
if it was cold or hot. And after a few minutes she felt
brand-new. And that's the way it happened every day. And
he always paid punctually: 30,000 *pessetes* for thirty seconds a day of pissing on her. And he never touched her.

I never liked Jacint. Stuck-up, taciturn, malicious . . . I
told her so, my Conxita. But she married him just to be
contrary. A lot of good it did her! A crazy man, that's what
he is, and a thoroughly bad person! And if she cheated on
him, so what? A woman has to have some pleasure too,
we're not made of stone. He was always sick, a weakling, a
wimp. . . . To tell you the truth, it's hard to believe she
could have cheated on him, because with the piety that
she caught from the nuns . . . and she was colder than a
fish, the poor girl. I could have sworn that she was incapable of it. But the evidence is too clear. With her in the

cemetery, and him in prison, I had to go take care of the
house and the little ones. At my age. . . . I've had bad luck
too! When I found it—the money—hidden in a little box
at the back of the pantry . . . a fortune: 490,000 *pessetes*.
She couldn't have gotten it honestly. And it has come in
handy, because I have plenty of work now, taking care of
three snotty kids. But when, and with who? Because it
can't have been Mr. Roura, he's been impotent—I know it
from a reliable source—for years. So when and with
whom? Aside from going to type for Roura—and the silly
fool thought I didn't know about that! When Gloria told
me I mentioned it to her because I knew that it would do
her a lot of good—and aside from going shopping, she
was always with Jacint and the kids. It's a mystery. Maybe
if at Roura's there had been a nephew, say, or a male secretary. But no, he would never have stood for it—and anyway, in that house there was only a maid and a cook.
Besides people are bound to have known. At the trial it
would have come out. And if I hadn't happened on the
money, I would have always thought she was innocent.
Conxita was so strict and pious. No, you can't explain it.
It's a real mystery.

From the bed he watched her dress. "She must be cheating on me. She's a different woman. She used to always go
into the bathroom to get dressed. And now she undresses
here in front of me, shamelessly. She must be cheating on
me. If I could only get out of this damn bed!"

Conxita was having a hard time getting her bra fastened.

"Come here, let me do it."

"Fine." And she backed over to him. He sat up a little to
reach it, and then he had an idea: he'd do something that
would give him proof. And if it turned out . . . it would be
better not to know! But what about that new dress? And
she had bought shoes for the three children last week—
she couldn't have had anything left. Those 3,000 *pessetes*

couldn't explain it. There's got to be something more. So he decided to do it.

"Can't you fasten it?" Conxita asked impatiently.

"There. That's got it." There were three hooks on the strap. He fastened the first to the second eye, the second to the third, and the third he left loose. She didn't notice a thing.

"I've got to hurry. It's 3:45."

He watched her leave and wave good-bye, and heard her saying, "Come on, Eulalia is waiting for you. . . ."

She was late returning that evening. It was unbearably hot. In Alcoi when it's hot, it's really hot. And the cold is just as bad. But he couldn't complain. The doctor had said, "If you were in a humid climate, then you'd really be in trouble." He didn't like it here. He had liked it at the time he met Conxita. Everything was so pretty. But now. . . . And then there was the language. He had been forced to learn it, because outside of camp, no one ever spoke to him in Spanish. Even though they knew it. Conxita wouldn't speak it at all, though she knew that speaking Spanish would make her more of a lady, more refined. But no one here could get used to it.

He thought a long time, and worked out a plan. Carefully he loaded his service revolver. He got up and washed his face, brushed his teeth, put on the new robe, the silk one, and instead of going back to the bed, which had become a torture for him, he sat in the bedroom armchair, with the light out and the blinds slightly open, so as not to be completely in the dark. He sat and thought. The two hours must have passed. He heard her come in.

"Hello! How are you doing? You've gotten up? And see how good you look, in your new robe! What about this hellish heat today?" She spoke in a rush, without looking at him.

"She's too cheerful," he thought, wrinkling his brow. "She's been making love: I know it." He could feel his pulse throbbing.

"I'll change my dress, since it's so hot, and run get the kids—they must be waiting for me, poor things!" She took off her shoes. Then her stockings. She unzipped her dress and let it drop to the ground; her slip, too, and turned to look for her housedress, that was on the chair, to her right. It was then that she turned her back to him. The hooks. The hooks were properly fastened: the first hook in the first eye, the second in the second, the third in the third. She stood with her arms in the air and her head buried in the dress, groping to find the sleeves. She stood there for a few seconds, showing him the hooks: the proof.

He put his hand in his pocket and gripped the pistol. "Conxita." His voice was so hoarse that she looked at him with surprise. "You're cheating on me." He said it softly, slowly, his eyes wide open, his forehead sweaty. And with a black veil, the color of despair, in front of his face.

"What!?"

"I know. I know you're cheating on me."

"Are you crazy or what?" But when she looked into his eyes she must have seen something that made her be quiet.

"I know. I have proof."

Now she was mad, and she looked up and shouted, "Proof? Proof? Of what? I've always been faithful to you, do you hear, and if you're crazy you ought to be locked up!"

He had an idea. He grabbed the crucifix from off the night table. Ramirez, his best friend, had given it to him when the first child was born. "You know how you've driven me crazy with the devotions, your Christianity, your faith? Now maybe they'll be good for something. Swear before God that no man but me has touched you." He raised his hand and the shadow of the crucified Christ fell across Conxita's face. The solemn gesture disturbed her, but she looked calmly at the crucifix, and knelt down.

"I swear before God, who is listening to me and watching me, that no man but you has touched me, Jacint." She said it slowly but with vehemence, pronouncing each word clearly.

"You've gone too far, Conxita. Mocking your religion . . . you've gone too far. I know—I said *know*—that you've deceived me. That I could have pardoned, but not after this oath. Tears with me and laughter with another? No, that won't do."

"But you must be crazy. Who do you think I've deceived you with? With Roura?"

"I don't know. It doesn't matter. You never liked for me to touch you and now you let someone else do it. For pleasure. Or for money. And there's a name for that: whore. Tramp. Slut."

And then he took the gun out of his pocket and aimed it. Conxita had a few seconds to think. She looked him full in the face. She thought, "what if I told him the truth?" But she looked into his eyes and saw clearly that nothing, nothing in the world, could save her. She knew she was going to die. And, without knowing exactly how, she found herself saying the Our Father to the image of the child Jesus from the holy card she had as a little girl. She heard the first shot. But Jacint's hand was trembling, and the bullet whistled past her. With the second she felt a pain and an intense burning in her stomach. She looked at him before she fell. He fired again, but it ricocheted into the carpet. Conxita was dead, doubled over, she died on her knees, drenched in blood that flowed like a fountain. And then he was the one to double over, crying and shouting at the top of his lungs, "Conxita, Conxita!"

Montserrat Roig

Montserrat Roig

Montserrat Roig *Barcelona, 1946*

Creative works *Molta roba i poc sabó*. Barcelona: Selecta, 1971. Short stories, winner of the Víctor Català prize. Translated into Castilian by Mercedes Nogues as *Aprendizaje sentimental* (Barcelona: Argos Vergara, 1981).

Ramona, adéu. Barcelona: 62, 1972. Novel. Translated into Castilian by Joaquim Sempere as *Ramona, adiós* (Barcelona: Argos Vergara, 1980).

El temps de les cireres. Barcelona: 62, 1977. Novel. Translated into Castilian by Enrique Sordo as *Tiempo de cerezas* (Barcelona: Argos Vergara, 1980).

L'hora violeta. Barcelona: 62, 1980. Novel. Translated into Castilian by Enrique Sordo as *La hora violeta* (Barcelona: Argos Vergara, 1980).

L'òpera quotidiana. Barcelona: Planeta, 1982. Novel. Translated into Castilian by Enrique Sordo as *La òpera cotidiana* (Barcelona: Planeta, 1983).

The best known of the new generation of Catalan women writers is undoubtedly Montserrat Roig, most of whose fame comes from her work in journalism. She has done

203

many interviews on Spanish television, and gathered together several collections of them in published form. She
has also written a book of essays on Spanish feminism, a
study of the Catalans in Nazi concentration camps, and a
report on Leningrad during World War II. Her creative
work consists of a collection of short stories and four novels, all published in Catalan and translated into Castilian.

Roig's journalistic training is reflected in her literary
style, which has a strong sense of contemporary chronicle,
and in some of her characters, who are either themselves
journalists or live in the world of publishing.

In her very successful first novel, *Ramona, adéu*, Roig in-
terweaves the stories of three women sharing the same
name and born into three successive generations of the
same family. One of the three uses a diary format, with
brief entries reflecting current preoccupations, somewhat
reminiscent of Roig's short columns for *El Periódico* and
other publications. In an integration of content and form,
she incorporates much information from her study of Catalans in Nazi camps into *L'hora violeta* (The Violet Hour), a
novel that also uses fragments of diaries written by the
characters. The narrative structure is somewhat disjointed
but nonetheless well managed, and leads to her masterful
fourth novel, *L'òpera quotidiana*, which succeeds in blend-
ing the lives of several characters by having them pronounce arias, cavatinas, and duets in the manner of a
musical opera.

The almost-simultaneous translations of Roig's recent
work into Castilian and her frequent television ap-
pearances have helped her gain recognition and popularity throughout Spain. But her work as a journalist is a
two-edged sword. In a 1977 interview, she said she was
still trying to find her narrative voice, but that she did not
write enough to make much progress. "I do too much
journalism and I have too many extraliterary preoccupations," she said, and went on to explain what happens to
all who feel the pull of nonliterary commitments: "I often

pull back, but sometimes I feel so involved, because in this country, we always have to be fighting history. I wish history would go on normally."

In an interview seven years later, Roig described the two facets of her writing career as two sides of her personality. At times she needs to write for the newspapers, and she likes the immediate dialogue established with the reader. At other times, she needs to write novels. She began her career by writing for the literary and art monthly *Serra d'Or* because she wanted to learn the craft, and of course, to support herself. Like Isabel-Clara Simó, she attributes some of her ability to write creatively to the apprenticeship of disciplined writing that journalism demands. She seems to have combined the two kinds of writing successfully; in 1986 she signed a contract to do a new television program for young people, and in 1985 she published a book on the siege of Leningrad during World War II, *L'agulla daurada* (The Golden Needle, Barcelona: 62).

Translated by J. M. Sobrer from *L'òpera quotidiana*, © Montserrat Roig 1982.

The Everyday Opera (Selections)

MARI CRUZ*   Ivonne had green eyes, bottle green, sparkling, and her hair, worn up, had a sheen the color of corncobs. Her hair was always poorly combed, the discolored bangs falling on her forehead. The day she showed me the ashes in the flask, the veins in her neck bulged as if they were about to burst. She goaded me with her gaze. I felt she wanted to turn me into a thousand pieces, smaller than her father's ashes. Me, like a scarecrow, with my palm extended, not knowing what to do. I was afraid I might scatter the ashes, the ashes that were perhaps her father's. I didn't quite understand why she called me that, fascist pig.

A few days later I asked the "poet of the phalluses" why his wife had insulted me. He explained to me that Ivonne was a little confused since she had learned all that had happened to her family, that at first they only told her that they had disappeared in a concentration camp during the German war, but that, little by little, she learned the de-

*Mari Cruz is a young Andalusian woman trying to survive as a maid in Barcelona. She cleans house for Senyora Miralpeix, whose boarder, Senyor Duc, she falls in love with. She also acts as maid/companion to Senyora Altafulla, and previously worked for "el poeta dels phallus" and his wife Ivonne.

207

tails, and that those details were hard to accept, because
no one can take lightly that their grandmother has been
converted into a bar of soap. And that their father is now
only a pile of ashes. And that, according to Ivonne, we
were all responsible. He too believed this, that those of us
who had done nothing to kill Franco when it was high
time to do so, were a bunch of fascists, and also a bunch of
pigs. But it didn't worry me much, to be called fascist pig
by Ivonne, and that the poet of the phalluses would believe it too, because when Franco died I was only twelve,
and at school they barely made a comment. And fascists
are these gentlemen who appear once in a while in the
newspapers, dressed in black, shouting a lot and brandish-
ing pistols. I thought it was truly a pity for a woman to go
berserk and go around with her father's ashes in a little
flask.

Because I have never had a father. I do not know what
he looked like, I have no pictures of him, no letter from
him; I do not know his name, I cannot hope to gather his
ashes in a little flask. My mother is from a village lost in
the geography of Spain; no one lives there anymore, or at
most a few old folks and a couple of children. My mother
always says that she has sponged it off clean, that the
house where she was born has faded in her memory, and
the animals they had, and the land dying of drought. She
claims it's better that way, that if you want to start a new
life you can't drag along the sorrows of all that you left behind. That her village is static in the past, in a corner of
Castile. Only barren land, a few ruins that used to be
houses, Mother says, and the wind whistling at night as a
vigil to the dead left alone in the graveyard. My mother
taught me to have no memories. Because my mother is
very different from Senyora Altafulla, who was chock-full
of memories, and from Senyor Duc who had them but
who did not want to share them with me.

One day, when I was three, mother told me that she
was fed up with so much poverty and that we would go to

Barcelona. Our grandparents were dead and she only had
two sisters, Aunt Florentina, who had married an As-
turian, and Aunt Angels, who was a hooker but my
mother said she was a good person. Aunt Angels had
come to Barcelona as a young woman, to be a maid in a
house in the upper part of the city. The brother of the
lady of the house went after her because my aunt had
been a very good-looking woman. My mother would explain to me sometimes that the train ride had been as long
as Moses' stay in the desert, and that she mostly wanted to
piss, she was so nervous. All I remember is that the moon
followed the train and that, from time to time, it would
hide behind some shreds of cloud. When it came out
again, it winked.

I will go quickly over what happened later because it is
not very important for this story. My mother became a
maid and she locked me up in a school run by nuns in the
neighborhood called Gracia. For ten years I did not leave
the place at all, not even in summers, my mother had no
vacations, and even if she had had them, well, we would
not have known where to go, the two of us alone. She
came to see me one Sunday every month. Once in a while
the aunties came, the one from Asturias, and the whore,
with makeup, looking like an Easter cake, with her tall
hairdo that seemed to have no end. Aunt Angels smelled
of lavender and gave me candy. Aunt Florentina looked
like Ivonne, she was very tall and had a parrot nose; from
my height I could only see her nose because she barely
had breasts. Aunt Florentina looked at me and said, poor
little one, what a pity, and she told me that I had to do like
her, I had to preserve myself in order to find a good husband, that then I could go through life with my head very
high and I would not end up like others who, because of
their carelessness, had "lost cattle and bells, if you know
what I mean." I did not understand very well. Later I
gathered that she referred to my mother who had me by a
man whose name nobody even knew. When my aunt told

me that, told me not to end up like others, and that I
should "keep my thing" for my future husband, my
mother always burst out crying, no one could stop her.
Aunt Angels looked furious and told Aunt Florentina to
stick her tongue where she could fit it; Aunt Florentina
told her to keep quiet; and as the two of them started
shouting at each other, my mother would blow her nose
and wipe her tears which were unstoppable. Then I knew
that the drama would last the whole Sunday afternoon
and I let my thoughts fly. Because, when my mother cried,
her face became like a tomato, as if they had slapped it,
and she would blow and blow her nose. My aunt who was
a whore would give her one Kleenex after another, but my
mother tore them all up, saying that she was not used to
blowing her nose with a paper handkerchief, and a whole
bunch of shreds always stuck to her fingers.

Auntie Florentina was the one with authority in the
family. She had as much authority as the old woman,
Senyora Altafulla, though I must admit that it was a different kind, perhaps because she was more elegant, I
don't know. Aunt Florentina was very proud of how things
had been for her, in life, mostly because she had a husband who brought home the cash and she did not have to
clean up other people's houses, like my mother. Her husband, Uncle Baldomeru, had gone to Argentina to strike
it rich. He came back poorer than a church mouse and
Aunt Florentina was very angry at him, said he was lazy.
Then she sent him to Switzerland, and there things went
very well, Auntie says, because there her husband couldn't
bum around or have bad women or drink, like he did in
Argentina, and he took to working and working so he
could come back sooner. He slaved like a mule until he
had enough saved. In a few years, with the savings, Aunt
Florentina decided it was time to go back to Asturias. Uncle Baldomeru never forgave her for having made him
sweat it out so much and thought, I'll get even. Aunt Florentina told her husband, you could be a barber, and they

opened a barbershop. And he told Auntie, you ought to open up a notions store. Next to the barbershop they set up one of those stores that sells everything, from pins to writing pads, thumbtacks, and toilet water. Uncle became fat, his belly grew round like a ball about to burst, because barbershops are a bad business now that men shave at home with electric shavers, and Auntie became so skinny that, as I said, you could only see her parrot nose. She looked like one of those old parchments, dry like a bone, and that was because her dime store was going very well. One day Aunt Angels whispered in my ear that Uncle Baldomeru had never seen his wife naked and that she was always saying her rosary when they were doing it. My aunt the whore added that with a woman like that a man must be unhappy no matter how you cut it.

Most of the girls in the school had no known father, and the nuns kept saying to us that we had to pray so that the souls of our mothers would not be condemned and go to Hell, where they would burn for all eternity. Our mothers, they said, were sheep that had been thrown to sin and vice, and we were the branches thereof, and we could as easily be saved as damned. But that Our Lord God had not abandoned us, and that was why we were in the school now, to be protected from all the evil in the world. And that once outside it would be very hard for us to preserve ourselves intact.

There were a few who did have one, a father, and every Sunday, during visiting hours, the girls without a father had to stand in line to be kissed by the fathers. There were fights; we slapped each other and scratched to be first in line, because we knew that the first kisses were warmer, they were bigger and the hugs tighter, and that the last ones would be the kisses of a tired father. The girls who had fathers were our bosses and during the week we had to obey them in everything, from giving them the candy we had received to making up their beds, unseen by the nuns. They even started a father-kisses business, selling them for so much a unit. To get the first place in line was much more expensive, and at times we fatherless girls would sell the numbers among ourselves. A first kiss from a father, for example, would cost about fifteen pieces of candy, and then you still had to copy the homework of the bossy girl. Once I spent a whole week scrubbing the altar of the Immaculate in order to earn the kiss of a very handsome father who, besides, stroked my cheek. Later the daughter of that father told me that wasn't enough, scrubbing the altar of the Immaculate for her, and that I had to give her the marron glacé that my aunt the whore would bring me. I got angry at her, I told her that it was not fair, that deals are deals, but there was nothing I could do. So I gave her the marron glacé in exchange for the first kiss of the father who, besides, caressed my cheek, which was like a tip. After a while I realized that Senyor Duc looked a lot like this father and the first time he kissed me I felt in my mouth the taste of the marron glacé.

Ivonne, after showing me the flask with the ashes, took to thinking that I was going to bed with her husband, and she followed me the whole day long. And the poet of the phalluses, all he ever did was explain to me the poem he intended to write, in which he would describe how the creation of the world had really happened, where we women come from, and men, and he would prove that all this theory of Darwin's was idiotic. He told me Darwin was a sage who had discovered that the earth was millions and millions of years old and that we the species had evolved from pure matter to become what we were, men. That is to say, rational beings. But it's poetry that says what we imagine as truthful, what science does not dare admit, and for this reason he intended to write a poem in which he would explain the whole truth about creation. As I was dusting with the feather brush he followed me and explained that we all proceeded from an enormous phallus that God had planted one day, at six in the morning, in the middle of the earth, a phallus that was made out of bark, covered with sea algae as if these were branches, and that's why the Bible spoke of the Tree of Good and Evil. But God got it wrong: instead of planting it in the middle of a garden He planted it in the desert and Eve, who had sprouted as a woman from some of the algae, was dying of thirst and spent a whole moonless night embracing the phallus. She began to lick it, to see if there was moisture in the bark, but little by little she fell in love with it and ended up eating the phallus. Then she was satiated. She was so happy that she did not realize until nine months later that she was pregnant, not by a man but by a phallus. According to the poet the phallus is the beginning of all created things, and that is why Eve felt a deep desire to swallow it in order to survive. And so the first child she gave birth to, a male, had a penis in remembrance of that phallus made of bark and sea algae. While he explained all of this, the poet had me caress an enormous white marble phallus, with purple veins, just like his own, he said, at once slippery and cold. Ivonne heard his mumblings and she started to scream hysterically; I grabbed the feather brush and went to dust the dining room paintings. For, to tell the truth, I couldn't care less about the history of the first phallus, creator of all things that have a soul.

That is how Ivonne started disliking me and chasing me through the house, you must clean real well, you must fix dinner, you forgot to buy butter. . . . Whew, I had had it up to here. She howled at me, her eyes ablaze, what you want—you—is to go to bed with my husband, how funny, she said, you'll see what a surprise, because his is smaller than a sparrow's beak.

I decided to go back. I was up to my eyebrows with Ivonne and with her husband's phalluses. I would look for work in Barcelona; the Paris adventure was over. All in all, young people want to have an adventure in Paris. Now that my mother had moved in with Heraclio, I could organize my life with no problem. Besides, in my *chambre de bonne* I just shivered with cold. Every morning I had to stand in line in that frozen corridor to wash myself after a very quiet Moroccan and a chubby Valencian who kept saying, "what a *rigolade!*" and spied on me through the keyhole while I was in the toilet. I was fed up with having to crouch in order to piss and not splash my legs, and with having to wipe myself with pages from magazines because I always forgot the toilet paper in my *chambre*. Because if I went back to get the paper, I would lose my place and would have to stand in line all over again.

The Dutch man tore me away from my thoughts by offering me another marron glacé. Then he told me he felt very lonely and I thought, here we go, please don't explain your life to me, he saw clearly that only women would understand him, because we knew how to listen. He asked for my address in Barcelona and I told him I had no home. What a pity, he said, what a pity, he repeated. He spoke, waving his fishy hands about and nodding as if he felt very sorry.

Then, so that he would leave me alone and so I could think quietly, I let him caress my left thigh a little.

HORACI DUC/SENYORA MIRALPEIX   "In the beginning, I would say that she not only accepted it but that she was happy with it. She liked me to tell her stories of people who had been in the war, and I may say that I invented many of them. She listened to me enraptured. She stared at me in such a way that I had to exaggerate a lot, to the point that I no longer knew what was true and what was false. In those times, to survive, you had to live in an ideal world."

"That's true of any time, Senyor Duc."

"I would get up very early, at six o'clock, and leave my room barefooted so as to make no noise. I looked at her in her sleep, like Sleeping Beauty she was, and I thought, when I come back, I'll kiss her like the prince and break the enchantment. She breathed so softly that she seemed a girl. My working hours were only a parenthesis and, when closing time came, I hurried to finish my last job, I left the counter without polishing it, my tools without sharpening, I felt so anxious. She waited for me on the balcony. The walk home from work was short, but it was a walk filled with strange feelings; I felt uneasy but all at once so happy. . . . Only when you are in love, Senyora Miralpeix, do you realize the existence of what they call time. My house was like a silver platter, I have never known such a tidy woman. The furniture looked like mirrors. And the little balcony was so full of potted plants that passersby stopped to look at it as if it were an exhibition. The asparagus plants bent almost to the ground, the carnations jutted up toward the sky, the geraniums a burst of color, the hydrangeas in bloom. . . . And she among the flowers, the princess waited for me among flowers, in that apartment like a closed-in paradise, away from the poverty outside, and now, just remembering it, I could cry. . . . Excuse me."

"Please, don't stop on my account, go on, go on. But have another piece of toast, please."

"That's how the first months went, fast as a thought. Because I, Senyora Miralpeix, have been a man without any companionship. My mother died of a heart attack just as the war ended. And my father, my father left one morning at dawn when the revolution broke out, and he never came back. In the neighborhood they said that he had left with a militia woman, one of those who practiced a free life. Stories of war. During the last year they almost sent me to the front. I wanted to go, but I was only fifteen. My mother said, do you think this is an adventure? But I wanted to go because they said that the Moors behaved like barbarians and also because everything was collapsing, and my father had told me that Catalonia is a country that hides when things don't go well and that it is reborn the stronger because of the suffering, but that a day may come when the blow would be so hard that we would no longer rise. . . . And I don't know quite how it happened that the day they came in, and people were shouting 'They are on Diagonal Avenue!' I found myself on the roof only wanting to look at the sky. With his hands on the roof railing he was also looking toward the sky."

"Who was he?"

"His name was Pagès. I went closer and glanced at him out of the corner of my eye. He was crying like a child. Like a child, Senyora Miralpeix. Tears came down his cheeks and he did nothing to hold them back. And to see such a strong man, so tall, crying like a child is something you cannot easily forget. I asked him nothing; I knew very well why he was crying, and he put his hands on my shoulders and, pointing to a place up in the sky he told me, they have defeated us, Horaci, but we must keep on, now we'll have to be quiet, but deep inside we must shout very hard. Remember this, Horaci, inside we must shout a lot so that they do not take away our words. And I looked toward the point in the sky and I could see nothing, but I imagined that God was there and that God had gone over to their side, He had abandoned us."

"God sides with no one, Senyor Duc. God is inside each one of us."

"God is with no one; but let's not discuss that now. I had a lot of trust in Pagès. In the very early days he had gone to the front as a volunteer. Pagès was our upstairs neighbor and a good friend of my father, even though he was younger. The day the Republic was declared they went together to Sant Jaume square with Catalan flags, and took me with them. Pagès placed me on his shoulders, and people were happy, flags were waving; grandfatherly Macià spoke to us from the balcony, he told us we had a Catalan Republic, and Pagès was shouting louder than anyone while holding my legs, and I felt like a man just like them, because I saw my father was laughing, he, a man always in a bad mood. He turned to Pagès and told him, now, now we can start working, and Pagès answered, you're right, Duc, now is our time!"

"That day I was very frightened."

"But my father left with that woman, and we stopped speaking to Pagès. My mother said that she didn't want to have anything to do with him or her husband's world. And that men had used the war as an excuse to hurt and to destroy families. I saw him when he came on leave and was dying to ask him how things were going at the front, but a mother is a mother. And so I met him on the roof, alone and crying like a child. He walked with crutches for he had been wounded in the war. I saw that he had aged a lot, even though for a boy of fifteen a thirty-year-old looks like an old man, and he told me that thing about shouting out loud inside, remember, Horaci. Since they had wounded him he did not want to escape to France and he was arrested. He spent a few years in prison, and when he came out he was once again that man from the day the Republic was declared. Was he made of stone? Once he came to see me when I was closing up the butcher shop. He said he wanted to talk to me. He had a bunch of leaflets because the Eleventh of September was approaching.* He told me, you must distribute them to the stalls in Santa Caterina market. He commanded me as if I was one of them. But years had gone by and I was very afraid. When I got home I burned them. And through this lie everything began. He had been in prison, but I had lived in the neighborhood. The neighborhood was not the same: many had disappeared, some looked like ghosts, others were just skin and bones. Nobody trusted anybody. Some had become rich by denouncing others. And my father, who never came back. The owner of the butcher shop told me, you'll have to be thankful to me for your whole life, you see, I'm giving you a job even though you are the son of a Red. But if I learn that you have dealings with Pagès,

---

*Senyor Duc refers to the Catalan resistance to Castilian domination, commemorated on the eleventh of September. On this date in 1714, the Catalans lost their bid for autonomy as a result of the War of Succession.

out you go. I took to being alone, as if it were a punishment. I thought, you've been condemned not because you are the son of a Red, but because your father left with a woman. That was the way things were, that's all. But I also wanted to live, I was young, Senyora Miralpeix, I had many years ahead of me, I wasn't an old man like I thought Pagès was. And that's why I burned the pamphlets. I didn't let him know. I was afraid of Pagès. Every year, when the Eleventh of September came near, he brought me phamphlets to distribute, and I burned them every year and threw their ashes in the toilet. I never dared tell him the truth because I had seen him cry like a child, he, who was so strong and tall. Those kind of tears make one more frightened than the threat of a beating."

"I think you're too sentimental, Senyor Duc."

"During our first married year I taught Maria to write correct Catalan. At night she would ask me, do you write 'amor' with an 'h' or without? She was teasing me; she thought it was very funny that the Catalan name for the letter *h* was 'hac.' I had her do homework. She wrote it down in a notebook with grid paper. Like a girl, she bit on her tongue while doing the exercises. That's how I transformed Maria into an authentic Catalan. I had done it all by myself. I had kept my inner words for her, just for her. I thought this was my contribution so that our country would not disappear, even if it was in the basement then, or in the sewers filled with shit, forgive me. And the day would come when I would show Maria to Pagès and would tell him: see? this is my trophy, my little work to help Catalonia become once again what it was. I have transformed an illiterate hick into an educated Catalan. I've paid my dues."

MARI CRUZ   The hut where the gardener kept his tools was made of red bricks and covered with an ivy vine that never stopped growing. The ivy covered the walls and a window as well.

If you wanted to see what was inside you had to draw the leaves apart. The outside leaves were light green and those inside were darker, almost black, because the sun could barely penetrate there. I don't quite recall what the gardener looked like, except that he had very blue eyes, yellow teeth, and a pockmarked face. He came to the school three times a week, he pruned the lemon trees and the pear trees; in the spring he planted summer flowers and winter flowers in the fall. He taught us to talk to the flowers, he said they had souls, souls smaller than ours because they were vegetable souls and, if we did not talk to them, they would wither and die. We told our secrets to the flowers and also whispered to them whose father was the most handsome.

I waited for the arrival of the gardener; he gave us licorice and told us news from the street. One day he called a few of us and told us to go to the toolshed during break, that he had something for us, something we would like very much, but to tell no one, for we were his pets. He closed the door and had us sit on the floor, on top of a pile of empty sacks. He showed us three pieces of candy, lollipops, round, strawberry flavor, and a bigger one in three colors blended like watercolors. We started to play with him, clapping our hands, and then we played Humpty Dumpty. We had to lie on his knees, face down, and guess how many fingers he was showing. After that he pulled up our blouses and undershirts and he pretended to play piano on our "rosary bones." He started to kiss us all over. He gave us the strawberry lollipops and he said that the three-colored one would be for the girl who took her panties off. I wanted it and took them off and then he put his hand on my little hole. I didn't complain because I was enjoying it, even though his hand was rough and calloused. But it smelled exactly as I felt the day I was on the Rambla with Senyor Duc, a moist smell but warm, even though it sounds strange. And while he

219

was caressing my hole, he told me, you have one like a flower, your little hole has soul. When you grow up they'll water it for you and you'll love it, you'll see.

We thought it was very amusing and became used to getting locked up with the gardener in the toolshed, all covered with ivy, while the other girls played in the garden. He told us not to tell anyone, that it would be a secret. We ended up calling it "the secret of the watercolor lollipop," because we all wanted it, the bigger lollipop. And we told no one, we just waited for the day the gardener came to get locked up in the ivy shed. One of the girls had a father and one Sunday she confessed to him that she had a very big secret but she couldn't tell him because, then, it would no longer be a secret. The father told her mother, and her mother wanted to know about it and spanked her daughter. The girl finally revealed the secret, the spanking was so hard. The mother told the father, and the father told the nuns, and the nuns got very alarmed and reported it to the police, and the police went after the gardener; but it seems that he had suspected it for he disappeared. The nuns called a very large lady, dressed in white, with breasts like cathedral domes. The fat lady had us all undress and examined us very well and said I don't know what to the nuns and what happened is that the nuns had us get up at six in the morning for a week. We had to stand without moving, with arms stretched in front of the main altar, to see if the Holiest would forgive us, now that we had lost our purity. The gardener was still in hiding, and the police were still looking for him. Everybody now knew the secret, the nuns told the other girls that we had been stained forever, that the stain we had would never go away because we had been sullied by the Devil who had come to earth in the body of the gardener. The other girls did not wave to us or speak to us, and chanted that jingle, I'm not your friend, to the world's end, if I see you in town, I'll frown, and I told them they were idiots because we were never in town and they could never frown at us since we were always locked up in the school, and that one day I would elope with the gardener, even if he were Satan himself. Weeks went by, we were locked up in the classroom or in the bedroom, forced to say prayers all day long to see if we could wash away the stain we had inside. The nuns said I was the worst one of all and that I would burn in Hell, just like my mother. Until finally everyone forgot about the gardener and, one day, one of the girls in on the secret of the watercolor lollipop climbed up the moist ivy vines that covered the window of the toolshed, and she let out a scream because there she saw a dancing shadow. It was the gardener who had hanged himself.

I was shaking all over while we were going up to the study. I don't know why, but the Rambla was an avenue filled with leaves. Senyor Duc told me that for a few years fall had been coming early, the sycamores in Barcelona had a strange disease that had come from outside, and they were slowly dying. It was almost the hottest part of summer and the streets were filled with dry leaves. It was sad. Senyora Miralpeix had told me that all those changes were provoked by the rockets they were sending into space, they were polluting the universe, and they made summer no longer summer and winter no longer winter. And the sky over Barcelona would never again be like before, it would now have a dirty and grayish patina, as if the city had put on a hat. I had always seen it like this, an overcast sky as if it were about to rain, and I was used to it. But Senyor Duc explained to me that summer showers cleaned the sky and then Barcelona would look like before, clean and jolly. And then it started to rain, a good storm with big drops, far apart; and he said it was summer heat and it would soon stop, and you'll see a truly clear sky, like a gift from the gods. From my house I can see the sky, I said. Let's go, he said, and his eyes became bigger and broader like the drops falling from the sky.

I was shaking because I felt a fire within, I was and was not afraid. While we climbed the little staircase to the study the image of the ivy-covered toolshed came to me, and I saw the gardener with yellow teeth and pockmarked face, I felt his fingers caressing my little hole and also his rusty voice saying to me, this flower, one day they will water it for you and you'll like it a lot, you'll see. And out of the blue a word Senyora Altafulla had used came to my mind: selvage. Selvage. I did not quite know what it meant, but I adopted it, as if I had invented that word. The gardener had touched my selvage, he had touched the bottom of my soul. Selvage. My little hole would get moist as I took the gardener's hand, time and again, I longed for his coarse and calloused hand smelling like the moist earth.

I didn't let the poet of the phalluses touch it, nor the man who took me to Tibidabo, but I was craving for Senyor Duc to touch it. Selvage. That word came down my throat, like swallowed honey. I wanted Senyor Duc to caress my soul, I longed to feel once again my cunt moist as when I was little and the school gardener touched it.

I didn't dare ask him to do it and we remained distracted for a moment, looking at the sky that was now clear and blue as Senyor Duc says the sky always is after a summer shower. I didn't want to look at the sky, I didn't care what color it was, I would rather have captured Senyor Duc's thoughts, make them go down toward my hole, to the moist cavern, moist like the ivy on the toolshed, I was thirsting to capture them well inside me, with the word selvage tickling me all over; I said, I would like you to caress my cunt, and I don't know how I told him, but the words came out of my mouth as if it wasn't me saying them but my body. He stood there motionless like a boulder, he took a while to answer me, and when he did he just told me, in great fury, where have you learned this bad word, Maria? Haven't I taught you to speak properly?

Be kind enough not to repeat it, I find it disgusting. My
body answered: it's a word that comes from deep within:
and I told him because the nuns used to punish me when
I pronounced it, because for a long time nobody told me
what it meant, only this, something that's very disgusting,
that was meant to designate ugly things, that which is un-
speakable, and because for a long time I thought it was a
word with no object, a bad word with no meaning, empty,
until I found out that the word cunt was the selvage of my
desire, all of me turned into desire, and for this reason I
wanted him to caress it until I would die; you're strange,
Maria, I don't understand you, he told me with a sorrow
beyond my comprehension, why do you want to tempt me
once more? It made me laugh, the idea that I wanted to
tempt him, I thought it was kind of cheap; but I just replied don't call me Maria, Senyor Duc, don't call me
Maria; and I grabbed his hand, warm like the gardener's,
and I made it go down to my sex, I want your hand here,
Senyor Duc, right now.

Everything changed. He said kneel down, and I knelt
and then Senyor Duc was transformed. He became a
magus, a haughty and powerful magus, standing on a hill-
top, and he pierced me with his gaze, as if the whole of
him wanted to invade me, I want you to suck my sex until
you die, just as you want me to do with you, I want to fill
you with my strength. I told him yes, that yes I would do it
and, then, I'll lick your cunt as I know you like it, and
you'll taste the sky, Maria, as you have never tasted it, or
like before, like when you were all mine, when you belonged to me, when you were thirsting for me to caress
you. On my knees I started to lick his sex with the tip of
my tongue, slowly at first, as if his sex were a flower about
to open, slowly, and I closed my eyes, to concentrate
deeper on what I thought was a new wonder, a pleasure
that had been hidden from me. I cast away the image of
the poet of the phalluses, all the marble phalluses, and the

great phallus in the desert, the beginning and end of all creation, because this sex belonged to me, I would suck it, I would destroy it, you are my little whore, and his whole sex filled my mouth, as if it could not get out, a piece of sky, a piece of earth, all mixed up, water and mud, teeth and tongue, inside my head, inside my head, and I no longer knew who was speaking, he or I, Maria, Maria, his sex said, I am Maria and I'll swallow you, like the bee sucks the flower's pollen and with my sting I'll kill you, Maria, Maria, you have to destroy me, and his sex was so deep inside me that it seemed as if I was all a part of him. The magus threw me to the floor, he made me open my legs and he kissed my selvage and then I tasted the sky, I wanted it to be him, all of him, I wanted him to come deep inside me, the magus was my cunt, he was mine, and I was the cave that would protect him, it was me, it was him, he-me, I-he, the two of us, the two of us until death, I wanted to disappear, and the magus told me, ride me, and I galloped on top of him as he pierced me with his sex and became a male animal and I a female animal, and in that way we lay for a while, just panting, shrieking, skin, sweat, no words, until he, all of a sudden, went away, far, so far that I couldn't catch him, come back, come back, love, but he had left without me, each one of us in a different world, two galaxies beyond understanding, irreconcilable, as if we spoke two different languages, come back, come back, love, and then he cried out frightfully, a sound that seemed to be of terror but that was of pleasure, as if he were a mortally wounded animal, and he became all distended, returning heavily to earth, as if forced, and his eyes went after mine, and he had me lie on the floor, and from behind he caressed my selvage and then it was I who shrieked with no containment, a long howl, as if an electric current ran through my backbone, an unstoppable current, unstoppable, until I felt like crying out for so much happiness and my shriek penetrated all the darkness of my forgotten past, of my demolished hometown that I had left as a child, of the nuns, of the father I did not have, and then I understood for the first time that I had fallen in love. I felt the joy of abandon, abandoned in that harmony that nobody had ever explained to me and that I, all by myself, had discovered. All I said was, thanks.

MARI CRUZ/SENYORA ALTAFULLA   Distracted, Mari Cruz was cutting Senyora Altafulla's nails, and she could barely hear the old woman scream, "But, girl, can't you see you're hurting me? Where's your head?" God knows where it was. She would have gladly severed her fingers with the clippers. She felt anger as she began filing Senyora Altafulla's claws, it was as if she were filing at her own heart, she wanted to see if what Senyor Duc had left inside her would disappear, that mixture of apprehension and joy.

Senyora Altafulla again asked her why she had only one earring. She was shouting. Filing away at her own heart she could not hear her. Finally she answered that she wore only one because she wanted to, trying to hold back the tears. She wanted by all means to hide her tears from the witch, come on, hold on. Oblivious, the old woman repeated that only one earring was very ugly, that you had to keep in mind the proportion of the human face, and so on and so forth. You'll leave me without nails, girl, don't pull so hard.

She had never felt sorry for herself; she thought that her life was laughable, like all lives, if you look at them closely. She had always felt untouched by the stories of others, she thought that over time people added a good dosage of fiction. Now she had to swallow her own sadness, not let the old woman see it. But there was no danger, her boss continued to mumble, that if we have two ears we must show them off, I can't stand so much carelessness, your poor aesthetic sense, girl. Mari Cruz hit her with the file.

"Look, Madam, I wear only one earring because I damn well feel like it, and leave me alone, damn it," she shouted.

Shocked, Senyora Altafulla was left with her hand hanging down and her nails spread out. She remained like that for a while, her hand in the air, her mouth open, not knowing what to do, ready to slap her. But she lowered her hand slowly and caressed the girl's cheek.

"Forgive me, my child, it was none of my business," she said.

She took hold of her chin and, little by little, inspected the girl's face. She gazed at her eyes and eyelids and perhaps realized they were moist. But she did not persist.

"You know that you are very pretty?" she said. "Your face is a perfect oval. And I like your eyes; they are pure eyes."

She was examining her face with her half-filed nails, as if drawing all its lines.

"Your features look like a Botticelli," she added, "I had not realized it before. A fine chin, a long neck, a svelte figure . . . and your lips . . ."

She followed her lips with her fingers and, all of a sudden, she stopped.

"No; I don't like your lips, your mouth is a bit too large. Let me see, show me your teeth. . . . Yes, your teeth are also pretty. . . . But you need your eyebrows plucked, they are too thick, and also your upper lip. A mustache is very unbecoming, for a girl like you. You seem older than you are."

For the first time since she started working for the old woman, Mari Cruz smiled at her. Senyora Altafulla detected a mixture of irony and friendship.

"Well, I mean that it could look as if you didn't wash," she specified, "and that makes you look older. You are a lucky one, all you need is a clean face."

"But you yourself don't wash a whole lot," Mari Cruz

answered in a relaxed way. "What you do is use a lot of perfume."

"We old women do not need to wash much," replied the old woman as she observed her nails, now completely filed. "And even more if we follow my habit of not going into the streets, to soil myself with dust, and with what they now call pollution. That way I preserve my silken skin. Have you noticed? See how soft my skin is? Touch it, touch it. . . . Move your finger on my face, my neck, my arms, you'll see how fine my skin is. The Colonel often told me. Caterina, he said, your skin is like a young girl's."

Mari Cruz felt her face while Senyora Altafulla held her hand. "Was Colonel Saura a man of his word?" she asked.

"Of course!" said Senyora Altafulla, looking into the box of the manicure set. "I don't know what color to choose. What do you think? Candide is a good evening color, but Grisant Fum Rosé is more delicate."

"The pink suits you better."

"The night we both were on top of the bluff and we could see the lightning pierce the sky, we sealed a pact without words. We knew that our relationship would be different. I won't deny that, at that time, I was seeing other men. And I am sure he was seeing other women. But, how can I tell you? We did not want to mix what we felt for each other with lust. . . . It was . . . as if we were both looking for our lost youth. I found in him the ideal of the male, the ideal I had built for myself when I was still a girl and wanted to leave my hometown. Perhaps he felt the same way. I am afraid you may not understand me, dear. At the time people did not understand us either. . . . My friend, Núria Campins wanted to found a family with a real man. And I did not want to be a mother, I had no wish for children. I wanted to preserve, untouched, inside me, the dreams from my early years, when you feel the world is made just for you, when you discover it in all its neatness. I resisted growing old. I was forced to, later. . . . That's why, the night on the bluff, I felt totally possessed by my Colonel at the very moment when he seized me by the waist. He was the lightning piercing my sky and I had no more needs. Who knows, if things had gone differently, our dream might have cracked open. . . . And later it might have become corrupted. Then we discovered, the two of us, that people had gone crazy and they were destroying the world's harmony and killing each other with no regrets. For this reason, one evening when we were strolling in Ciutadella Park, when the birds had left the linden trees in the avenue, we said good-bye to each other so that our relationship would never become a routine. . . .

Mari Cruz listened to the beginning of Senyora Altafulla's last monologue. She had heard it many times, but now she captured every word. A Minorcan colonel, Albert Saura, smiled at her from afar and his image, which had been blurred and distant before, grew, becoming solid, tangible, real. With him she strolled down the avenue of the linden trees, on a birdless day. And for the first time she understood that she did not have to grow up the way they wanted her to. Because now she had inside of her an image that would never fail her.

Instead of applause Senyora Altafulla heard the voice of Mari Cruz asking, why didn't you marry the Colonel? Senyora Altafulla took a moment to answer, she liked to feel the ecstasy, transported to an imaginary state, and Mari Cruz's question did not fit the scenario she had created. Without changing her dreamy tone she replied, why should I marry him? How ridiculous! . . . We were two free and independent spirits, we had an inner life, just like Verdi and his beloved Giuseppina Strepponi. They never married either. They faced the sharp tongues of Busseto, they faced the Parma authorities. In a letter to Barezzi, his father-in-law, Verdi had written: "Neither she nor I need render any account for our actions and, besides, who knows what our relationship is like? What is there between us, what ties? Who can tell if these are good or bad? Why shouldn't they be good? And in the event that they were bad, who has the right to pronounce an anathema? . . ." Senyora Altafulla sighed. We too liked a solitary life and did not have to account for our acts to any one. . . .

Mari Cruz wanted to know more things and she spewed forth questions, without thinking much. She was so happy on account of Senyor Duc's telephone call telling her he wanted to see her. . . . And she felt no surprise at her own attention now to a story that she had heard so many times and the end of which she knew by heart. . . . She was so happy that she continued to question the old woman. And what happened to you both when the war was over? Heavens, girl, what can I tell you; Senyora Altafulla continued with her gaze half-lost; I was holed up in the Pirelli factory, working like a mule, making ends meet as best I could. I spent the summers in Caldetes, with Raul and Antonieta, who had made it and pretended to be aristocrats. . . . God, how boring they were, those summers! Until I retired and became my own mistress I wasn't able to relax. With theatrical tenderness the old woman placed her fox stole around Mari Cruz's naked shoulders. See? Who would have guessed, she said, how the picture changes with some furs over your buxom décolletage. . . . Or would the llama-wool dress suit you better?

But Mari Cruz persisted; and the Colonel, what happened to the Colonel? Without interrupting her appreciation of the effect of the fox stole on the buxom décolletage, Senyora Altafulla removed from one of the drawers of her Jacobean dresser an old photo album with frayed edges. In it there was an envelope of foreign origin and she gave it to Mari Cruz. The Colonel went to his island, my dear; for all his bravery and courage in the affairs of war, deep down, he was a peaceful man. . . . Do you know what? I think it is better if you wear the fox to go to the opera; I want you to be the prettiest of all. . . . But Mari Cruz had already opened the letter and had begun to read what it said. It was handwritten in an English hand, in almost perfect Catalan:

In Mexico we live well, the worst is over. At first I myself had to do the cooking, but now I have two maidservants, can you imagine! They are very inexpensive here. We have bought a villa in Cuernavaca; Ricard makes a very good living at the laboratories. If our parents could see us; they did not want me to marry a man in the military! My sister writes often from Chile, and it seems they are also doing well. . . . We were very lucky, Caterina, to take off before they came in; I do not know what would have happened to Ricard as he was a career soldier. . . . We heard so many stories, later. . . . I am sure he would have ended up like that poor soul, Colonel Saura, the Minorcan. . . . Do you remember him? How we used to laugh at him because he was so sloppy, and stiff as a fence post. You were always the first to make fun of him, you said you could not understand how he could be an officer, so short and small-chested. Ricard used to say that he had gotten into the quartermaster corps to avoid the front lines and that he was so naive that he did not see the disaster coming. I must say that he did not deserve that death; it was a pity for him to be executed. At any rate they shot him because he was an idiot and a coward; who told him to stay in Spain? He had never hurt a fly. . . . Well, you may not remember this Saura; I think you did not meet on many occasions, did you? I hope you will write now that you know our whereabouts. A big hug from your friend, Núria Campins

She read the letter twice. First because she was not used to reading in Catalan and then because she could not quite believe what the letter said. She repeated, to herself, some of the terms: "sloppy, short, fence post, coward. . . ." She could barely hear the rustle of Senyora Altafulla's voice. She had not stopped speaking all that while; I told you, darling, the Colonel went to his island because he was a man of peace, even though he had courage to spare. You don't know how much I am looking forward to going to the opera tonight, mostly because they are putting on *La Traviata*. You and I will be the most beautiful; we each have a different style and we look so chic, don't you think? . . . At times, when I was young and felt sad, for I felt sad once in a while, I would murmur to myself the duet with Alfredo and Violeta, when they say:

Amor e palpito
dell'universo intero
misterioso, altero,
croce e delizia al cor!

For love is this way, child, at once a cross and a delight. . . . But, you are listening to me, aren't you? If you go on so distracted you won't understand a bit of the performance. In order to understand opera you must have a special disposition. You may begin with this one, this is an easy one, and little by little I'll explain others to you, you'll see. . . . I tell you, you'll learn a lot with me, you are just a young sprout and I an excellent teacher, you can be thankful for that. . . . Let's see, to begin with I'll tell you how Verdi composed *La Traviata*. He had been to Paris and had seen *La Dame aux Camélias*, and since at Busseto they didn't much like Giuseppina Strepponi, his beloved . . .

Mari Cruz came down from her thoughts and interrupted her: No, Senyora Altafulla, tonight I can't go to the opera with you, I'm busy. . . . But, what are you saying? the old lady did not quite get it; is that why you dressed up? Come on, don't laugh, you must think that going to the opera is like having a date with the Colonel, with our Colonel. . . . No, Senyora Altafulla, it's no joke, I can't go, I have a previous engagement with . . . another person.

Her dress was uncomfortable, the underwires were digging into her flesh under her breasts, the fur was suffocating. She put the letter back in the album. She felt that she had to forget something that was hurting her and could

not remember what, she wanted to go with Senyor Duc,
Senyor Duc who waited for her on the corner of Hospital
Street. The old woman, now hysterical, was screaming:
what do you mean you cannot come? Do you want to miss
Traviata? No, this cannot be, you are out of your mind,
dear. There is still a lot for you to learn, you'll see what
you feel when the tenor starts that part "Libiamo,
amore"—Look, I'll translate it for you:

> Let's drink, love, for in the glass
> One finds the most ardent kisses
> That love ever offers!

Your body will fill with a new breath, she went on now
with a dreamy voice, as if it were filled with air. . . . She
looked tenderly at the girl; OK, I'll let you wear my pearl
necklace, I'll go without. Mari Cruz paid no attention to
Senyora Altafulla's insistence—I can't, I told you I have a
date. Then the old woman became her boss once more:
What do you mean? I am telling you to stay here, after all
I've done for you, after all that I've given you! You'll never
amount to anything, do you hear me? You will go through
life like a toy top, like a valise, like a . . . And right now, I
want my furs back, this very minute. She looked at her
with teary eyes: And besides, you smell!

Mari Cruz was laughing while Senyora Altafulla was
crying like Mary Magdalene. Come on, Madam, you have
no demands on my free time, the comedy is over. The old
woman was still trying to retain her: Comedy? Yes, this is
nothing but pure theater, nothing of what you tell me exists, it has never existed; "your" Colonel Saura, that
phony, the Royal Café, the woman you say loved that man
Verdi; you're way off, you're . . . dead, do you hear?
They're all dead. Mari Cruz threw the fox fur on the bro-
cade bedspread as she fled from the room.

Senyora Altafulla carefully picked up the fox stole and
started to pet it. Theater? Did you hear, Colonel? She says
this is all theater. . . . She will never understand opera, she

will never understand life. She turned around slowly and looked at herself in the mirror with delight. Her lips insinuated a smile, a smile as soft as the grimace of a fish just caught.

MARI CRUZ   She spoke openly, until it was dark and I couldn't see her face, and I thought it was not Senyora Miralpeix who spoke but the shadows of all the old people I knew. They were laughing at me, like the gardener with yellowish teeth and a pockmarked face. They told me their secret and I felt all smeared with it.*

When she finished talking I let out a scream, it was a shriek that came out from my entrails, long imprisoned there. I went to the toilet and vomited, as if my guts came out of my mouth and, with them, all my memories.

I was enraged at Senyora Miralpeix. I didn't want to know. And she seemed to enjoy it, telling me those stories. The Colonel, I mean Senyor Duc, had made me love this land almost without my realizing it. He had made me notice the color of the sky over the city and he had helped me understand that I had a body. I don't care what he had done before. Older people, at times, give that too much importance.

Senyora Miralpeix was now observing me with her gaze made out of bark and, as she held my forehead to help me vomit, she said, you see? I told you, you should have taken some herb tea. . . . I have not invented what I told you; if I know about it, you must know too; this man has left it on top of me, like a tombstone. . . . With my hand I asked her to be quiet, but she went on, you must clean it with a sponge, don't you see that he only looks at you with his memory for the other woman?

But I didn't remember what she had told me, because I

---

*Senyora Miralpeix has just revealed Senyor Duc's darkest, haunting secret to Mari Cruz, as well as the news that he has left her.

know today's Horaci Duc; through him I discovered the word selvage, with him I became the mistress of words. I will look for him. And when I find him I will no longer have to stand in line to be kissed by the fathers of the other girls. The Colonel will be mine alone.